BEYOND THE SILENCE

Kennedy took a deep breath, then said, 'Would you be surprised if I told you that there are people in SIS and elsewhere who suggest that your loyalty was questionable?'

Carling laughed. 'Which particular loyalty?'

'Loyalty to this country.'

Carling smiled. 'Oh that. No, it wouldn't surprise me at all. Everybody from directors-general down has suffered unfounded stories about their loyalty. The likes of me are fair game . . .'

'We need to know the truth . . . It would be done very discreetly and in confidence.'

Also by Ted Allbeury and available in Coronet paperbacks:

As Time Goes By
The Line-Crosser
Show Me a Hero
Other Kinds of Treason
The Dangerous Edge
A Time Without Shadows

About the Author

Ted Allbeury was a lieutenant-colonel in the Intelligence Corps during World War II, and a successful executive in the fields of marketing, advertising and radio. He has been writing since the early 1970s: he is best known for his espionage novels but has also written one highly successful and highly praised general novel, *The Choice*, and a short story collection, *Other Kinds of Treason*.

BEYOND THE SILENCE

Ted Allbeury

CORONET BOOKS
Hodder and Stoughton

First published in Great Britain in 1995
by Hodder and Stoughton
A division of Hodder Headline PLC
First published in paperback in 1996 by
Hodder and Stoughton
A Coronet Paperback

10 9 8 7 6 5 4 3 2 1

British Library Cataloguing in Publication Data

Allbeury, Ted
Beyond the Silence
I. Title
823.914 [F]

ISBN: 0 340 64907 0

Typeset by Phoenix Typesetting, Ilkley, West Yorkshire

Printed and bound in Great Britain by
Cox & Wyman Ltd, Reading, Berkshire.

Hodder and Stoughton
A division of Hodder Headline PLC
338 Euston Road
London NW1 3BH

Here richly, with ridiculous display,
The Politician's corpse was laid away.
While all of his acquaintance sneered and slanged
I wept: for I had longed to see him hanged.

Hilaire Belloc, *Sonnets and Verse* (1923)
'Epigraph on the Politician Himself'

The spirit of liberty is the spirit
which is not too sure that it is right
Judge Learned Hand

ONE

CHAPTER 1

Old habits die hard and Kennedy had paid off the taxi at Victoria Station and walked the rest of the way to Ebury Street. As he crossed the road to number 25b he wondered if it really was the chaos back at Century House with Facilities planning the move to the new HQ, or was it because he rather liked the pretty safe house itself, that had made him choose it for the meeting. It was no longer a safe house. Some joker at the Soviet Embassy had sent a 'Get well' card addressed to the Director-General 'care of' 25b Ebury Street. But the rent had been paid until the end of the year so they might as well use it until then.

He pressed the door-bell and when the door clicked open he walked slowly up the steep, narrow stairs, aware that security cameras had watched his progress from when he crossed the street, and that now the internal circuit had taken him over.

Maggie was waiting for him on the small landing at the top of the stairs.

'Mr Farmer and Mr Shelley are in the side room waiting for you, sir.' As he thanked her and turned she said, 'Will you sign the chit, sir, please?'

He sighed and read the card. It confirmed that Angus Roffey, Signals Section, had checked the whole house at 14.00 hours that day and it was electronically clean. He signed the card and Maggie said, 'I've told them it's either tea or coffee until after the meeting.'

He smiled and headed for the side room. It was bright, walls and ceiling Dulux Brilliant White and Venetian blinds at the windows overlooking the street. Farmer and Shelley looked bored already.

There was no tape recorder and no notepads. It was not a meeting of record. Kennedy had told them briefly already what he wanted to discuss. In fact he had already made his mind up about what to do, but a little support from other sections would do no harm; it might even spread the load if the whole thing went down the pan.

He took off his jacket, hung it over the back of the chair and sat down.

'Thanks for coming, both of you.' He paused. 'Let me just outline the problem.' He paused. 'Our old friend Carling. Lord Carling. Ex-SIS and suspected by several colleagues of having played footsie with the Russians during his time with us. Maybe even before.' He paused. 'And maybe even after he left us.'

'Why the sudden interest in him now, Freddie?'

Kennedy hesitated for a moment, then said, 'Two reasons. Maybe even more. The timing is because we have strong indications that one of the tabloids is considering one of its "investigatory" pieces on SIS. You know the stuff. They want to hang it on to the Carling business. Mole in the heart of SIS. Lax security. Who was protecting him? Heads must roll – and all the usual crap they dish up.'

Farmer said quietly, 'I gather you've got some scheme in mind—'

Shelley interrupted. 'First things first, Freddie. You say some of our people suspected him.' He paused. 'On what grounds? Where's the evidence?'

Kennedy shrugged. 'I've had long conversations with the DPP and he says we have nothing that would stand up in court. And we *could* end up with a libel writ.'

'So could the tabloid, Freddie.'

'Fair enough. But old Carling's in his late sixties. May even be seventy already. The tabloid could be waiting for him to kick the bucket. Just putting the bits together as they come in.'

Shelley said, 'It must be old stuff now. You say some people suspect that he's still playing footsie with the Russians. Glasnost and perestroika will have ended those games. He can't be important enough for them to risk running him now.'

Farmer shook his head. 'I'm always reading about him on trips to Berlin, Vienna, Prague and Budapest. He hasn't stopped those.'

Kennedy said, 'He'd claim that it's just his work for the Arts Council.' He smiled. 'Or could be.'

Shelley laughed softly. 'It's a bloody good cover anyway.' He looked at Kennedy. 'I gather you've got something in mind?'

'Well. The obvious alternative to prosecuting is to do a deal. He tells us all and we give him immunity from prosecution.'

Shelley nodded. 'So?'

Kennedy sighed. 'The snag is – we've got so little evidence that I wonder if what he's got to tell us is worth the immunity.'

'Go on.'

'I had in mind having a chat with Carling. Tell him about vague suspicions here and at the tabloid. Tell him that there's pressure building up to expose him and we'd be prepared to do a deal, but we need to know roughly what he's got to tell us before we can make a decision.'

Farmer frowned. 'And what if he just tells us to get stuffed?'

Kennedy shook his head. 'Put yourself in his place, Dickie. An aristocrat, a popular and well-known figure, an icon of the arts scene. He won't want to go through the mill of a court case or being done over by one of the tabloids. You know what they'd make of it.'

Shelley interposed. 'And what they'd make of us too. Nothing definite – "high-level sources suggest" – "a well-informed ex-officer says" – "who is protecting the traitors?" – it's all been done before, with far less to go on than in this case. Even now I ask myself: if our people had suspicions why the hell didn't they do something about it?'

Kennedy shrugged. 'First of all the suspicions are only with hindsight, and secondly – like I said – the DPP says we'd be out on our ears as soon as the judge had heard the opening statement and read the file.' He paused. 'It's going to take some time even if he co-operates. Whoever does it will have to decide whether Carling is telling us the full story or just a cover-up.'

'Who've you got in mind?'

'One of my own chaps. Name's Mathews. Wasn't even born when our friend could have first started playing games with the Russians. He can get alongside Carling without the luggage of prior knowledge or old prejudices.'

'How long's he been with us?'

'Five years officially, another three years before that on loan from the I.Corps.'

'Positively vetted?'

'Of course.'

Farmer shrugged. 'You seem to have got it all worked out.'

Kennedy smiled. 'Can you think of something better?'

'No. It just seems a bit – I don't know what – airy-fairy. We ask our friend to spill the beans but promise him nothing definite. Why should he trust us?'

Kennedy, still smiling, said, 'It isn't us he'll be trusting, it'll be Mathews.'

There was a long silence and then Kennedy said, 'Shall we vote on it?'

Farmer shook his head. 'No. I'll go with it for want of anything better.'

They had hung on, gossiping, for another ten minutes and then gone their different ways. Only Kennedy went back to Century House.

CHAPTER 2

Kennedy knew George Carling from Carling's last few years with SIS and had subsequently met him from time to time at meetings at the Foreign Office. He decided that he ought to meet His Lordship alone to get the thing moving, before briefing Mathews. There were ways of presenting the possible deal that he felt he could best put to Carling himself. He phoned him and arranged a dinner meeting at the Reform.

The conversation during the meal was amiable and amusing as Carling gave him the inside story on the fine-art forgeries that had recently been exposed. He obviously enjoyed the discomfiture of the so-called connoisseurs and experts. It seemed in character that Carling was so obviously on the side of the forger.

They took their coffee in the members' lounge in comfortable armchairs in a corner that gave them some privacy. Kennedy ordered malt whiskies for them both and as he lifted his glass to Carling, he said, 'I need your help, George.'

Carling was obviously surprised. 'Really. What sort of help?'

'We need your co-operation.'

'Who's we?'

'SIS.'

'Sounds ominous.'

Kennedy smiled. 'Not really.'

'What's it all about?'

'You.'

'Me? For God's sake. I've been away from that game for a decade. What help can I give you?'

Kennedy took a deep breath, then said, 'Would you be surprised if I told you that there are people in SIS and else-where who suggest that your loyalty was questionable?'

Carling laughed. 'Which particular loyalty?'

'Loyalty to this country.'

Carling smiled. 'Oh that. No, it wouldn't surprise me at all. Everybody from directors-general down has suffered unfounded stories about their loyalty. The likes of me are fair game.'

Kennedy said quietly, 'We have information that one of the tabloids is trying to put together a story that suggests you had contacts with the KGB over a number of years.'

Carling smiled, shaking his head. 'But they couldn't prove it.'

'They don't have to. They print the story and their sales go up. They can keep it on the boil for weeks and months. You've seen what they've done recently to quite insignificant politicians. And you're very well known to the public.'

'And you're afraid that SIS will be accused of being lax and inefficient.'

'That's part of the problem.'

'What's the other part.'

'We need to know the truth.'

'Go on.'

'We thought it might be prudent to go over the past with you.' He paused. 'And then, if it satisfies us, grant you immunity from prosecution in exchange for your co-operation.' He paused again. 'It would be done very discreetly and in confidence.'

'So what's the problem?'

'First, that you may not agree to co-operate, and secondly, that you give us a heavily doctored account of whatever happened.'

Carling smiled. 'Not get value for money, yes?'

'I suppose you could call it that.'

'And if you're not satisfied, what then?'

'We go back to square one. To the situation as it is today.'

'All bets off.'

Kennedy shrugged but said nothing.

'Who would I be talking to?'

'One of my best officers. Timothy Mathews. Mid-thirties, wide experience. I think you'd quite like him.'

'It sounds an interesting exercise. What is it you people used to call it? "Walking back the cat?" Seeing what really happened and how it had influenced your old colleagues when they'd made the wrong moves and wrong analysis.'

Kennedy, relieved, smiled. 'We call it damage limitation these days.'

'So when do you want to start?'

'As soon as possible and when it's convenient to you.'

'I'll have to go, Kennedy.' Carling stood up. 'I'm due at the Festival Hall. Tell him to phone me at home.' He smiled. 'I'm sure you know the number.'

Mathews put the tea bag in the mug with the sugar and reached for the bottle of milk, his hand hesitating before it grasped the bottle. He tried to remember what his father had always said about the only way to make a good cup of tea was to put the milk in last. Or was it first? He poured in the boiling water. As he stirred in the milk he realised how hopeless he was domestically, now he was on his own. His solicitor had said it would be easy. A 'no-fault' divorce. No lies about either party. Just an acceptance that she'd wanted out. Out for him and in for Roger Thomas, a local solicitor. A real creep of a man, self-satisfied and, as they say, with a reputation with the ladies. And, standing on the sidelines, trying to take it all in, eight-year-old Tony, the Mathewses' son. Care and custody to the mother, Pamela, reasonable access for the father. The court had said that as they seemed reasonable people access could be left for the parties and their solicitors to settle. His chap had said that the best he could get him was every other Saturday, 9 a.m. to 6 p.m. The first two Saturdays had been no problem but the third Saturday Pamela said the boy was going to a Cub camp and would have to miss out. And as he started to protest she had hung up.

When the phone rang he was careful not to give his name or the number.

'Yes?'

'The deputy would like to see you, Tim. Soon as possible. He suggests three this afternoon.'

'Where?'

'Do you know the Special Forces Club?'

'Yeah.'

'He's having lunch there. He'll be waiting for you.'

'Any idea what it's all about?'

'No idea. But I'm sure it's frightfully important.' And he heard her soft laugh cut off as she hung up.

He wondered what it could be. Kennedy was his immediate boss and had been for two years. Tough but fair and had been over all the same hurdles in his time.

He wouldn't call him back from his week's leave unless it was either urgent or important.

Mathews paid off the taxi at Harrods and walked the short distance to the Special Forces Club. Kennedy signed him in after the club steward had checked his ID and then took him upstairs to a private room. When they were sitting Kennedy looked across at Mathews.

'How's things?'

'Much as usual.'

'I've got a special assignment for you. It might help to keep your mind off the domestic problems.' He paused. 'What do you know about George Carling – Lord Carling to give him his proper title?'

'Is this the Arts Council guy? The one who's always on TV?'

'That's the one. He used to be SIS. Some years full time and then a kind of unofficial consultant on Eastern bloc intelligence.' He paused. 'We've always had our suspicions that he was playing games with the KGB. All circumstantial. Virtually nothing we could use in court.' Kennedy looked towards the windows and then back at Mathews. 'We've done a deal with him. We've formed a small committee to control it. Myself, Shelley and Farmer. Let me tell you what we want you to do.'

Kennedy spent ten minutes explaining the deal he had done with Carling and the background that had prompted it.

'He's actually agreed to do this?' Mathews said with obvious disbelief.

'Yes.'

'Maybe he'll just try and string me along. And we'll end up knowing no more than we know now.'

'Could be. But it'll be up to you to decide if he's just wasting our time.'

'Do you think he's guilty?'

'I'm sure he is but I not only couldn't prove it in court, I doubt if I could convince anyone who matters in SIS either. They don't like suspicion, most of them have been under suspicion for something or other at some stage in their careers. They only want facts.'

'How long have we got?'

'As long as you need. It's going to take time to get to know him well enough to judge whether he's telling the truth or not.'

'What about the newspaper?'

Kennedy shrugged. 'They'll be more cautious than we need be. Their lawyers will see to that. They'll probably wait until Carling dies.'

'How old is he?'

'Late sixties, could be seventy even.'

'Looks younger on TV. Who's got his "P" file?'

Kennedy reached in his briefcase and brought out two videotapes. 'I suggest you don't read his file unless you absolutely need to. These are videotapes of programmes he's been on and a few clips of black and white surveillance material. Most of it stills.' As he handed the tapes to Mathews he said, 'It's better to go in with a clean slate and no prejudices. Feel free to contact me any time you want.' He shrugged. 'Some sort of sitrep weekly will do, even if it's a nil report. OK?'

'OK.'

CHAPTER 3

Despite Kennedy's warning about going in without prejudice, Mathews had a look at Carling's entry in *Who's Who*. There wasn't much. Born 1920, which meant he was about seventy. Not married. Served for five years in Intelligence Corps during the war. Rank, Captain. Foreign Office, which meant SIS, from 1945 to 1960. Then nothing but various consultancies. Arts Council, British Film Board, Tate Gallery, and the London Symphony Orchestra as fund-raiser. Hobbies listed as photography, ham radio and reading. Education, Harrow and Trinity, a 2:2 in modern languages, German and French.

The videotapes were mainly TV interviews. He was a frequent guest on programmes about the arts including a solo interview with Melvyn Bragg, where they seemed to get on well together. There was a slightly acerbic *Late Show* where Carling was amiably defending one of the London orchestra's performances at the Festival Hall against a reviewer who was angered by 'fluffed notes on the horns, mistimed entries by the brass and jagged string playing.'

The surveillance clips in black and white showed Carling and another man strolling around the lake in St James's Park, Carling getting out of a car at the Polish Embassy in Portland Place, Carling and what looked like a casual meeting but had all the signs of a contrived meeting, with a woman at Gatwick in the Burger King. There were a number of other photographs, none of them apparently significant unless you knew who the people and places were.

Mathews looked at the card that Kennedy had handed him giving Carling's home telephone number. It gave a code number that he didn't recognise and he phoned Facilities to check where it was. It was a Tunbridge Wells number. He rang three times before he got a reply and then it was Carling himself who picked up the phone.

'Carling.'

'My name's Mathews, sir. I was told to get in touch with you.'

'Who?'

'Mathews, sir.' When there was a long pause he added, 'Century House.'

'Ah yes. Of course. You want to see me, I suppose.'

'When would suit you, sir?'

'Come down tomorrow. Not before 9 a.m. I'm not an early riser. You know where my place is?'

'No, sir, I don't.'

'You car or train?'

'Car.'

'OK. Take the Frant road out of Tunbridge Wells but don't go to Frant, turn off left to the Bayham Road. Through Bells Yew Green and on to a sign for the trout farm. Turn left through the gates and go on about a mile and you'll find my house on the right-hand side of the road. There's a sign says Lake Cottage. You can't miss it.'

'I'll be there about ten, sir.'

'Good show.'

And Carling hung up.

*　　*　　*

It was the last day of March, a Saturday, and the roads were busy as Mathews drove through Tunbridge Wells and turned off at the Pantiles. Fifteen minutes later he saw the sign for the trout farm and the wide open gates. Five minutes later he was at Lake Cottage. It wasn't Mathews' idea of a cottage. It looked as if it had once been at least four terraced cottages before they had been converted. Beautiful stone and large old-fashioned windows. A brick path led through a front garden with two magnolia trees already in bloom despite the weather, and masses of daffodils across the two lawns with primroses in flower each side of the path. The solid oak door was ajar but he rang the brass bell and waited.

A young woman came to the door and when he gave his name she smiled and said, 'His Lordship is in his study. I'll take you to him.'

Mathews barely had time to notice the rooms but he was conscious of antique furniture, a Steinway grand in the sitting room and walls everywhere lined with books. The girl knocked on a solid door and then opened it and ushered him inside. She smiled at the man in the leather armchair. 'Mr Mathews to see you, sir.'

Carling held out his hand without getting up and nodded to another chair facing him. 'Good journey?'

'No problems, thank you.'

'You need the loo or a cup of tea or anything?'

'Not at the moment, thank you, sir.'

'So. How do we start?'

'Can I ask you how I should address you?'

Carling smiled. 'You make me sound like an envelope. Not My Lord for heaven's sake. Let's start as you started, with 'sir' in deference to my age. When we've got to know one another it can be George.' He paused. 'Let me start, eh?'

'Of course, sir.'

'I gather you want to talk about my life, so I'd like to know a bit about you. Where you come from. Your background. What you've been up to in SIS. OK?'

'I'm thirty-five. Recently divorced—'

Carling intervened. Eyebrows raised in query. 'The job? Never around when you're needed and all that?'

'No. Not really. She met someone else, more successful. A solicitor.'

'Bastards. All of 'em. I wouldn't trust any one of them an inch. Go on.'

'A son. She has him. I'm fighting for access.' He paused. 'I was born in Erdington in Birmingham. Went to King Edward's and then St Antony's, Oxford. My father has a music shop. Sells instruments, pianos and sheet music. My mother gives piano lessons. He likes jazz and she likes Schubert and Chaminade. In SIS I did the usual two-year training and probation and I've had postings in Berlin, Paris and Vienna and a year in Washington.' He paused and shrugged. 'That's about it.'

'What a splendid summary. I assume that when you say Washington you mean Langley and the CIA?'

'Yes.'

'How did you get on with the Americans?'

'I liked them.'

'Why?'

'Oh. I found them generous and optimistic. They don't really understand Europeans but they mean well.'

'Interesting.' Carling shuffled around in his chair and tossed a cushion to the floor. 'And now. What do you want to know about me?' He paused and looked at Mathews.

'By the way, do you believe all those stories about me having a relationship with the KGB?'

'I've no idea, sir. I don't know much more than that there *were* rumours.'

'Fair enough.' He laughed quietly. 'This is going to be like a long version of *This Is Your Life*. They were planning to do me on that show but Julie stopped them. By the way, Julie looks after me. Supervises the cleaning and cooking and all that. She's very attractive but I don't sleep with her. She came from an orphanage and I'm very fond of her.' He paused looking at Mathews. 'You *did* wonder if I slept with her, didn't you?'

Mathews blushed and said hesitantly, 'I guess it passed through my mind. But only fleetingly,' he added.

His Lordship laughed heartily. 'Well done.' Then more seriously: 'How about you. Do you have a girl you sleep with?'

'Just girlfriends. One or two.'

'Good show. Always be discreet.' He sighed rather theatrically. 'Now me. Where shall I start?'

'How about you do your background as I did? Just briefly.'

'I inherited the title when my father died. We didn't get on well together but I admired him. He was brave and a great patriot. Was our ambassador in Vienna for a few years. He was also a snob, and what we would now call a racist. He didn't like foreigners and he didn't like Jews. He thought we made a great mistake not going along with Adolf Hitler. Despite all this he had great charm, that's why my mother married him. She was Austrian. A great singer. I don't know how she stood him. But she did. She loved him, poor woman.' He paused and sighed. 'She loved me too. Protected me. He thought I was a sissy. He caught me reading a Left Book Club book called *Guilty Men*, about Tory politicians who voted for rearmament because they had shares in the companies who made the arms. He burned the book in a kind of ceremony. Echoes of the Nazis. I hated him and I was frightened of him. And of course it made me what they'd nowadays call a typical left-winger. I think I would have been anyway but he made the idea even more attractive. I was about seventeen then.

'I was at Trinity when the war broke out. I joined up. The army. I went into the I.Corps because of my languages. I was bilingual German and had decent French. I served here in the UK and a short time in Italy and then in Germany. Denazification and all that. And then I was approached by SIS. With everybody being demobbed they were short of people. It was typical of their attitudes that they just looked for the sons of people they deemed loyal and trustworthy.' He smiled. 'The old-boy network, you know. Society had not got around to realising that sons sometimes want to be the opposite to their fathers.' He paused and sipped from a glass of water.

Mathews said, 'Were you positively vetted before they recruited you?'

Carling smiled. 'No. They hadn't even invented it in those days. For them my father was proof enough that I was the right kind.'

'Apart from your father, what was it that first made you decide you were left wing?'

'Well, I didn't know then that having those thoughts made me left wing. I'd never even heard the words.' He closed his eyes, thinking, for several moments and then said slowly, 'I guess it was a photograph that started it all.' He stood up. 'I've still got it. Let me show it to you.'

It was almost ten minutes before Carling came back with a file and a piece of a newspaper. He put the picture on the low table between them. 'It's from the *Daily Herald*. I've never got it out of my mind.'

The picture was brown round the edges with age. It showed row on row of ill-clad men with hopeless faces trudging through the rain in a grim street of some industrial town.

Mathews looked up at Carling. 'Who are they?'

'They were the Jarrow marchers, unemployed men from Tyneside who had been thrown out of work. The woman at the front was a Labour politician, Ellen Wilkinson. Later, somebody lent me a book she wrote called *The Town that was Murdered*. Very sad. Very disturbing.' He went on. 'A miner in those days, after long hours down the pit, took home two pounds and four shillings a week. Even the poorly paid workers in the cotton mills earned more.'

'And you wanted to do something about it?'

'I wish I *could* say that. It made me angry and sad but it didn't enter my mind that I could do anything about it.' He smiled. 'I showed the book to my father. He just said the marchers had been wasting their time. And that led to our first big bust-up. But in fact he was typical of most of his contemporaries.'

'So what did you do?'

Carling shrugged. 'Nothing. Absolutely nothing. Except be uneasy and unhappy about those men and others like them. And in less than a year I was in the army.'

'Well at least you were doing your bit against Hitler and fascism.'

Carling sank back into his chair, shaking his head. 'Not really. Nothing so rational. I just joined up, because that was what most of my university friends did.' He shrugged and smiled. 'Let's say I was aware of the human predicament but not of politics. I guess that didn't start for another couple of years.'

'How did it start?'

He laughed. 'This is where you'll prick up your ears. It started because I was terribly impressed by the tremendous sacrifices of the Russians. Rather naïvely I wrote a letter to the Soviet Embassy praising their resistance to the Nazis.' He smiled and looked at Mathews. 'I got a letter back almost immediately. Thanking me for my letter and inviting me to an official cocktail party they were giving for Allied officers. I was on leave after doing a training course at the depot in Winchester. I was a lieutenant then. The party seemed quite formal, interminable toasts and around forty officers, most of them Brits including two brigadiers and several colonels.

'There was a young Russian captain introduced himself to me and said he had heard my mother sing at a concert in Vienna. He was a pleasant chap and we arranged to have a meal together. We went to an Italian place in Frith Street. He had noticed my I.Corps cap-badge and green flashes on my arm and he asked me the usual questions about when I thought the war would end and if I was going to stay on in the army. He told me about his family in Kiev and he spoke about the terrible casualties and the brutalities of the Germans in the areas they had captured.'

'What was your job at that time?'

'I was part of a team at GHQ Home Forces covering the German Order of Battle.'

'Did he ask about your work?'

'I guess we'd had three or four meals together before he asked me for any information.'

'Can you remember what he asked you?'

'Not exactly, but he was mainly interested in the movement of German troops from France to the East Front.'

'So that they had ammunition to pressure Winston
Churchill about mounting a Second Front?'

'I guess so.'

'You must have realised that you were committing an offence in passing military intelligence to a foreign national?'

'A foreign national who happened to be an ally. An ally
who was actually fighting our mutual enemy. Doesn't that
make a difference?'

'That's surely for other people to decide, not individuals
who only have one small piece of the jigsaw?'

'To my mind our people should have been passing that
information themselves to the Russians. How could it
affect our forces for our allies to know what the enemy
was doing?'

'That's not really the point. You were doing something
that you knew was an offence just because *you* decided it
was the right thing to do. Did it never strike you that you
may be endangering the lives of our men?'

'Tell me how it could do that?'

'I don't know. No more did you.'

'Do you think it might have saved some Russians' lives
to know where the Germans were moving up troops to
attack them?'

'I suppose so.' Mathews paused. 'Did they pay you for
the information?'

Carling looked shocked. 'Of course not.' He paused
and looked across at Mathews. 'Haven't you ever broken
the rules because you thought that the rules were stupid
sometimes?'

It was several moments before Mathews replied. 'I don't
think I have to answer that.'

Carling laughed softly. 'You're pleading the fifth, aren't you? That's the coward's way out.' He paused. 'Does the truth have to be only for me, my friend, but not for you?'

Mathews half smiled. 'OK. Yes, I have sometimes ignored orders or bent the rules when it seemed better to do that.'

'I rest my case, m'lord.'

Mathews laughed and then there was a knock on the door and the girl came in with sandwiches and coffee, placing them on a low table between them.

'Smoked salmon, beef and cheese. There's more if you want it,' she said.

'Thank you, Julie. How about you join us?'

For a moment she hesitated and then she said, 'I'd better not. There are things to do.'

Carling smiled at Mathews. 'She's going to make someone a wonderful wife.'

As she turned to go, Carling said, 'Hold on, my dear.' And turned to Mathews. 'Why don't you stay the night?'

'I didn't bring anything.'

Carling said to Julie, 'Give him my old study bedroom and find him a razor and the rest of it.'

'Right, sir.'

As she left Carling said, 'She's such a honey, that girl. Just does things. Nothing's too much trouble.'

'How long has she been with you?'

'Eat up. Help yourself.' He paused, thinking. 'I'd guess it must be – let me see – she was sixteen when she came here – must be five or six years.' He laughed. 'You don't remember dates and things too well at my age.' He paused. 'I say, she's given me some brie. I love brie.'

'How did you find her?'

'I often get asked to give talks. You know – Rotary and the WI. They insist on giving me a fee and think I'm being snobbish if I don't take it. There's an orphanage between Tunbridge Wells and Eastbourne and I get them to send the fee there.' He munched at his sandwich and then said, 'Saves all the bloody palaver with the Inland Revenue. It's seldom more than fifty quid.' He paused. 'Where was I? Why am I going on about all this?'

'The girl, Julie.'

'What about her?'

'How you found her?'

'Of course. What a fool.' He sighed. 'She was being a bit of a nuisance at the orphanage. I go there about once a month. They asked me to talk to her. Seemed reasonable enough to me. I don't think anyone had ever listened to her before. Been in care, fostered, the usual routine. But she was bright as a button. I fixed for her to have a tutor to get her a bit civilised. I gave her the job here about a year later. I had an old biddy who looked after me then. She was a motherly old soul and the girl loved her. Then the old lady died after about a couple of years and Julie has been on her own here ever since. She has a help two or three times a week and we've got a part-time gardener.' He looked at his watch. 'Let's have a break and Julie can show you your room.'

To Mathews the room seemed big. There were leaded windows along one wall and the other walls were lined with books. A comfortable-looking bed was under the windows and there was a hand-basin with a mirror and an electric razor on a glass shelf under the mirror. There was a white towelling bathrobe draped across the bed and a small table with a reading lamp at the head of the bed.

Mathews looked at a small pile of paperbacks on the bedside-table. There was Len Deighton's *The Ipcress File* and a couple of Linda Barneses, and Sue Grafton's *A is for Alibi*. At the bottom of the pile was an Ed McBain and John O'Hara's *A Rage to Live*. The books on the shelves were mainly reference books, dictionaries and a number of books in German. There was an old edition of *Encylopaedia Britannica* and a shelf of travel books and maps.

Mathews turned and walked to the windows. The late afternoon sun cast long shadows across the lawn from the budding fruit trees. Immediately below the windows was a paved area with a small formal pond already garnished with yellow marsh marigolds. Mathews opened one window and leaned with his arms on the stone window-sill. There were the sounds of sheep and lambs not far away. He wondered what he would have been doing if he had gone back to London. He'd probably have phoned Joanna or Mandy and taken her out to dinner at one of the Soho restaurants and then back to bed. They were both quite recent relationships. He hadn't messed about when he was married but he was determined now to make up for lost time but not be long-term committed. On the whole he decided that he was quite happy to be where he was. The house and its garden had a timeless air, a feeling that nothing would go wrong here. It reminded him of a painting by Monet, or was it Renoir?

He took off his jacket and stretched out on the bed. Somebody was playing the piano downstairs. Quiet, gentle, flowing music. The kind his mother loved so much. A few minutes later he was asleep.

CHAPTER 4

Carling had insisted, despite her protests, that Julie sat down to dinner with them. She was part of the family, he said. As they talked through the meal Mathews could see how Carling had built the young woman's self-confidence. His Lordship aired his views on *Coronation Street* and *EastEnders* but left it to the girl to point out the finer points of the characters and criticise where she thought *EastEnders* often went too far in its desire to be topical. They were both regular followers of *The Archers*. Mathews had listened with some amusement at the man who regularly appeared on TV arguing with great erudition the similarities of Satie's music with Picasso's painting.

When the meal was over, Julie discreetly disappeared and Carling had sat at the piano, thinking for a moment and then smiling, said, 'Let me play a piece of your mother's Chaminade. Is your mother a feminist by the way?'

'No. Far from it. Why do you ask?'

'Well, Chaminade is no longer popular and it wasn't until fairly recently that the feminists realised that she was a woman not a man. However . . . let me have a go at her. See if you recognise it.'

As Mathews listened he recognised the music. It was a song his mother often played, singing quietly as she smiled at his father. When Carling finished he turned to Mathews, smiling. 'I'm sure your mother will have played that for you.'

Mathews smiled back. 'I think she played it more for my father than for me.'

'Do you remember what it was called?'

'Was it "The Little Silver Ring"?'

'Well done, well done. Simple music but I like the words. The woman looking at the silver ring her lover gave her and thinking that the ring encircled all her life.' He smiled. 'They call it schmaltz but it's more than that.' Carling stood up. 'Anything more you want to know about what I've told you?'

'I'd like to know about your unit that covered the Order of Battle of the Germans. How did you get the information?'

Carling moved back to the armchair. 'SIS had agents in Europe and SOE had people in France and the Low Countries. We had people who read local newspapers – road accidents involving military vehicles, some sergeant in a unit who played football for a local team and then plays somewhere else when the unit moves elsewhere. Even radio request programmes of music for the Wehrmacht. Then there was photographic reconnaisance by the RAF. There was a continuous flow of small details that were analysed by our staff.'

'Did you ever ask your Russian friend about the Soviet forces?'

'A kind of quid pro quo, you mean?'

'Yes.'

'No.' He shrugged. 'It didn't seem likely to matter to our people where some Soviet tank brigade was stationed.' He paused. 'The war in Russia appeared to be in another world. It was a different war. We had enough of our own problems. We were glad that they were fighting the Germans but that was all.' He laughed softly. 'It was like my father and his friends who said you don't have to worry about the poor, they were used to being poor and you just let them get on with it.' He paused and looked at Mathews. 'Do you ever go to church?' He smiled and held up his hand as if to calm the surprise on Mathew's face. 'I ask because there's a performance of Fauré's Requiem at one of the churches in Tunbridge Wells tomorrow. It's one of my favourites. I chose the Kyrie when I did *Desert Island Discs*. I thought perhaps you might like to join me.' He smiled. 'You don't have to.'

Mathews hesitated for a moment and then said, 'I'd be glad to go with you.'

Carling looked at Mathews. 'Do you miss seeing your son?'

'Yes. A lot.'

'What's getting in the way?'

'My wife. I mean my ex-wife.' He paused and shrugged. 'It's just spite. A way of getting back at me.'

'Why should she do that?'

'God knows. It's probably Thomas, her solicitor and her intended new husband.' He paused. 'Everybody thinks he's very wealthy but he isn't. He's in debt up to his ears and he's also being looked at by the Law Society for misuse of clients' funds.'

'How do you know all that?'

'I've checked up on it myself.'

'You must have bent a few rules to do that.'

Mathews shrugged. He hadn't noticed Carling's half-smile. 'So what? It's my son who's going to suffer when it all goes wrong.'

'It must be a great worry for you.'

'It is.' He paused. 'That reminds me. That Left Book Club book you mentioned. Where did you get it?'

Carling laughed, softly. 'I was still at Harrow then and there were books passed around that could cause trouble if you were caught reading them. There were three or four circulating in my circle. The Left Book Club book was one of them, then there was *Lady Chatterley's Lover* and a lesbian novel called *The Well of Loneliness*. I can't remember the other one. They were all pretty innocuous by today's standards. I found them pretty boring even then. A few taboo words. Much ado about not very much.' He paused. 'Why did you ask?'

'It seemed that was really the start for you. The picture in the paper and then the book. I wondered how the spark was ignited.'

'Don't read too much into it. There were many young men who had similar thoughts to mine. Some were influenced enough to eventually become politicians.'

'But politics didn't interest you?'

'Not the slightest. I'd seen and heard them at home. My father's friends. I detested them.' Carling stood up. 'I think I'll get off to bed. Have a good night's sleep and breakfast's at about nine on Sundays.'

In his bedroom Mathews tried to collect his thoughts. Carling seemed a strange man but he had a lively mind despite his age. He wondered if Carling had ever been married. Apart from his title and possible wealth, he guessed he must be the kind of man that women would find very attractive. He wasn't handsome but his was a lived-in face and the features were the kind you saw on sculptured heads – a Roman face. But it was the eyes and mouth you would remember. Big, brown eyes and a full sensual mouth made wider by the smile creases each side of it. And above all you would remember his modesty. He listened intently when you spoke. Mathews felt in a way that Carling had been as much learning about him as the other way round, and he felt he had learned something from his talk with Carling but he wasn't sure what it was. He could understand now why Kennedy had briefed him not to rush things and not to leap to conclusions.

CHAPTER 5

They drove to the church in Carling's beautifully preserved Rover 3-litre, vintage 1963. When they were leaving after the service, Mathews realised how well-known His Lordship really was. It was slow progress back to where the car was parked as Carling had to stop at several groups of obviously admiring ladies. There were a bold few who even asked him to autograph hymn sheets and New Testament fly leaves. And Carling chatted amiably to all of them as if they were old friends.

Julie had put out an array of drinks for them in the conservatory where, as the back of the house faced due south, it was both warm and sunny despite it being barely the start of spring.

Carling sat with a glass of red wine and Mathews had a sherry.

'Well, Mr Mathews, what did you think of poor Fauré's Requiem?'

'I thought it wasn't bad for amateurs.' He paused. 'Why *poor* Fauré?'

'He never heard it sung. I think the first time it was performed was at his funeral.' He smiled. 'The French never like new ideas. But great on monuments to politicians.' He laughed. 'Just think of what they did for poor old Pompidou.' He paused. 'But they never take to new boys until they've become world famous. But at least they pretend to be civilised, which is more than our lot do.' He put his glass down on the white table-top, turning to look at Mathews. 'But I wouldn't trust that bloody parson with a fiver.' He emphasised his point with an extended finger. 'Never trust a man who uses words like "whomsoever". They hide behind words like some men hide behind beards. It's a sure sign of deviousness.'

'What were you doing when you were in Germany?'

'That was mainly counterintelligence. And, of course, denazification.'

'Did you keep in touch with your Russian friend in those days?'

Carling reached for his glass and turned it slowly, watching the wine swirling in the glass. Then he looked up at Mathews. 'In the last year of the war my contact was somebody else. Somebody more senior. I kept that contact when I was in Germany.'

'What information did you pass to them at that time?'

'In the last year of the war I was still in London and I kept them informed on what we and the Americans were planning about post-war Europe. And in Germany I passed them any evidence that came my way about Nazi war crimes against Soviet citizens, mainly civilians. Sometimes I could identify Russians and Ukrainians who had collaborated with the Nazis.' He paused and looked at Mathews. 'And no. They didn't pay me. They did give me a Leica IIIb, but that was, I believed, a genuine gift, not a reward. I could have got one myself in those days for a carton of cigarettes.'

'How did you pass the information to them?'

'In London it was the normal rigmarole of dead-letter drops and chalk marks on park benches for meetings in different places.' He smiled. 'They rather liked the James Bond bit. I suppose it was necessary. Our people had them under surveillance most of the time. Not always the right people, of course.'

'What sort of places did you use for meetings?'

Carling sighed, closing his eyes, thinking before he replied. 'It's hard to remember. It was a long time ago.' He paused, obviously trying to recall. 'There was a place in Frith Street, a printing place. A house in Finchley, the house of a Party member, a Scot.' He sighed. 'A prostitute's pad in Shepherd Market. A Joe Lyons café in Leicester Square. A shed on an allotment on Hackney Marshes.'

'You must have been a high-grade informant to rate that sort of treatment.'

'Yeah. I think I was. What I gave them was very useful to them. But it didn't harm us, their knowing.' He paused. 'You've got to remember, these people were our allies. Churchill presented Stalin with the Sword of Stalingrad on behalf of the British nation. What I passed to them ought to have been given to them by us as a matter of routine. It maybe saved thousands of lives, but what did Whitehall care?' He shrugged. 'The Russians were used to dying. It was a national pastime.'

'And in Germany?'

'No problem. I was in Hamburg and Berlin. In both cities there were Russian liaison units. The British Army treated them like genuine allies. They respected them. They were all serving soldiers. There were pretty wild parties every night of the week. Good food, lots of booze, and lots of pretty girls. Of course, SIS and Whitehall didn't feel the same way about our gallant allies and it was barely a year before the Cold War set in on both sides.'

'Who was your contact?'

'There were three or four depending on the material concerned. They were all military officers so far as I could tell.' He smiled wryly. 'Maybe they were NKVD but I don't think so.' Carling stood up. 'Let's have a bite to eat.'

'Is there any reason why you haven't named any of your contacts?'

Carling shook his head slowly. 'No reason at all except that on the one hand I don't remember their names and on the other hand it's not likely that the names they used were real.'

After they had eaten Carling said that he was going to take a nap.

'Meantime, my friend, make yourself at home.'

Mathews drove to the nearby village of Lamberhurst and tried to phone Kennedy but there was no answer. Knowing as he did it that it was stupid, he dialled what had once been his home number and it was Pamela who answered.

'Hello.'

'Hi. I just wanted to know how Tony is.'

'You've got a bloody nerve. You know you're not supposed to contact me except to make arrangements for having Tony.'

'So is it OK for next Saturday?'

'Your solicitor wrote to Roger complaining that I was trying to stop you seeing Tony. Roger's advised me to withdraw our voluntary agreement and get it settled formally by the court. And until it's been heard there's no access.'

'Do we really need to make a dogfight out of me seeing my son?'

'It was your solicitor who set the ball rolling, not mine.'

'What about Tony's interests?'

'He's got to get used to new circumstances. Roger has

explained it all to him.' She paused. 'After all, Roger will soon be his father.'

'You really are a bitch.' And he hung up, trembling with anger at the thought of Roger Thomas working hard to alienate his son from him. For a moment he touched his forehead to the coolness of the glass panel of the phone box until an old lady knocked on the door of the kiosk, gesticulating that she wanted to use the phone. As he held the door open for her she looked at him. 'Are you all right, young man?'

Confused, he said, 'I'm fine, thank you. It's a bit hot in there.'

He walked to his car trying to keep back the tears in his eyes because it was the first time in many months that somebody had shown even the slightest interest in how he felt.

The three of them had dinner together but Julie had taken out the dishes and left the two men together, still sitting at the table, with a bottle of Marks and Spencer's '91 Margaux between them.

Carling looked across at Mathews and said, 'I think it's time you called me George, and it's Tim, isn't it?'

'Yes, sir.' Then he laughed. 'It'll take me time to get used to it.'

Carling shrugged. 'A lot of nonsense anyway.' He paused. 'What's your next question?'

'You said you were never interested in politics because of the politicians you saw at your father's house. Does that mean you don't ever vote?'

'I voted Labour in 1945 like everybody else in the forces. Time for a change and all that. I felt they had the right ideas.'

'What made you stop voting Labour?'

'Well, Labour did a good job – in my opinion – for about six years. But they became, for me, the proof that our kind of politics in ridiculous.'

Mathews smiled. 'I don't follow the reasoning.'

'They made election promises about what they'd do if they were elected. They were elected. And they did what they promised to do.' Carling laughed softly. 'And then they had to get on governing the country and it was no longer a plan. Just responding to events. A bandage here and a Band-Aid there.' He shrugged. 'So they did stupid things, the bigots and extremists muddied the waters, and that for me was the end of Labour. They were just men desperate for power like all the others.' He paused. 'I don't think I've ever met a politician I'd really trust. To me they're suspect right from the start. Why do they want to be in politics? Not to do the rest of us good but to have the power to control our lives. I suspect all men who have power over people's lives. Judges, lawyers, priests, prison-warders, police, bosses of any kind. People who can sack a man just to save money or because they don't like him. Power is the corruption, not money. Remember the old adage – "money is the root of all evil"? It's always misquoted – First Epistle of Paul to Timothy – it's "*love* of money is the root of all evil". And the same applies to power. It's the love, the lust for power that is evil.' Carling laughed. 'My God, I'd better shut up. I'm beginning to sound like Billy Graham. Forgive me, my friend, but when the subject is politicians I tend to let rip.'

For Mathews it had been very revealing, an oldish man with such intolerance in one area where otherwise his character was so easy-going.

'I found it interesting. What are your views on lords?'

Carling thought for a moment. 'For those like me who

inherit the title – we're just stuck with it. But we generally have an advantage. We're either rich or fools. Seldom both – they tend to be self-cancelling. They've got enough money not to grind an axe for reward and a good many have been trained from childhood to responsibility for others who work for them.

'You can see it in the House of Lords. When some party egoist is given a life peerage he begins to relax. You'll hear more good sense spoken in the Lords than in the Commons. Even the front benches avoid the open lies and deceit that go on in the Commons.'

'What would you have liked to be if you weren't born to be a lord?'

Carling leaned back in his chair. 'What an interesting question.' He closed his eyes for long moments. When he opened them, he said, 'It's impossible to answer. All the bits and pieces contradict one another.' He shrugged. 'And I have no skills, no qualifications. Or at least, the only qualifications that I have are what everybody has but few people use.'

'What does that mean?'

'Most people look without seeing, listen without hearing and have only enough love to love themselves. I think for some reason I'm not like that. But such talents as I have are not virtues but just how I was born.'

'So where are the contradictions you spoke of?'

'Contradictions?' Carling looked puzzled. Then, 'Ah yes, contradictions.' He smiled. 'I've often wished I was a Jew. A member of a community that never had a square deal from the world in general. I've got a need to fight for oppressed people.' He laughed. 'And I'd hope that being a Jew would have made me a great musician.' He paused. 'The contradiction is that I'd also like to be an Italian.' He looked at Mathews. 'That's surely contradiction enough?'

'Tell me. Why Italian?'

'I just like Italians. They're alive, they wear their hearts on their sleeves, they love music and art and all things artistic. Not just the upper classes but working classes too.' He smiled. 'And they like old people and kids.' He reached for the bottle. 'One last glass, Tim?'

'I've had enough, thanks. Thanks for making it easy to talk to you.'

Carling smiled. 'We've got a long way to go, my friend.'

CHAPTER 6

———————————

Mathews was buttering his last piece of toast when Carling joined him for breakfast. There were untouched copies of *The Times* and the *Daily Mail* at the side of Carling's place.

'Which do you want?' Carling said. 'The *Mail* or *The Times*?'

'Neither thank you. I'm going to London for the day, is it OK if I come back tomorrow?'

'Of course. I never move from here if I can avoid it.'

'Is there anything I could get you in London?'

'Let me think.' He paused for a moment. 'They've just issued a new CD of Korngold's fiddle concerto. I'd be grateful if you could get me a copy. Do you know Korngold's music?'

'Didn't he write film music?'

'Well done. Yes. So the poor man is despised by all the cognoscenti. But in fact he was a fine musician.' Carling grinned. 'Could be me, my alter ego, despised because I make good money writing popular music and ostracised because I'm a Jew.'

Mathews said quietly, 'What kind of friends do you have?'

'Friends?' Carling was silent for a moment. 'Good friends – none. Pleasant, interesting contacts and acquaintances –

scores of them. All over Europe. But not friends. That's too much responsibility. Sometimes you let friends down.'

'Have you ever let a friend down?'

It seemed a long time before Carling answered. Then he said quietly, 'I can think of two occasions when I let a friend down. I still regret it.'

'Who were they? What happened?'

Carling shook his head. 'I wouldn't want to talk about it.'

As he reached for the marmalade Carling said, 'You know music makes strange bedfellows. Did you know that when he was a young man Nye Bevan was madly in love with a young woman cellist?'

'No. I didn't know that. Seems out of character. Both the loving and the cello.'

'They're very popular, lady cellists. They all seem so very beautiful.' Then as a seeming afterthought Carling said, 'And it *is* a lovely instrument. Beautiful to listen to and lovely to look at.' He smiled at Mathews. 'We do go on, us old fogeys.'

Mathews laughed. 'You'll never be an old fogey, that's for sure.'

For a moment Mathews thought that Carling looked surprised, or sad. He wasn't sure which.

Mathews stopped in Sevenoaks and made three phone calls, all to London numbers.

His meeting with Kennedy was relaxed and Kennedy smiled from time to time as Mathews reported on his stay with Carling.

When he finished, Kennedy said, 'You seem to have laid out the foundations of a relationship. What did you think of him?'

Mathews shrugged. 'Hard to describe. Definitely left wing although he claims he doesn't know what left wing means. Seems too easy-going to be playing games with the Russians.'

'He's admitted to you that he passed restricted information to a Soviet contact during the war?'

'But the onus in court would be on us to prove it. Anyway, most people today would probably approve of what he did.' He paused. 'You said at my briefing that he was suspected of other things. What were they?'

For a few moments Kennedy seemed absorbed in checking the date and time on his digital desk clock, and then he said, 'Remember way back when the media were always going on about the so-called Fourth Man? And in the end poor old Blunt was left with no chair to sit on when the music stopped?'

'I remember it vaguely.'

'The media decided that whoever the Fourth Man was he had tipped off Burgess that we were closing in on him. In fact we knew exactly who had tipped off Burgess and it certainly wasn't Blunt. Nor was it anyone in SIS. It was a politician's stupidity. Anyway it was obvious that Blunt was going to carry the can as the Fourth Man so we did a deal with him. Trading what he had been up to in exchange for immunity. A bit like you're doing with friend Carling. Except that in Blunt's case there was virtually nothing to tell us that was significant. But we knew all along that Burgess, Philby and Maclean weren't the only ones working for the Soviets. We reckoned there were at least three others. Blunt was one of them. There was an academic of sorts and there was Carling.

'We had enough to take both Burgess and Maclean to court and know we would win and they'd get long sentences. But they had done a bolt to Moscow and were no longer in our jurisdiction, so they were out. The DPP and the Attorney-General himself said that despite all the stuff we had on Philby it wouldn't stick in the High Court. Philby wasn't sure how much we'd got on him so he didn't resist when we quietly moved him out. After SIS he worked as a journalist in the Middle East for *The Economist* and one or two newspapers. There were hard feelings in high quarters in SIS about Philby, and Nick Elliott was sent out to pressure Kim in Beirut to get a confession that would stand up in court. Philby admitted everything but lit out for Moscow a few days later.' He paused. 'There are still people in SIS or who have retired who think we should be looking much harder at Carling.'

'Are you one of those people?'

Kennedy hesitated and then said, 'I guess I'd like to know what *did* happen way back. And, if I'm truthful I'd like to know if friend Carling carried on after the Philby gang had been dealt with. But I don't go all the way with some of them when they talk of prosecution.' He smiled. 'That's why I was glad to get approval for my suggestion that you carry out this little exercise to test the water before anybody starts splashing around.' He looked at his watch. 'I've got to go, Tim. Next year's departmental budgets.'

Mathews' meeting with Latham, his solicitor, was in Hampstead and as he drove there he went over in his mind his talk with Kennedy. Kennedy had seemed satisfied with the rather disjointed and inconclusive report on his time with Carling. It still sounded a bit of a wild-goose chase, but if that's what they wanted, so be it. As he parked his car and walked up to the High Street, he wondered what Latham would have to say. It always seemed to him as if

Latham had more sympathy with the other side. It had been an easy ride so far. No great conflict over the divorce and the financial settlement. But now she was playing games about access he needed somebody who was totally on his side.

When Mathews was settled in the visitor's chair, Latham said, 'I'm sorry you're having problems about access to the child. How often has it happened?'

'Three times so far.'

'In what period?'

'Ten weeks.'

'Any idea why she's playing up?'

'I assume she gets a kick out of being bloody-minded.'

'What reasons has she given?'

'A Cub camp, a cold, and some other engagement.'

'Any offer of an alternative access?'

'No. She just hangs up on me when I protest.'

'I've had a letter from her chap suggesting that it should be settled by the court and meantime that there should be no access. What do you feel about that?'

'How long before it could be heard?'

'Ten to twelve weeks at the moment.'

'What alternatives do I have?'

'I had an unofficial word with the other party's solicitor but there was no joy there. He said his client had given him firm instructions to go back to the court. Not very co-operative, I'm afraid.'

'Why should he be co-operative?' Mathews said angrily. 'He gets his costs out of my pocket and screws her into the bargain. And they both get a kick out of harassing me.'

'Don't make comments like that elsewhere, Mr Mathews, or we shall be facing a writ for slander and we couldn't prove a thing.'

'I've checked a dozen times in the last three months. His car was in the drive all night.'

'You mean you checked on them yourself?'

'Yes.'

'Mr Mathews, I must advise you very earnestly not to pursue this – this matter. We should be on very thin ice. Very thin ice indeed.' He paused. 'Remember, in the eyes of the court she is entitled to have a relationship with anyone she chooses. She's a free woman now.'

'She told me that she will be marrying him shortly and to remember that the bastard will then be Tony's father.'

'You mean she intends marrying Roger Thomas?'

'So she says.'

Latham took a deep breath. 'It's best I make no comment on that but she's talking nonsense about your son. You're his father and always will be. Even if she does marry him, which I very much doubt, they couldn't have Thomas adopt him without your agreement.'

'Which they'd never get.'

'Quite. I'd still like to suggest a policy of wait and see – for at least a few weeks. There's little else we can do.' He stood up, holding out his hand. 'Sorry to seem so negative but I want the court to see that we have kept to the rules. I'll write a pressing note to Thomas, just for the record.'

'Do you know him personally?'

'Yes, I do. Off the record I can assure you he won't be marrying your ex-wife. That's for sure.'

'Is this because of the Law Society enquiry?'

Latham turned his head quickly to look at Mathews. 'How on earth do you know about that?'

'I checked up on him.'

'You or a private investigator?'

'Me.'

'Well, for Chrissake don't tell me. I don't want to know.'
He shrugged. 'I'll send you a copy of my letter to Thomas.'

The estate agent had described the flat as being in Chelsea
but in fact it was well into Pimlico. Nevertheless, it was
pleasant, with a distant view of the Thames. It had two
rooms with kitchen and bathroom, newly decorated and
with fitted carpets supplied by the landlord.

There were half a dozen letters in the box. The one
Mathews opened first was his bank statement and for
once he had more in his account than he expected. There
was an offer for double-glazing, two insurance offers and a
brochure from BUPA. The last letter was from his parents.
Nothing startling. He smiled to himself as it went through
his mind that letters from his mother were what would be
classed as nil reports in Century House.

When the phone rang he picked it up as he went on
reading his parents' letter.

'Hello.'

'Hi, Tim, Joanna. Do you still want to see that stuff
from our morgue?'

'Yes, please. Are you OK?'

'Yeah. If you could come round now you could have an
hour with it.'

'Where?'

'*Daily Mail*, you eejit. Northcliffe House. Yes or no?'

'Yes, please. I'll get a taxi. Will you be there?'

'Of course. And you'll owe me a decent dinner. See you.'
And she hung up.

He had only known Joanna for about three months.
She was twenty-five, exceptionally pretty and worked as
a researcher for the gossip and showbusiness sections of
the *Daily Mail*. Her aim was a column of her own, which

almost certainly meant a move to another paper. She was modest but slightly bossy, which he put down as part of her job specification. They had met at the wedding of mutual friends and she had slept with him that first night. She made it seem rather like being awarded the *Good Housekeeping* seal of approval.

She was waiting for him in the entrance hall of the newspaper offices, giving him a peck on the cheek as she took him to stairs leading down to the basement.

'I've had a quick look through the file in the morgue. Why are you interested in this old boy? He looks quite intriguing. A milord who seems to be permanently agin all kinds of authority is a rare bird.'

'I just need a bit of background, honey. And I've booked us a table at Jardin des Gourmets for eight. By the way – am I allowed to make notes from the cuttings?'

'Of course. It's all run-of-the-mill stuff.' She opened a door. 'Here we are. The files are on the table with the reading lamp. I'll be back in an hour. If anyone asks you what you're doing, you're working on some research for me. OK?'

'That's fine.'

'Any problem, my extension number's in the internal directory by the phone.'

The Carling records were housed in three old-fashioned box-files labelled with the periods they covered. He started going through the latest material.

As Mathews riffled through the cuttings it was obvious that until recently Carling had been an avid writer of letters to editors, mainly to *The Times* and the *Guardian*. They were usually provocative and against the grain, defending some writer or painter or performer who had been the victim of some excoriating review. What was interesting was that Carling's letter always evoked a torrent of letters in support of his views.

One of his recent letter campaigns had been his suggestion that what the country needed was another Festival of Britain to remind the world and the country of all the successes in science and the arts that the nation had achieved in the last three decades. The correspondence had gone on for weeks and *The Times* had eventually not only supported the idea but had subtly taken it over as if it had been their original thought.

The harassment by the media of politicians and public figures for their alleged sexual or financial indiscretions had been another of Carling's targets. We are all sinners, was his theme, but most of us don't get found out. There was an unusually sharp letter about the behaviour of Lord Wigg and the part he had played in the Profumo affair. It was clear that George Carling was always on the side of the losers and victims of media or political hypocrisy. Despite this he seemed to be admired by the very people he criticised.

There were brief pieces about two different betrothals over the years. One to a distant relation when he was in his early twenties, and the other in his mid-forties to a Polish film actress. From the grainy pictures the only thing they appeared to have in common was that they were both exceptionally beautiful. From the typed chronology on the cover of the files it was clear that there had been no marriage in either case.

There were dozens of photographs with brief captions of Carling at first nights of plays and films, standing in line to be spoken to by the Queen or some other member of the royal family. Almost half of the photographs were of Carling at similar functions in other European capitals,

Warsaw, Prague, Budapest, Vienna and Berlin, where his status seemed to be as an unofficial representative of the Arts Council or as a guest of the government concerned.

There were a few interviews for women's magazines by women journalists who mainly asked questions about what it was like to be an earl. The tone was always friendly and only one interviewer had asked him about his time in intelligence. He had, it seemed, laughingly dismissed it as the mistaken patriotism of a rather naïf young man. It was obvious that the ladies had taken to His Lordship. One of them had suggested that he looked rather like Peter Finch in the Oscar Wilde film.

There was nothing worth copying and when his hour was up and Joanna came for him, the box-files were already closed and put to one side.

They had a long, pleasant meal at Jardin des Gourmets and then took a taxi back to her flat in Chelsea.

As she poured them drinks and handed him a glass, she said, 'Why are you interested in Lord Carling?'

He shrugged. 'Just a routine check-up. Why do you ask?'

'There has been talk about one of the papers doing some sort of exposé on SIS and Carling's name was mentioned.'

'Which paper was it?'

'I'm not sure but I think it's the *Sun*. It came up at our own editorial meeting last week. They didn't give the name of the paper or the source of the rumour. But I think it was being taken seriously.'

He smiled. 'Let's go to bed.'

As they sat at the table after dinner, Carling said, 'What are you reading at the moment?'

Julie smiled. 'You're just checking on whether I'm reading that paperback you gave me.'

'Which one's that?'

'*Aristotle on Ethics*.'

'Ah yes. What d'you make of it?'

'A load of rubbish for people who've got nothing better to do than sit around nit-picking about what is courage or happiness.'

'You don't feel it helps to analyse the various types of courage or happiness?'

'No way. We all know what courage is and we all know what happiness is. It's like when you take me to posh restaurants and the waiter asks me whether I want it on or off the bone. What does it matter? Either way it's just a piece of fish.'

He smiled. 'I like that, my dear. Courage – on or off the bone.' He paused. 'Speaking of virtues, what do you think of our young man?'

She shrugged. 'He doesn't trust anyone. And I don't trust him either.'

'Give me an example.'

'I can't. I just know it. Feminine intuition.'

'He's very bright.'

'But not much heart.' She paused and looked at him. 'Don't trust him, Georgie. I don't know what you and he are up to but he's not as innocent as he looks.'

He smiled and reached over, covering her hand with his as he said, 'Don't worry, my dear. We'll make him human between us.' He paused. 'By the way. Do you think he's handsome?'

She nodded. 'Yeah. Very. That's his only virtue in my book. He's very attractive especially as he doesn't seem to realise it.'

He laughed. 'There's philosophy for you. Who needs Aristotle?'

CHAPTER 7

They were sitting on the trunk of a tree that had come down in the long-forgotten hurricane. It was on the edge of the woodland and warm from the spring sunshine.

'How did you get transferred from Field Security in Germany to SIS?' Mathews asked.

'Well, when the war was over there were lots of officers who wanted to get back to civilian life as soon as possible before all the jobs had been taken,' said Carling. 'I was interviewed by a couple of chaps, one who knew me well, and we had three or four meetings and then they offered me a job in SIS.'

'Doing what?'

'They didn't specify my duties but I was put on the German desk with special responsibility for the Russian Zone that eventually became East Germany. Then for several years I was a kind of interface, as they called it, between the German section both West and East, and the Soviet desk.'

'You must have had contact with Philby at that stage?'

'I already knew Philby. We had met when we were visiting lecturers at Beaulieu for SOE.'

'What did you lecture on?'

'The war was still on then, of course. Philby dealt with the structure of the Nazi Party and its organisation, and

I talked on the German intelligence services. The Abwehr, the Gestapo, the SD and Gehlen's organisation, Foreign Armies East.'

'How did you get on with Philby?'

'I liked him. He was sociable and he played the piano very well – Jerome Kern, Irving Berlin, Gershwin – that sort of thing. But I didn't spend much time with him. I wasn't, as they say, "into" drinking and the party games.' Carling shrugged. 'Most people liked him. He was very charming. Except to his women, of course. He treated them very shabbily. Not, perhaps, a man to admire.'

'How often did you come into contact with him?'

'Three or four times for SOE and fairly regular brief contacts at meetings at Broadway. Much later I saw him a couple of times in Washington when he was at our embassy and I was visiting Langley.'

'Were you surprised when he turned out to be a traitor?'

'Nobody was ever able to substantiate that he was a traitor. Only he knows what he did or didn't do.'

'Him and Nick Elliott, of course.'

'All that Nick ever got was what Kim Philby told him. Who knows what the actual truth was. Senior SIS men, including at least two directors-general, have been accused of treason by the media.' He smiled. 'But only after they were dead.'

'If that suggestion was made in the press about you, what would you do? Would you sue them?'

Carling said quietly, 'Let's wait and see, shall we?' They walked over to the ornamental pond and stood looking at the fish. 'I used to have plenty of koi but the herons from Bewl Water take them. Maybe I should just keep to the goldfish and frogs.'

Mathews hesitated and then said, 'Do you mind me continuously asking questions?'

It was a moment before Carling replied. 'I think you've been very diplomatic, dear boy. It could easily have slipped into an interrogation rather than a stroll down memory lane.' He laughed. 'It's a bit like our old friend Proust and *A la recherche du temps perdu.* No. You carry on asking. The only thing you have to bear in mind is that that was then and this is now. It was a long time ago. And the world was very different then.'

'You said you didn't like politics because of the politicians you met at your father's house. Was that the only reason?'

'If I said I didn't like politics that was a mistake. It's politicians I don't like. Not just ours but all politicians. It angers me that a quite small group of power-hungry men can decide the fate of millions of young men.' He paused and then said, 'OK. Let them decide on war but on one condition – that the next day they will all be shot or hanged.' He laughed softly. 'We old boys can be terribly bloodthirsty under our Marks and Spencer's woolly sweaters.'

After sandwiches for lunch, Carling went up to his study bedroom and pulled the leather chair to the windows that ran from ceiling height to floor level.

Mathews had shown him the picture of him with Oleg in Shepherd Market. As always with surveillance pictures it was taken on 35mm fast film and the print was hopelessly grainy. His own face was only just identifiable. Mathews had said that they thought the shot was taken somewhere near Broadcasting House. He had said that he didn't recognise the other man in the picture. Poor Oleg. He was a born loser and his compatriots had used him ruthlessly, swearing that they valued his contribution to the war effort. But all they had wanted was to establish a working relationship so that they could insert Panov. Panov was more sophisticated. He had worked for them in Paris before the war and for a time in Australia. He understood how to use the idealism of foreign sympathisers. Never wanting more than was reasonable, and trading the gossip of NKVD intelligence headquarters in return. Not averse to a sly joke about Stalin or some lesser Kremlin figure. Never an offer of money or valuables but just building the feeling of being comrades in a cause that was going to liberate the poor and oppressed, the workers who created the world's wealth. Carling wondered how far up the ladder of Soviet life you had to go to find the men who actually knew that it was all no more than a dream.

The problem was that it was a highly desirable dream. It's not easy to abandon a dream. The indications that it was all a myth could perhaps be mistaken. Analyse it how you will, the men who created that dream had had good intentions. There were simpler ways just to grab power. Why such an elaborate scenario? It was no more than a variation of those loving words on the Statue of Liberty – 'Give me your tired, your poor, Your huddled masses yearning to breathe free . . .' Maybe the Americans hadn't lived up to those generous sentiments, but way back they must have meant them and that was a similar dream. These days, with the benefit of hindsight, people said it had all been nothing but a dream. But they were wrong. Underneath it all was that longing for a better life for everyone. Why should that be just a dream? Why let it all go? Perestroika and glasnost mustn't wipe out the dream.

The young man Mathews was sharp and observant, but Carling wondered what sort of life he led. Mathews seemed too controlled, lacking in enthusiasm for being alive. A man without a goal to reach for. Earthly but not worldly. Hard-working but not creative. He'd have to work on him. How could he explain to a man like that what had motivated people like Philby? In the end, of course, Philby had gone too far and arrogance had taken over.

Poor Philby had always dreaded the thought of ending up in Moscow. He spoke no Russian and he knew all too well that once you were no longer in a position to supply them with intelligence you would be of no use to them. They'd treat you well. A decent flat and even, perhaps, a dacha at Peredelkino. A life status equivalent to that of a general, but stuck with Burgess and Maclean and a few KGB 'friends' involved in your interminable debriefing. For a defecting double agent could even be a triple agent. And Kim was, in any case, a dyed-in-the-wool Brit. Even in Washington he had to know the latest Test match score. He had avoided Moscow for so long and taken such risks in so doing that Moscow had wondered about his commitment. The SIS conclusion was that a drunken evening and his confession to Nick Elliott had left him no choice. He didn't even return to the dinner party he had left. The Order of Lenin would be no consolation for Kim Philby. And with the boredom and monotony of his useless life he ended up ruining the lives of a few more women. Somebody had once described Kim Philby as a romantic shit. But Kim was never really romantic. Charming yes, but romantic no.

Carling sighed as he wondered how long the business with Mathews would have to go on. Kennedy obviously wanted to make sure that he was going to get his pound of flesh before he did a deal, so the longer he himself could drag it out the better. And the longer he could keep them in the past the safer he would be. He could choose his own cut-off point. Give them enough to see it as a confession for past deeds and do a deal and Kennedy would be satisfied. He smiled to himself at the thought of using them instead of them using him.

CHAPTER 8

━━━━━

'Julie and I are going over to the orphanage. Would you like to come with us? It's all very informal.' Carling smiled. 'It gets them a couple of inches in the local rag and that helps donations.'

'Are you sure I won't be in the way?' asked Mathews.

'Of course not. It's just a flying visit.'

As they drove down the Eastbourne road, Carling related how the orphanage had been given the big house in an old lady's will and £500,000 for its upkeep as an orphanage for girls. The money had been wisely invested and they now had a reliable regular income. He said that the director of the orphanage was a very Christian woman and Julie had laughed and said, 'That's how he always describes people he doesn't like. She ought to be running a prison. She's a great believer in retribution.'

Carling smiled. 'I think it would be fair to say that she runs a very tight ship. But she has her problems. Not every girl is like our Julie.'

As the car crunched to a standstill on the gravel drive, the massive oak doors of the house stood open and a young girl waved to them from the steps. As they approached she gave a little curtsey to His Lordship and said, 'Madam's compliments, m'lord, and she's waiting for you in her room.'

In her comfortable room, Madam, a grey-haired woman in her late fifties, welcomed them and invited them to sit. There were sponge cakes and glasses of milk on a low table placed strategically between them. Mathews had been introduced as a friend. Proceedings followed what was obviously a well-tried formula. She related and detailed new donations and details of girls who were receiving instruction in domestic and commercial skills and finally a few details of problem girls. Problems ranging from disobedience to defiance, from promiscuity to pregnancy.

There was, it seemed, one special problem. Her name was Gabriella, surname not yet established. Parents unknown both as to names and circumstances. Intelligent guess said that she was part West Indian and part Spanish or Italian. She had been in institutions since being left in a cardboard box on the steps of a police station in Liverpool. She had been passed from one foster parent to another. None of the relationships had been successful and now, aged sixteen, she had a six-month-old child. Girls with babies or children were not accepted at the orphanage and Madam was at her wit's end. The girl refused to go into the Council hostel. Madam described her as both feckless and irresponsible, and blamed the West Indian blood. She accepted that the girl loved the baby but she had to go where the authority decided was suitable. Would His Lordship persuade her to do as she was told. His Lordship said he would talk to the girl. The last item of news was that three of her girls now had full-time jobs locally and were soon to leave the orphanage for their own places. There were a dozen names on the Council list for three new girls to fill the vacancies at the orphanage. There was a touch of Miss Jean Brodie about Madam.

*   *   *

In the small room with its cot and single bed the young girl was sitting watching the sleeping baby. She stood up as Madam introduced them all before she left. Mathews was amazed. The young girl was so beautiful, with a mane of black hair, big dark eyes and a wonderful, dazzling smile.

Carling sat beside her on the edge of the bed. She talked animatedly with delicate movements of her hands as he chatted to her. The baby's name was Carlotta. No, that wasn't anything to do with the father's name. She spoke as if the father were of no importance.

When Carling said gently, 'You obviously very much wanted this baby, am I right?' she beamed.

'She's all I shall ever want.' And her hand went between the bars of the cot to touch the sleeping baby.

'Why is she so important to you?' Carling said quietly.

For a moment she looked at the baby and then she turned to look at Carling. 'All my life I've longed for somebody to love me and to have somebody to love myself. That's why.'

Mathews saw Julie looking at Carling's face. For a moment they were all silent and then Carling said, 'You know Julie, don't you? She used to be here. Now she looks after my home for me. She needs some help. There is a small flat over my garage that was meant for a chauffeur. You could have that and a small wage for helping Julie. Would you like that?'

There was a long silence and then she said softly, 'Do you really mean that?'

'Yes. If you want it.'

'When? When could I come?'

Carling looked at Julie, eyebrows raised in query. She laughed and shrugged as she nodded. And Carling said, 'I'll have a word with Madam, Gabriella. You and Julie collect up all your things and the baby's things. I'm sure Madam will let us borrow the cot until we get one of your own.'

She flung her arms around his neck, kissing him like small children kiss people who have just given them a highly desirable present. His Lordship seemed to enjoy it.

When they arrived back at Lake Cottage there was a large black limousine parked in the lane and as they turned into the drive there was a uniformed chauffeur.

'Good afternoon, milord. BBC.'

'BBC?' Carling said. 'I don't understand.'

'The arts discussion show.'

'But that's not until the thirtieth.'

'It's the thirtieth today, sir. But we've got plenty of time. No hurry at all.'

Carling stood transfixed and then turned to Mathews. 'My God, Tim, I'll have to go. Can't let them down. How about you come with me?'

Mathews grinned. 'I'd enjoy it.'

Carling turned to Julie. 'Can you make our new young lady at home, my dear?'

She smiled. 'Of course I can. But have a cuppa before you go.'

It was over an hour before they both left for the drive to London. Carling had insisted on checking out the rooms over the garage himself and had gone over with Julie the things to be brought from the house that Gabriella and her baby daughter might need that night.

There were four participants in the discussion programme and the producer, a woman in her early thirties, briefed them all after they had been to make-up.

'As you all know, the subject for this evening is government funding of the Arts.' She smiled a professional smile. 'Is it enough? Is it distributed effectively? And does the taxpayer get value for money? As much controversy as you want. No holds barred. Let the chips fall where they will.' She handed over to another woman who said, 'Cars have been laid on immediately after the show for those who have asked for them but there's a meal available for those who can stay.' She smiled. 'Best of luck. Enjoy the show.'

One member of the group was a senior spokesman for the Arts Council, a man who knew exactly how much money had gone where from government funding. His opposite number was a musician from an orchestra whose funding and future existence were in doubt. The third participant was a left-wing journalist whose carping criticism of the government was too obviously political. The programme had followed its expected course. The Arts Council man and the orchestral musician were at loggerheads from the start. And Carling intervened from time to time in support of either argument.

It was in the last five minutes of a diatribe by the journalist that Carling took him on.

'Do you seriously suggest that there should be no funding of the Arts in this country? The second biggest earner of tourist currency?'

The journalist sneered. 'I should have thought that I had already made that clear. The answer to your question is yes. Not a penny. The prices of theatre tickets, concert tickets, opera tickets make them an entertainment for the rich not the man in the street.'

'And what would you suggest the money be spent on instead?'

His face suffused with anger, the man said, 'Have you

seen the disgracefully poor figures of our aid to Third
World countries?'

Carling smiled. 'My friend, I have a definition of aid to
poor countries – aid is poor people in rich countries giving
money to rich people in poor countries.'

The producer recognised the perfect ending that could
hit tomorrow's headlines and signalled to the presenter to
close the show.

In the hospitality room, the man sitting next to Mathews
said, 'He's a real bastard, that man.'

Mathews shrugged. 'He's just a journalist grinding his
axe.'

'I don't mean him,' the man said. 'I mean that stupid
old fart Carling.'

They didn't stay for a meal. Carling said he was tired
and wanted to get back home.

It was after midnight and there wasn't much traffic but
they were held up by a garbage truck. Carling looked out
of the window and suddenly said, 'My God.' He spoke to
the driver. 'Is this Drayton Gardens?'

'Yes, milord. It is.'

Carling turned to Mathews. 'That house across the street
there. That is where Kim Philby's mother's flat was. That's
where he gave the press conference after Macmillan had
cleared him in a statement to Parliament.'

Mathews followed Carling's gaze. It was just beginning
to rain and the old Victorian house looked grim and
forbidding with its bay windows and net curtains. It passed
through his mind that Carling must have known it very well
to have recognised it. Carling was still looking at the house
as the garbage truck moved on to release them.

Mathews saw the tiredness on Carling's face as he sat

with his head back, the streetlights turning his big hand-some features into the face of a Roman statue. Then Carling said quietly, 'Do you think she'd have settled in all right?'

'I'm afraid I never knew her.'

Carling opened his eyes and turned his face to look at Mathews. 'Never knew who?'

'Philby's mother.'

'I meant the little girl – Gabriella. One more strange place after a life of being shunted from one ghastly place to another.' He sighed. 'And you have a baby so that you've got somebody who'll love you and who you can love.'

'She seemed pleased enough with her new home.'

'Poor soul,' Carling said. He gave a deep sigh as if for the whole of humanity. 'I'm going to take a nap, old chap.'

As he lay back in his seat with his eyes closed he could still see the house and he wondered why Kim had always lived in such gloomy places. The place that was now the orphanage had been the training school for radio operators in the war and it had been chosen because it was handy for Philby's house at Crowborough. Another grim building. He'd seen a photograph of it when *The Times* was doing one of its pieces on Philby, years ago. He could remember when Philby was so much at odds with Aileen, his wife, that he was living in a tent in the back garden of that wretched house.

CHAPTER 9

It was a bright sunny day and they had walked down to the ruins of an old abbey, Bayham Abbey, about a mile from the cottage. Julie had given them each a Mars bar and as Mathews unwrapped his he said, 'How did Philby get to know Burgess and Maclean?'

'Do you know about Litzi?'

'No.'

'I'll have to go back a bit to Cambridge. Philby was first spotted as having either extreme socialist or mild communist leanings by a don at Trinity named Maurice Dobb. He was a more or less open communist and on his last day at Trinity, Philby spoke to him about joining the Party. Dobb realised that he was too potentially useful to have as a mere member.

'Dobb gave him a lead to a group of communists in Paris who passed him on to Vienna. There was a lot of trouble there with Nazi sympathisers eager to integrate with Germany. Philby threw himself into the fight against them, acting as a courier and getting hunted communists over the border into Czechoslovakia. He was sent to stay with a chap named Israel Kohlman who was a committed Party worker. Kohlman had a young daughter in her early twenties. Her name was Alice. Alice Friedmann. Everybody called her Litzi. She'd already been married and divorced.

'In the end she was on the Nazis' wanted list and the simplest way to get her out of the country was for Philby to marry her. They were lovers already, but I think the marriage was equally a marriage of convenience.' Carling smiled. 'Hugh Gaitskell and his wife were the witnesses at the marriage in Vienna.

'They came back to England and Kim started a fund to raise money for Austrian workers who by then had been totally defeated by the Nazis. He gave a fund-raising talk at Trinity and that was when he first had contact with Guy Burgess who was on a fourth-year research scholarship.

'For a short time Philby was quite openly a communist. People just accepted it.'

'So why was he recruited for SIS with a background like that?'

Carling shook his head. 'With hindsight it's incredible. But it's the old, old story. With a war coming or actually started you had to recruit new people in a hurry. There's no litmus paper for loyalty, so you turn to the old-boy network. The old boys themselves are too old and they've all got other responsible positions. So you go for their sons. Philby's father was a well-respected man. An explorer, an Arabist and all the rest of it. His son, Kim, had been a first-class games player and a very successful scholar. What more do you want?' He paused. 'Nobody looked into his background at that stage. And by the time they started looking, he had created himself a right-wing background. Reporting from the Franco side for *The Times* when Franco was killing socialism and socialists in his own country in a dress rehearsal for World War Two.' Carling smiled and went on, 'Forgetting any suspicions of helping the Russians, I still wouldn't be recruited by SIS today. I'm not good enough by any standards.'

'What happened to Philby's wife?'

'Litzi? They divorced and she just faded out of sight. She got into films in East Germany. Was disappointed in their lack of progress towards communism. Moved to West Berlin and then to France where, as far as I know, she lives today.'

'Who actually recruited Philby for the Russians?'

Carling turned his head, looking at the distant hills for long moments before he looked at Mathews again.

'Let me just say that it wasn't a Russian who recruited him. He's still alive. Never been under any suspicion. He's near the end of his days. He deserves to die in peace.'

'Why?'

'Why what?'

'Why should he die in peace?'

'Dear boy, you're doing what they all do. You're looking down the wrong end of the telescope.'

'I don't understand.'

Carling reached down to pick a daisy, looking at it carefully and Mathews saw for the first time a look of anger on the old man's face. It went quite quickly as he turned back to Mathews.

'If you ignore Philby's contacts with the Russians, he had the kind of war record that would have got anyone else at least a medal, maybe a knighthood. His work to defeat the Germans was incredibly effective. Long hours, great energy and consistently good planning and execution of everything he handled. That was the core of his work during the war and it can't be just swept under the carpet.' He wagged his finger at Mathews. 'And remember what I said, the Russians were our allies. He wasn't helping our enemy.'

Mathews half smiled. 'I'm sorry. I've obviously annoyed you.'

'I wouldn't say that.' Then he smiled. 'Yes, you have annoyed me. But you weren't there at the time. You can be forgiven. But there are people who were there who still distort the facts for their own reasons.'

'What reasons?'

'Who knows, Tim? Who knows? If you ever discover them, please do tell me.' He paused. 'Jealousy, maybe. Just look at what they did to poor old Blunt. Offered him immunity in exchange for a full confession and then let it leak to the press. And then, the shameless muck-raking by the media – like sharks with a piece of meat. And what was he, for God's sake? Just a messenger boy. Nothing more. But away from his so-called treason he had risen to an important position by his own skills. Loses his title, his job and his character.' He shook his head like a dog coming out of water. 'Hypocrisy is our national vice these days. And . . .' he said bitterly, '. . . They'll do the same to me if they get half a chance.'

'That's not my impression.'

'Tell me.'

'I've nothing to tell. It's just instinct.'

'Tell me. Tell me more.'

'There really is nothing more. I just have the feeling that there's some game on the chessboard but you're only one of the pieces. An important one but not the king anyway.'

Carling looked thoughtful, pursing his lips, then saying, 'Let's walk back and have some lunch.'

Mathews felt that Carling had had enough for one day and he drove up to London after lunch. He stopped at Sevenoaks to telephone Century House and make an appointment to see Kennedy.

*   *   *

Mathews got the impression that Kennedy wasn't very interested in what he had to report. His comments were brief and he looked at his watch several times.

'The way he talks about Blunt sounds as if he's a bit wary about doing a deal.'

'I think he'd have thrown me out by now if he was totally against it.'

'Maybe. Anyway, keep plugging away. There's no hurry.'

'What about the tabloid?'

Kennedy smiled. 'We took the editor out for lunch and I think they'll put it on the back burner for a bit.' He paused. 'His proprietor's going to have some problems himself if they go ahead.'

'Any particular phase you'd like me to concentrate on?'

'Not really, Tim. You're on a fishing expedition and it means dipping in where you can.'

'You think it's worth it?'

Kennedy looked surprised. 'Don't get me wrong. It's worth it all right. Keep going, fella.'

Kennedy had just agreed to having his mail redirected to a Post Office Box at the main Tunbridge Wells post office but Mathews went back to the flat to check that all was OK and to collect his recent letters.

It smelled dusty and stale and he opened all the windows to let in some fresh air and then looked through his post.

There was the usual letter from his parents, a TV licence reminder, a quarterly service charge from the landlord and an official-looking foolscap envelope. He opened it carefully and took out the folded document and a letter from his solicitor. The letter was brief.

Dear Mr Mathews,
I enclose a statement by the petitioner regarding access to your son Anthony James. I shall need to take a statement from you in response. Please contact me to make an appointment. The hearing is not until September so there is plenty of time but we may also need to have statements from witnesses to support your statement.
Yours sincerely,
P. Latham.

The folded statement was eight pages long and on the outside it said,

IN THE MATTER OF THE CHILDREN ACT
1989
IN THE MATTER OF ANTHONY JAMES
MATHEWS
BETWEEN
PAMELA JOAN BAILEY   PETITIONER
AND
TIMOTHY MATHEWS   RESPONDENT

This is the statement of the oral evidence of Pamela Joan Bailey to be at the hearing of the above mentioned matter.

He wondered why she had gone back to her maiden name but he read on slowly, growing more angry and frustrated by the minute. It had all the vitriol that legal terms would find acceptable and was obviously concocted by Roger Thomas.

Mathews had, apparently, taken little interest in his son during the marriage and had pressed her to have an abortion when she found she was pregnant. He had been violent and abusive to her in front of the child. On the occasions when he had had access he had not kept to the agreed time for his return and the child had been seriously disturbed after each visit to him.

Shaking with anger, Mathews phoned Latham who was busy, but sensing Mathews' pent-up anger he agreed to see him as soon as he could get up to Hampstead.

Latham leaned back in his swivel chair until it creaked as he listened to Mathews' diatribe about his ex-wife's statement.

When it eventually came to an end, he said, 'Let me give you some advice, Mr Mathews. These statements fly around before a case is heard. They annoy whoever's on the receiving end but that's about all they do. They don't impress the judge because he's heard it all before. Divorce cases and custody cases are about the only occasions when a person's character can be kicked around in the court as a means of stating a case.' He pointed at the copy of the offending statement on his desk. 'I've seen hundreds of statements like that in my time. They don't cut any ice with a court unless the plaintiff can produce witnesses or evidence to back up the statements.

'Now even if everything that she says was proved, the court operates on the basis that a father should have access to his children. He can have a criminal record as long as your arm, he can have been a violent husband but that alone doesn't make him a bad father. At the very worst your wife will have to agree to regular access. Bearing in mind the unproven facts she relies on, I think that you will be given reasonable access. One day, Saturday or Sunday, every two, or maybe three weeks.

'So I strongly recommend that you play it very cool, Mr

Mathews. If the other side do indulge in spite, it's not much fun for them if you don't rise to the bait. So do me a statement. There's no hurry. End of next week would be fine.'

'I'm sorry if I overreacted. I'll do as you say.'

Latham smiled. 'I'm on your side, Mr Mathews, even if it doesn't always look like it. I've been through it all hundreds of times. I've seen what happens if it's done the wrong way.'

Back at his flat, Mathews took his cellphone and spare battery and battery charger and then went down to his car. He wondered what Carling was doing. It was getting late. He looked at his watch, it was almost nine o'clock and the moon was already up.

Carling, Julie and Gabriella had eaten together in the big old-fashioned kitchen with its copper pots and pans, the thick oak beams and an Aga cooker. The baby was asleep in her carrycot near to the warmth of the cooker.

'So,' he said, 'tell me what you've been doing today, the two of you.'

Julie had a list beside her plate. 'Fixed Gabby a TV and one of your old radios but we'd like you to look at the aerial. We got some baby clothes from Oxfam in Tunbridge Wells and some clothes for Gabby.' She looked at him, smiling. 'That's about it. And Gabby's cleaned all the inside windows.'

He looked at Gabriella, smiling. 'Are you happy, young woman?'

She smiled shyly. 'I love it. I can't really believe it.' She paused for a moment. 'When will I have to leave?'

'Never, girl. This is your home now as much as it's Julie's and mine.'

There were tears on her cheeks and her voice quavered as she said, 'You don't know how happy I am.'

He turned to Julie. 'Let's try that lovely Pavlova I saw in the refrigerator. Let's celebrate. Then we'll clear up and I'll play you a bit of music.'

When the crockery and cutlery were in the dishwasher and the kitchen table smooth and bare again except for a small glass vase with four or five dandelions, they all went into the sitting room.

He put a CD on the Technics hi-fi without telling them what it was. It was Nigel Kennedy playing the Mendelssohn fiddle concerto. He played them only the first movement but they had sat entranced by the lush and loving music.

After that he sat at the piano and started to play, singing the words in German. And then he stopped and looked at them, smiling.

'I don't know if you know it but my dear, dear mother was Austrian. From Vienna. And she was a concert singer. But there was one of those lovely romantic old Viennese ballads she really loved. She used to sing it to me . . . It's about a Viennese word – *Servus* – which means "goodbye" but not really goodbye . . .' He played softly and sang the words

> *'Sag beim Abschied leise Servus*
> *Nicht Leb' wohl und nicht adieu*
> *Diese Worte tun nur Weh . . .'*

He sang a couple of verses then closed the piano lid carefully and stood up.

'I'll walk you home, Gabby, and carry Carlotta for you.'

He shone the torch ahead of them as they walked through the small orchard to the garage and he lit the way for her up the wooden staircase to the flat.

Inside he switched on the light and looked around to check that all was well. He put the carrycot on the sofa and took Gabby's hand. 'You won't ever have to leave, my dear, so just relax and enjoy it. Everybody loves you.'

As he walked back threading his way through the fruit trees there was a carpet of pink petals on the grass from the wind-blown blossom. He stopped, and switched off the torch, standing in the darkness, his eyes closed.

The little girl was so like her. The long mane of black hair, the big brown eyes, the neat, upturned nose and the full sensual mouth. She could have been their daughter. He wouldn't ever forget her. Not a day passed without thinking of her. 'Dear, lovely Rachel, I wish you were here.' Despite everything they could have the rest of his life for just a day with her again.

He realised that he was talking to himself aloud, and he switched on the torch and walked slowly back to the house. He shouldn't have played them the Mendelssohn. It was unbearable but it was so beautiful that he wanted them to hear it. Like splashing them with holy water. Despite his dark mood he smiled to himself at the thought. You don't splash nice Jewish girls with holy water.

CHAPTER 10

———————

Mathews had hesitated between Robertson's Golden Shred and Tiptree coarse-cut marmalade. He reverted back to childhood and took a spoonful of Golden Shred to spread on his toast. Carling was leaning across to see the headlines on *The Times* front page.

He turned to Mathews. 'I liked it better in the old days when they had classifieds all over the front page. All sorts of stuff. Wonder cures for anything you could think of. Offers to make you a millionaire for a fiver. Even the sleaze was nicely done. Beautiful young girl needing help with fees for art studies. Anything considered.' He smiled. 'We need a bit of sleaze to keep us lively. You don't have to do anything. Just use your imagination.'

'Kennedy said that I ought to arrange some payment they can make you for my keep while I'm here.'

Carling laughed. 'You know why he said that, don't you?'

Mathews shook his head. 'No. Only the obvious reason that it would be at least a gesture.'

Carling smiled. 'And if the chips are ever down he can't be accused of abusing my hospitality.' He paused. 'You look a bit down this morning. Something to do with that laddie of yours?'

Mathews told him the latest chapter from the saga and

Carling listened intently. When Mathews finished his tale, Carling said, 'Tell me about the lady. What's she like? Pretend you've only just met her.'

Mathews laughed. 'I wish I had. She's very pretty. Blonde, blue eyes, nice shape. It was our temperaments and attitudes that weren't right. We married too young to realise the differences. She was real middle class. Like her parents. You go by the book. You do what the rules say. You read the *Daily Mail*, not the *Mirror*. You wear Barbours and pearls. You play tennis, or cricket if you're a chap. You like musicals but not opera.' He stopped and shrugged. 'That's about it.'

'And your side of the trouble?'

'Well, I wasn't definable. Part working class. Don't leave the lights on when you're not in the room. Taxis are for crises or coming home from a week at Rhyl. Repairing clothes not chucking them away. Home cooking not microwave. And on top of that a strange outlook on life. Money doesn't really matter nor does doing the right thing by other people's rules. Liking classical music. Liking Lloyd Webber songs but liking Puccini even more.'

'An interesting analysis. What's her name? And where does she live?'

'Her name's Pamela, she uses her maiden name apparently – Bailey. And she lives in what was our house in Esher in Surrey.'

'You miss seeing the little boy, don't you?'

'I do. It's crazy. When it rains I wonder if he's got his mac. But when I did see him I didn't use the time sensibly. You can't, you know. You can't ask how his mother is or it's prying. And you don't have a background. So it's the Science Museum, the National History Museum and the cinema. I take him from a real life with a constant background and give him a few hours of what seems like a temporary and phoney life. Mine.'

It was several minutes before Carling spoke. What he had just heard had changed his mind about Timothy Mathews.

'We must talk about this. See if we can't work out something better.' He smiled. 'What do you want to talk about today?'

'Shall we go in the garden. You like it there, don't you?'

'I do, my boy. How perceptive of you. The garden gives me a better perspective. Not just the view. But the feeling of things going on from year to year. Trees that were here before I was born and will be here long after I've gone. Wondering if the daisies on the lawn aren't really more beautiful than those fine Dutch tulips.'

He stood up and walked to the open French windows and Mathews followed him to the wooden bench by the pond. When they were both comfortable, Mathews said, 'In the last days of war what was your actual job?'

Carling smiled. 'Some people saw me as just a messenger boy and that suited me quite well. Philby's section was based at St Albans and then it was moved to Ryder Street. The place was torn down after the war and it's now *The Economist* offices. I was a kind of liaison between Philby and our old headquarters in Broadway. There was a lot of office politics by then, with people trying to make sure that they were kept on when it was all over. Philby was determined to stake his claim for a senior position and there was a lot of information in HQ that would help Philby and the Russians. It was my official job to look for what might be of use to Philby's team.'

'And what were you doing for the Russians at that time?'

'You have to realise that this group – Philby, Burgess, Maclean, Blunt and, I guess, Cairncross too, were all committed to communism. Each knew that the others were committed but didn't know how much and in what way they served the Russians, if at all. I was the only person who knew what was going on. I was there to keep an eye on them all for the Russians and report on them to my control.'

'Why you and not one of the others?'

'Because they trusted me more than they trusted the others.' He smiled. 'And strangely enough because they knew I wasn't a committed communist.'

'You mean they didn't even trust Philby?'

'They didn't trust any of them. Not completely.'

'Why did they trust you?'

Carling was silent for a few moments and then he said, quietly, 'It was something that happened. I can't tell you what it was. Maybe later, when I know you better, but not right now.'

'And Philby obviously came out top in the reshuffle after the war.'

'Yes. He certainly did. Underneath all that charm was a born conspirator and it worked in offices just as well as in his work. But what actually made certain he'd be kept on was a genuine piece of intelligence evaluation on Philby's part. He bothered just that bit extra and it paid off.' He paused. 'I don't want to bore you with the details.'

'I'd like to hear them. They sound interesting.'

Carling sighed. 'On your head be it. I'll make it as brief as I can.' He closed his eyes for a moment before he started speaking. 'There was a lot of pressure on Philby from the Soviet side to make sure that he consolidated his position in SIS.'

'How do you know that?'

'It was I who passed their comments to him.' Carling shook his head impatiently. 'Anyway. A German Foreign Office Ministry official named Kolbe, walked into the British Legation in Berne, in Switzerland. Said he was an anti-Nazi and offered to provide copies of secret documents. He even brought some samples. Our chap was so stupid that he didn't even read them, so the German went to the Americans, Allen Dulles, OSS. He proved to be a real find for them. The Americans said he was the best agent they'd ever had.

'OSS routinely passed copies of the documents to SIS, but Dansey was sure they were a plant and passed them to Cowgill and I mentioned their existence to Kim. He asked the cypher people to check the documents against the Ultra intercepts of German Foreign Office messages and they matched. They were genuine. The cypher people, the army, the navy and the RAF were desperate for all they could get. Kim passed it all to the Foreign Office, by-passing his boss, Cowgill, who, when he found out, was furious. So when it came to who was going to head up Section Nine it lay between Cowgill and his assistant, Philby. Well, Kim got the job and Cowgill, who was an avid anti-communist, resigned in a huff. It was incredible. Philby was safe, he'd got to be head of the section that covered all anti-Soviet operations and he'd got rid of a potential trouble-maker.'

'The Russians must have been very grateful for your part in it.'

Carling smiled. 'You don't understand how Russians think.'

'What's that mean?'

'The KGB, or the NKVD as it was then, like treason but they don't like traitors. You must have found this,

Tim. All espionage organisations are the same. They use traitors but they neither admire them nor trust them.'

'Did they see you as a traitor?'

Carling shrugged. 'It's hard to say. I was different from the others and that was always a problem for the Russians.'

'In what way were you different in their eyes?'

'Well, the others had all been members of the Party. They were traitors by conviction. But I'd never been a communist and was never interested in communism. And on top of that my father was an earl.' He smiled. 'I think they were rather impressed by the earl bit.'

'Was it a calculated decision never to join the Party, to give you better cover?'

'No. I told you earlier that communism never appealed to me. I helped the Soviets in the first place because they were fighting our war and I slowly got to feel that their attitudes to people were better than ours.'

'In what way?'

'The capitalist world works on the basis that we must all look out for ourselves. Get rich so that the world can't get you. The Russians never lived up to their constitution of brotherhood but at least it was what they set out to do.'

'Did you really prefer a dictatorship to democracy?'

'Now you're talking politics again. For me, all political systems are useless.' He paused. 'How can you have democracy? Why should what the majority want always be right? There are countless thousands of people in this country who can neither read nor write a sentence and who never give a moment's thought to politics or ethics but they still have a vote and influence the way you and I live.'

Mathews smiled. 'You're better at arguing a case than I am.'

'You're making my point, my friend. A man may win

an argument or a debate but that doesn't necessarily make him right. Maybe he's just a better debater.'

'When did you stop your contact with the KGB?'

Carling laughed. 'Why not ask me – when did I stop beating my wife?' He paused, still smiling. 'Let's say I'm pleading the Fifth, and maybe the Fourth too.' Carling stood up. 'Let's go and find Julie and some drinks.'

They all had lunch on the patio at the back of the house, with Julie and Gabriella, and the baby asleep in her carrycot in the shadow under the circular table. Joe, the gardener, was eating a cheese sandwich as he sat in the sun with his backside ruining a spread of aubretia on the rock garden.

'How's the vine this year, Joe?'

'Gonna be a record year, milord. I've done a bit of thinning out.'

'Any problems?'

'Yeah. Two. Those damned herons have taken the last of our koi. I think you ought to have one of them plastic herons to keep 'em away.'

'I talked to Sir John about that. He says they don't work after a couple of weeks. Says we need wire all round the edge of the pond. But I'd rather have no fish than that. You said two problems, what's the other?'

'That there aerial on top of your radio shack as you calls it. The pole's getting covered with lichen on the weather side. I don't know if it makes any difference. I can have a go at cleaning it if you wants.'

'No. It's not a problem, Joe. It's only the bits at the top of the pole that matter. And they're aluminium.'

'I'll be off then, milord.' Joe pointed at Gabriella. 'That one's been helpin' me with the weeding. Cleared out all the forget-me-nots. They was beginning to get mildew.'

Carling looked at the girl, smiling as he said, 'Well done, Gabby. You've made a conquest there.'

As Joe hobbled away, Julie said, 'At least he didn't call you Your Worship.'

Carling laughed. 'He used to call the judges at the County Court Your Grace.' He turned to Mathews. 'Let me show you my shack.'

The radio shack was about fifty yards beyond the garage and Gabby's new home.

'At one time it was a pigsty and then it was a storage place for apples. We give the apples away these days and I had it tidied up so that I could use it.' He smiled. 'Julie calls it my playroom. I suppose it is in a way.'

There were heavy locks on the door and it was dark inside. There were no windows but when Carling switched on the lights the interior was bright and spotlessly clean. Walls and ceiling were painted white and the floor was terracotta tiles.

There was a bench along the facing wall with the usual pieces of equipment that ham radio people go in for. Two ICOM transceivers, microphones, extension speakers. Shelves with rows of audiotapes and a pegboard with carefully laid out cable connections with different plugs and each properly labelled.

Carling pointed at the right-hand end of the bench. 'That's what they call an M-7000. A communications terminal. I can plug it into a short-wave radio and it takes Morse or other codes and converts them into normal alphabet characters. Covers ship-to-shore – aircraft – press agencies, embassies, all sorts of things.'

'How often do you come here?'

'Most days I have a play around. All amateurs have networks. Radio fanatics arguing about equipment and antennae, the latest discovery of some amateur in Thailand or the Yukon. There are magazines about the hobby.'

'What's the attraction?'

Carling grimaced. 'For some it's the technicalities, the chaps who build their own equipment . . .' he laughed '. . . they believe in valves, not transistors and chips. For some, I suppose it's the kick you get out of listening to something that's nothing to do with you.' He shrugged. 'For me I know nothing about the technicalities. I just buy the equipment and have fun with it.' He paused. 'Did you ever do a radio course?'

'We had a couple of days in the course on radio and communication generally but nothing technical.'

Carling smiled. 'I can remember doing my course. The Morse training school was on the top floor of Dickens & Jones, the department store. Gave perfect cover in wartime for us walking in and out. We each had our own instructor. Mine was an ATS girl. First class. She went to get me a cup of tea one day and I had a quick look in my "P" file. On the radio form it said, "Describe characteristics of operator when sending Morse under stress," and she'd written: "This officer always transmits as if he's under stress." ' He laughed. 'I never mastered Morse, I'm afraid.'

'Did you ever need to use Morse?'

'No.' He laughed. 'The main attraction to Morse was that you got extra pay if you passed the tests. But it was considered rather infra dig. Morse was for trades-men rather than us brainy types.'

Mathews pointed out an aerosol can marked 'Blower'. 'What's that for?'

'It's air under pressure. Photographers use it a lot to keep dust off negatives. I use it to keep the radios clean. All those knobs and switches seem to attract the dust and dust can ruin electronics in no time.' He smiled. 'I've got a similar aerosol in my bathroom and I use it to clean the head of my electric shaver.'

As Mathews made his way downstairs for the evening meal he realised that it was Carling who had been questioning him as they sat out on the patio in the afternoon sun. Asking him about his life with Pamela and about their son. He seemed to listen carefully but he made no comment and offered no advice. Which was at least a change.

Carling and Mathews took their coffees out to sit in the last of the sun on the patio and it was Carling who got them back to what it was really all about.

'You know, one thing always puzzles me. You and all the others. Even those who were around in the old days always seem to take for granted that Philby was the one who mattered to the Russians.'

'Who *was* the one who mattered if it wasn't Philby?'

'Have you ever heard anyone mention the codename "Orphan"?'

'No. Who was Orphan?'

'He was the one who mattered. Orphan was Maclean.'

Mathews was genuinely surprised. 'Why Maclean?'

'Well, he was the first of the Cambridge crowd that they recruited. Apart from that he had several virtues so far as the Russians were concerned. First of all he hated America and Americans, and secondly he moved and worked in much more delicate areas than Kim Philby. Philby on his own was useful inside SIS. He could abort actions against KGB agents and he could inform the Russians on the internal workings of SIS, including any agents SIS managed to run inside the Soviet structure.

'But the espionage that really matters is only one level.

It's what governments do or are thinking of doing that really matters. Maclean was a top Foreign Office man. He saw all the papers crossing an ambassador's desk wherever he might be. When Maclean was in Washington, Stalin himself read everything from Maclean.'

'What about his drunkenness and his crazy behaviour?'

Carling smiled. 'No Russian has ever thought ill of a man who drinks too much. They do themselves. From the Kremlin itself down to the beggars in the backstreets. It's a national pastime. They don't see it as a vice. And the behaviour . . .' Carling shrugged. 'Inside the Kremlin walls their behaviour was just as outrageous. And in any case they saw that our people both tolerated Maclean's behaviour and covered up for him.'

'Why *did* our people tolerate him? All those drunken and violent exhibitions in public and all that stuff?'

'The old-boy network, my friend. Good backgrounds. Officer fathers, public schools, Cambridge and so on. You have to remember that when they were starting in life, they were all very bright. Good at sports, excellent scholars and lots of charm. Charm counted for a lot in those days, no matter how spurious it might be. Kim Philby never drank when he was a young man. Lived very abstemiously. They made their way because they all had genuine talent.

'Philby didn't get to be a Section Head in SIS by anything other than talent. Nobody pulled any strings for him. Maclean didn't get to be First Secretary at our embassy in Washington without being a very clever chap. Even poor Burgess. He won the Roseberry and Gladstone history prizes at Eton and he won his scholarship in history to Trinity. But they were all human beings. They just happened to have flaws in their characters.'

'What were the flaws?'

'In the case of Burgess and Maclean they had the burdens of being alcoholics and homosexuals.' He paused. 'But Philby was different. His flaw was a lust for power and an incredible arrogance. He was not just efficient, he was ruthless. Ready to sacrifice other people's lives if it suited his plans. And of course they were all flawed by their passion for a political system that was nothing like they thought it was.' He shrugged. 'But plenty of so-called intellectuals fell for the same myth. We even had a "red" Dean of Canterbury, a man who openly avowed his communism.'

'But you seem to have rather liked them.'

'What makes you think that?'

'The way you speak about them. You try to emphasise their good points.'

Carling sighed, the deep sigh of contained exasperation. 'My dear Tim, what you've heard about these people is a one-sided view. If it had been like it's retold now, SIS would have had these men in court.' He paused. 'Just imagine what it would have looked like if it did get into court. Prosecuting men for treason whose crime was to pass on information to our then allies. Information that could maybe save tens of thousands of lives. The media would have a field day and the public would be on the side of the accused. Put it back down all those years when it was happening and the pro-Soviet feelings would have been overwhelming. There was no Cold War then.' He paused. 'They broke the rules, they were disreputable in their private lives but they took risks in what they thought was a righteous cause. Only one of them did us harm.'

'Was that Philby?'

'Yes. Read up the records on the Albanian operation. At least fifty men walked into a trap that Philby and the Soviets had contrived. They were all executed on the beaches where they landed. I have no respect for Philby, he *was* a traitor, by any standards. The others – in my opinion – were not.'

'And you?'

Carling shrugged, unsmiling. 'You must make up your own mind on that score.' He looked at his watch. 'I'm going over to have a chat with Gabby. I'll see you tomorrow.'

Up in his room Mathews undressed slowly by the light of the bedside reading light. It suddenly seemed crazy to be spending his days talking to a man about things that had happened before he himself was born. There was something wrong about it. Maybe not wrong, but at least it was strange. It was time he had another meeting with Kennedy.

CHAPTER 11

Kennedy's secretary had shown Mathews into his office and told him that Kennedy was on his way. He'd just called in on his cellphone from somewhere around Victoria Station. He wouldn't be more than five or ten minutes.

The strict internal security at Century House made his invitation to wait for Kennedy in his office a small sign of privilege and approval. And that same security-mindedness made him wonder what he'd done, or would have to do, to warrant the *Good Housekeeping* seal of approval.

Kennedy came in fifteen minutes later. Full of energy, jacket slung over one shoulder, tie loosened, pointing to one of the visitors' chairs as he sat down at the other side of his desk.

He leaned forward, elbows on the desk. 'How's it going?'

For about ten minutes Mathews detailed the various episodes that Carling had talked about. At the end Kennedy leaned back in his chair and Mathews wondered if it was a sign of disappointment or just a need to think about what had been said.

Then Kennedy leaned forward again. 'Did he actually admit to tipping off Philby about the German stuff from Switzerland?'

'Well, I wouldn't say *admit*. I didn't force it out of

him – he just said it in the course of talking about Philby being ambitious for the top job.'

'That's very interesting.' He paused. 'Has he ever asked you if you were wired?'

'No. He seems to trust me as – I was going to say as a friend – but that's probably going too far. Let's say that he treats me as a neutral.'

'You say he despises Philby because of the Albanian business. How does he feel about the others?'

Mathews shrugged. 'Tolerant, I guess. But quite sure that it was Maclean the Russians valued, not Philby.'

'D'you think he's gay?'

'Who? Carling? No. I'm sure he's not.' He hesitated. 'Well, maybe not sure, but my instincts tell me he's not.'

'There are two areas I'd like you to move on to if you can. Details of his KGB controllers and then his contacts with them after the war. Later on I'd like you to fish around what happened when he broke off with them. Indeed, did he ever break off with them? I can't believe all those trips to the Warsaw Pact countries were just for the Arts Council. Why just those countries? There were no visits to South America, Asia, the Middle East. But dozens of visits to Prague, Moscow, Budapest and Berlin.' He paused. 'Anything I can do for you?'

'Just one thing. I'd like to meet somebody who was in SIS when Carling was in. Just to get another angle. Somebody near his age.'

Kennedy closed his eyes, thinking for a moment and then he reached for the internal phone and pressed a button.

'It's me. Have you got a current address for an old boy named Powell – no, not him. This one's – let's see – Arthur, a major. Must be retired. No. I'll hold.'

Kennedy tucked the receiver under his chin and said,

'I've sent a decent cheque to His Lordship.' Then he turned back to the phone. 'Yeah – that's the one – write out his address and phone number and give it to Tim.'

Kennedy hung up. 'Carling must have been a pretty good operator when you look back on it. He wasn't suspected like the others. In fact nobody raised even the vaguest suspicion until about five or six years ago.'

'Why then?'

'There was a report from our chap in Prague. Seems that Carling had been seen at some reception at the Soviet Embassy. Seemed very much at home and had left with a known KGB man in a KGB car. After that people started remembering odd things and it looked very suspicious. There have been other reports of contacts that we don't like.' He shrugged. 'Nothing you could rely on.'

Kennedy stood up to end the meeting and walked Mathews to the door. Mathews picked up the slip of paper from the secretary.

CHAPTER 12

The address was in Chichester. One of those small but beautiful houses in The Pallants. The woman who opened the door was trying to calm a German shepherd dog that was barking aggressively.

'Quiet, Tessa.' She smiled faintly at Mathews. 'She won't do anything. Just doesn't like strangers. Can I help you?'

'I was hoping to have a word with Major Powell.'

'He's in the garden. If you'll wait I'll get him for you.'

She left the door open as she led the dog away and a few minutes later a man appeared. Tall and thin, wearing a panama hat and a cream-coloured linen suit.

'I'm Powell. What is it you want? If it's British Legion Tubby's looking after that these days.'

'Freddie Kennedy gave me your address.'

'Kennedy, Kennedy. Who's he?'

'He works at Century House.'

Powell seemed to hesitate and then said reluctantly, 'I see. You'd better come in. We'll go in the garden.'

It was a small garden, but carefully laid out to give both privacy and a feeling of space.

They sat in wicker chairs under a lilac still in bloom.

'And how is Freddie these days? Still screwing everything that moves?'

'He's fine, but I don't know him as well as you obviously do.'

'Don't know how he got away with it. Part of his training, I guess.' He paused. 'And what can I do for you, young man?'

'I wanted to ask you about George Carling. Lord Carling. Freddie said you knew him in the old days.'

'George, eh? And what's he been up to?'

'Nothing so far as I know. I just wanted to get somebody else's view of his background.'

'Most of the time when I knew him was in Washington. I was at the embassy. Passport Officer or some such bloody title. And George was liaison with Langley.' He peered at Mathews. 'You been to Langley?'

'Yes.'

'Well, Georgie boy was our liaison chap with the CIA.' He shrugged. 'Did a good job as far as I know. Seemed to get on with them better than his predecessors.'

'Was Philby in Washington when you were there?'

'The whole bunch of 'em were there. Maclean, First Secretary at the embassy. Then Burgess came as Second or Third Secretary, I've forgotten which. It seemed he didn't want to come. Hated Americans but he'd caused so much embarrassment in London that it was Washington or the boot.'

'How did the others get on with the Americans?'

'The Americans detested Burgess from the start. He was openly anti-American and his drinking and sexual habits were outrageous. He stayed at Philby's house when he first came over. Aileen, Philby's wife, loathed him. Philby was a smoothie and a dedicated traitor. Angleton, the head of counterintelligence at the CIA, rumbled him right from the start. Didn't trust him an inch. Maclean . . .'

he shrugged '. . . he covered himself publicly, but in private he was anti-American.'

'What was your role?'

'When London realised that Angleton was gunning for Philby, they sent me in as official CIA/SIS liaison.'

'So what was Carling doing?'

Powell shrugged. 'I never knew. But whatever it was he wasn't part of the embassy staff. He had his own place in town. He was working with the CIA but I don't know any details.' He smiled. 'The Americans were a bit cagey about him at the start but he soon got his feet under the table and they loved him.'

'What did you think of Carling yourself?'

Powell hesitated. 'Why are you asking me?'

'Just to get an impression of the man from someone who knew him in the old days.'

Powell was silent for a few moments and then he said, 'You're doing some sort of check on him, aren't you?' He paused. 'I suppose if Kennedy gave you my name and address it must be official.' He paused again. 'They've left it a bit late, haven't they?'

'Who knows?'

'OK. Back to business. I liked Carling. He was generous. I don't mean money. He was generous about people. He didn't rush to judgement. And whatever he was doing I always reckoned that he did it well. But there was something odd about him. He was extrovert but a loner at the same time. He listened but you never knew what he was thinking.' He paused. 'What did he say about me?'

'I haven't asked him anything about you.'

'Does Kennedy think Carling was playing games?'

'I think some people have some doubts.'

'If he was playing games, then you can take it from me

that he was much more dangerous than Philby and his gang.'

'What makes you think that?'

'Just instinct. No flaws that I could see. But if he put his mind to something he'd make it work.'

'What kind of thing? You mean like Philby and the others?'

Powell shrugged. 'Could be. I've no idea. Not a clue. But I've been in the business a long time.'

'Would you trust him?'

Powell smiled. 'I don't trust anybody. Twenty years in SIS puts you off trusting people. Let's say I'd trust him with my wife, with my money, maybe even with my life but I still wouldn't trust him. There's something odd there but I've no idea what it is.' He turned to look at Mathews. 'Somewhere inside that man there's conviction. Not of politics or religion. It's as if he worked it all out a long time ago. And he's stuck to it ever since.' Powell wagged a finger at Mathews. 'I've always thought he ought to have been a priest, but not belonging to any religion. They made martyrs of that kind of man in the old days. Broke their bones on the rack. Burned 'em at the stake.' He smiled and shrugged. 'And nowadays, all over the world, we put them in prison and leave them to rot.'

'Did Carling have any particular friends when he was in Washington?'

'He didn't have much to do with the Brits. His main contact was – Jesus, one of those American names, Chuck or something.'

'Hank?'

'Yeah, that's it, Hank, Hank Henney. He was CIA. The CIA was quite new, came out of OSS, and I think Carling was there to help them organise recruitment and define targets. When he eventually went back to London I know the Americans raised hell to get him back, but London wouldn't play. A mistake in my opinion.' Powell looked at his watch. 'Let's have a cup of tea before you go. My Muriel makes wonderful sponge cakes.'

It was a Friday evening and by the time Mathews had followed the coast road past Arundel, the weekend traffic from London was already building up. Couples off for a weekend in the sun, families with tents and barbecues, buckets and spades. He envied them the set patterns of their lives. He wondered what Tony was doing for the weekend. He must get down to writing that bloody statement for his solicitor. Maybe he should buy a boat and moor it down at Chichester. Have something that the boy enjoyed so much he'd raise hell if she tried to cancel his outing with his father. His mind went to his ex-wife and he wondered what the hell she saw in that creep Thomas. There was a time when he could do no wrong so far as she was concerned. There must have been something that changed it all. But he had no idea what it was. He could remember it now. Another sunny day, and he'd parked his car in the drive because they were having a baby-sitter and going out for dinner. She was sitting there in the living room and he knew from her face that something was wrong. Tony had had an accident? He'd been hurt? He was in hospital? And then she'd told him. No reasons, no discussion. Not even a row. She was moving out to her sister's for a week so that he could collect his things. She was divorcing him. She was going to marry Thomas.

Mathews had stood there like an idiot. Dumbstruck. Watching it like some episode in *Neighbours* as she picked up her handbag and coat and swept from the room. He could remember that she was trembling as she sat there saying her piece and his instinct had been to comfort her but it was as if he were paralysed. It seemed so unreal.

The house was scrupulously clean and tidy and she had left him a meal on the kitchen table. Ham and a dish of salad. The next few days had been like a bad dream. A mixture of lethargy and bursts of angry activity. Finding a lawyer, closing bank accounts, packing his belongings, sure that he could leave most of them as she would never be allowed to take over the house and throw him out after having walked out on him without any excuse or reason. Three weeks later she was back in what was now referred to as 'the matrimonial home' and he was required by law to continue paying the mortgage and the bills. There was little that he could put in his counterstatement. He had no complaints about her that were worth recording. He'd have gone on with her happily enough and he would have tried to put right anything that she complained of. But she hadn't complained.

Back at Lake Cottage Mathews had chatted for a few minutes to Julie and then gone to his room. Carling was on the train back from London where he had been on a TV programme discussing the exhibition of Bill Brandt's black and white pictures at the Photographers Gallery.

He had almost finished his legal statement when Julie came in with a tray. Sausages and mash, half a Gallia melon steeped in brown sugar, and a pot of coffee. She was surprised when she noticed the trace of tears at the edge of his eyes as he thanked her for bothering to get him a meal.

*　　*　　*

It was midnight when Carling got back to the cottage. A side window had been smashed on his much-loved Rover and the radio stolen.

'You know, Julie,' he said 'it would be more sensible and less expensive to leave the car unlocked with a notice saying, "The car's not locked so don't break a window but the radio's ten years old." '

She smiled. 'I've poured you a whisky. A Glenfiddich. There's ice and water if you want it.'

As he sipped his whisky she said, 'The boy's back. Looks very miserable. I made him supper and his light went out half an hour ago.'

'He's upset about not seeing his son.' He shook his head. 'I'll have to do something about that. It's crazy. Always remember: never get in the hands of lawyers. They'll cause more troubles than they solve and they'll rob you blind while they're doing it.' He sighed. 'My God, I'm tired. I shouldn't have to do all this running around at my age.'

She smiled. 'Go on, you know you love it.'

CHAPTER 13

As she brought in the coffee-pot Julie announced that His Lordship was having a long lie-in. Mathews drove to the village and posted his statement to his lawyer. By the time he got back to the cottage Carling was sitting at the table in his dressing gown, going through his mail. He looked up as Mathews sat down opposite him.

'I'm going to be away for three or four days next week. I'm on the panel for the young musician of the year competition in Prague. You're welcome to come along but Century House would have to fund your travel and subsistence.' He smiled. 'My favourite city, Prague. So beautiful, like all Europe used to be. Even under the communists it was a city of culture. Great orchestras and queues for every concert.' He smiled. 'Mahler and Dvořák – the local boys who made good. What more could you want?'

Mathews smiled. 'I'll speak to Kennedy but I don't think he'll feel it's necessary.'

'What's the position with your boy?'

Mathews told him about his statement and Carling frowned. 'Doesn't make sense. It's got locked into a crazy situation. We'll have to think of some way of getting it back to normal.'

*   *   *

Carling and Mathews were in the garden when Julie came out and said that there was a phone call for Mathews.

The call was from Kennedy, who wanted to see him as soon as possible. They settled for lunch at the Special Forces Club.

They talked cricket and the Derby as they ate and took their coffees out into the main room at a table by one of the windows.

'Tell me about your meeting with Powell.'

When Mathews had said his piece about Powell, he raised the possibility of a trip to Prague with Carling. Kennedy had turned it down out of hand. Their man in Prague could cover Carling's movements and contacts. Mathews then raised the possibility of a quick trip to Washington to talk to the man who Powell had said was Carling's CIA associate.

Kennedy thought about it for several minutes and then he said, 'Why not? How are you going to trace him, he'll have been out of the game years ago?'

'I was thinking of contacting Maguire, who was my opposite number when I was in Langley.'

'OK. But not longer than three days. Check with Maguire that he can actually locate Carling's guy. What was his name?'

'Hank Henney.'

Kennedy looked surprised. 'I've heard of Hank Henney. I think I attended a lecture by him at Langley on running non-national agents in overseas countries. Something like that anyway. Looked like Walter Matthau but sounded more like a drug-runner. OK, I'll get Facilities to fix you up.'

'Any chance of saving time by flying Concorde?'

Kennedy laughed. 'You must be joking. And Economy, not even Business Class.'

Mathews looked at his watch. It was midday Washington time and he put through a fast-track call to Langley. When he got through it seemed Maguire was now based in New York but the CIA operator was able to transfer the call. It was a secretary who answered and when he asked for Maguire she asked his name, which he gave, but when she asked his business, he told her frostily just to put him through. A few seconds later Maguire came on the line.

'Maguire. What can I do for you?'

'It's Tim Mathews, Joe.'

'I'm sorry, I don't . . . Jesus, where are you calling from? I thought it was a local call and I didn't recognise the name out of context. How are you?'

'I'm OK. I'm coming over in the next few days. Just a quick trip. I wanted to contact a guy named Henney. Hank Henney.'

'Official or unofficial?'

'Official, but nothing desperate.'

'You're lucky. He's been retired for years. He's no longer in Washington. He lives here with his daughter in Queens. When are you coming?'

'Is tomorrow OK? I'll change my flight from Washington to New York.'

'Fine. Send me a fax of your flight number and I'll meet you in.'

'Thanks.'

High winds had delayed the landing for an hour but Maguire was waiting for him at the luggage carousel and had taken him through Immigration and Passport Control and then on to the car park.

The rain was beating down as Maguire headed for the city.

'It's a bit late to contact Hank today but I'll take you over tomorrow morning and leave you with him. You can phone me at the office for a lift back. Or get a cab. Where did you book in?'

'There's a dump I used to stay at near Madison Square Garden. I've booked in there for a couple of nights.'

'OK. We'll drop your bag there and then head for the clubs.'

'Does your old lady let you go to clubs?'

Maguire grinned. 'My old lady's somebody else's old lady now. Took a fancy to an insurance guy and I didn't stop her. How's yours?'

'Same as yours but mine went for a lawyer.'

'Fuck 'em all, Timmy boy. We're well rid of 'em.' He laughed. 'We'll celebrate tonight.' He paused. 'Here's your hotel. Hop out, take your bag and I'll find somewhere to park. No, I tell you what, I'll go back to my place and freshen up and I'll come back to you in a couple of hours and we'll hit the town, OK?'

Mathews smiled. 'Anything you say, Joe.'

Mathews signed in and took his bag up to his room on the tenth floor. He had slept on the flight but he needed a bath and a shave.

Room service had brought him orange juice and a beef sandwich and as he towelled himself dry he walked over to the TV to switch it on. There was a short, sharp shock as he touched the switch. He had had a similar shock when he closed the door to the bathroom. He phoned down to the housekeeper and asked for an electrician.

The big black man tried the TV and the door handle but there was no shock. Mathews insisted, and when he touched the switch again himself the shock was obvious. There was even a small burst of blue light. As he looked at the electrician, the big man shrugged. 'It's just static, buddy. That's all.'

'So what can you do about it?'

The man looked at him and shrugged. 'Maybe you need to get laid.'

Maguire obviously shared the electrician's diagnosis and they had done the rounds of a dozen bars and clubs before going back to Mathews' room at the hotel with two girls in tow. Mathews had no idea the next morning as to what time his companions had left but Maguire had turned up in time for breakfast looking alert and at ease as they talked about Hank Henney.

It seemed that Hank Henney was a bit of a mystery man even inside the CIA, but that wasn't abnormal. Gossip and some informed guessing suggested that he had been responsible for communications with CIA field agents in Europe and the Middle East. He had been an officer in OSS when it was being dissolved and had been recruited into the newly formed CIA a few months later.

'I can't tell you much about him. We don't ask other employees what they do. I expect it's the same with your lot.'

'You're right.'

'Shall we go?'

'OK. Are you sure he'll be there?'

Maguire sighed. 'He's got a bad hip joint, so he doesn't get around much. He's due to have a replacement any day now. They've got a small balcony at the back. He sits there in the sun. When there is any sun.'

As they drove over the bridge to Queens, Maguire said, 'I'll leave you with him and come back in half an hour. You can have another session with him this afternoon or tomorrow. See how it goes. Don't wear the old boy out.'

Hank Henney was in his mid-sixties but he looked younger. He was handsome and there were only streaks of grey in his thick black hair. When Maguire had introduced Mathews to Henney and his daughter, Anna, he then left.

'Would you like to see my ID, Mr Henney?'

Henney smiled. 'No. Joe Maguire says it's OK. And that's enough for me. What can I do for you?'

'Arthur Powell gave me your name. He spoke very fondly of you.'

Henney smiled. 'Fondly, eh. A nice English word. And how is Arthur?'

'He's fine. He's got a nice house in Sussex. Not far from the sea and he seems to be a keen gardener.'

'And how did my name come up?'

'He said you were a good friend of George Carling – Lord Carling – when he was working with the CIA in Washington.'

'D'you know George Carling?'

'Yes. I've been staying with him for several weeks.'

Henney grinned. 'A lovely man. Wants to put the world right all on his own.' He paused. 'But he must be long retired by now.'

'He is but he still lives a very busy life on TV and radio, and in the newspapers.'

'Has he got over the girl?'

Mathews looked surprised. 'What girl d'you mean?'

Henney shook his head. 'Doesn't matter. Shouldn't be talking about it anyway.' He paused. 'So. How can I help you?'

'I was interested in what Carling was doing when he was over here.'

Henney's bushy eyebrows went up. 'But he was an SIS man.' He paused. 'How come an SIS man is asking *me* what another SIS man was doing? Your people must know what he was doing.'

'There doesn't appear to be any official record of what he was doing.'

'Has all this been cleared by the brass?'

'You could check with London if you want.'

'I mean has it been cleared by Langley?'

'Why should Langley need to clear information about an SIS officer?'

For long moments Henney was silent and then he shook his head and said, 'How long have you known Joe Maguire?'

'I met him about five years ago when I was posted over here to Washington as junior liaison with Langley.'

'How long were you here?'

'Just short of two years.'

'And what were you working on?'

'I was controlled by the Deputy Director for Operations.'

'Go on.'

'I was at the HUMINT Requirements Tasking Center.'

'You'd better level with me, boy. Why are you checking on George Carling?'

'It's just routine.'

'Don't give me that bullshit. Routine what? Checking on a guy who retired – what was it – fifteen, sixteen years ago?' He paused. 'Those bastards in London are trying to pin something on him, aren't they?'

Mathews heard the door-bell and prayed that it was Maguire. It was, and five minutes later they had left with a further session arranged for the afternoon. Mathews said nothing about his conversation with Henney and they went for a sandwich at a café near the local police precinct.

They had got to the hot chocolate when Maguire's bleep went. He stood up, still sipping his drink.

'Won't be long. I'll use the house phone.'

He put down the empty mug and wiped his mouth with the back of his hand, looking around for the phone. He walked to the counter and the girl pointed down a short passage. Mathews watched Maguire press the buttons for the number and then called the waiter for the bill.

It was nearly fifteen minutes before Maguire came back, lowering himself slowly into his seat before he looked at Mathews, frowning.

'What the hell were you talking about with Henney, for Christ's sake?'

'Nothing special. I just asked him about a man who used to work with him.'

'A Brit?'

'Yes.'

'SIS?'

'Yes.'

'I am in deep shit, boyo.' He stared at Mathews. 'I've got orders to escort you to Kennedy and check that you board the plane.'

'When?'

'Right now. Somebody's gone to your hotel to pick up your stuff and a driver will bring it here. And off we go.'

'Can I phone London?'

'No. My guy said if you make any difficulty and don't co-operate you'll not just be sent off, you'll be handed over to Immigration for your visa to be cancelled.'

'On what grounds, Joe? What the hell is going on?'

'I've no idea, but according to them you're stamping around on some very thin ice.'

'Have they contacted London?'

'Not yet. But I'm sure they will. They're really doing their nuts. Hollering about your people going behind their backs and God knows what else.' He paused. 'There's the driver now. Give me a couple of minutes with him and then come over. And don't, repeat don't, say anything in front of him.'

'Did they tell you why they were doing this?'

'No. They just wanted to make sure that whatever it was, it was all my fault. If anything happened I was going to be the fall guy.'

'Who did Henney speak to at Langley, do you know?'

'No idea. It was my boss who talked to me. Asked what the hell I thought I was doing.' He paused. 'And believe me, he was shaking in his shoes.' He turned and looked hard at Mathews. 'Who was this guy you asked Henney about?'

Mathews, still surprised and angered, said softly, 'Let's leave it, Joe. I'll get London to assure Langley that you know nothing about any of it.'

Maguire sighed. 'Thanks. Maybe it's better for me to just be righteously indignant and ignorant and ride it out.' Maguire looked towards the driver standing by the bar. 'Let's get on our way. We've paid your hotel bill. Your seat's booked already.' He laughed softly. 'The airline had to chuck off some crappy pop star to get you on so you're going First Class.'

They sat in silence as the driver made his way to JFK. The driver handed over Mathews' case and the flight ticket to Maguire, who walked with him to check-in and escorted him past passport control and on to the flight assembly waiting room.

Fifteen minutes later they were put through the final checkpoint and Maguire went with him to his seat at the front end of the plane. They shook hands without speaking and Mathews saw Maguire speaking to the chief cabin steward before he left the plane.

As he settled back in his seat after they were airborne, Mathews closed his eyes and tried to make some sense out of what had happened in less than a day. On the surface it was legitimate enough for the Americans to stop him from talking with a retired CIA man. What made it extraordinary was the speed and crudity with which they had reacted. And the fact that Maguire had told him originally that his section head had seen no problem. It was all in the business, whatever it was. And Hank Henney was long out of the business. He guessed it must be just the CIA resenting not being put in the picture. It would be interesting to hear what Kennedy had to say about one of his senior men being escorted out of the USA. It was just as well that he'd cleared his trip with Kennedy. And because the CIA had arranged his return flight at least SIS could cash in his return ticket.

CHAPTER 14

———

Dickie Farmer was waiting for him at the end of the tunnel from the plane. He looked amiable enough.

'Kennedy wants to see you at Century House. I've got a car.'

'How did you know what flight I was on?'

Farmer grinned. 'I understand Freddie got a call from the States. What the hell's going on?'

'I've no idea. I got the bum's rush. Escorted on to a plane. I was there less than a day.'

'What did you do, for Chrissake?'

'I just talked to a CIA guy. He was a friend of a Brit who worked in Washington way back. They both retired years ago.'

'I'm on Freddie's committee dealing with Carling. You've no need to talk in code.' He paused. 'What did you uncover?'

'Nothing. Absolutely nothing.'

As they got to the Hammersmith flyover Farmer concentrated on the driving. The early morning traffic was already causing long tailbacks and it was forty minutes before he dropped Mathews at Century House.

'Go on up. He's waiting for you. Take your kit. I'm not signing in today.'

'Thanks for the lift.'

'You're welcome.'

*   *   *

It was only when Mathews saw that Kennedy was wearing an open-necked blue denim shirt and blue jeans that he remembered it was Saturday.

'Well,' said Kennedy. 'sit down. Glad to see you got back. Seemed you might have ended up in Rykers.' He paused. 'Tell me what happened.'

'There's not much to tell you.'

'So tell me what there is.'

It took only ten minutes for Mathews to cover everything that had happened in New York but he could see from Kennedy's face that he was taking it very seriously.

'Let me get this quite clear. You told Maguire that you wanted to meet this guy Henney who'd been mentioned by Powell when you interviewed him. But you didn't say why you wanted to meet him?'

'That's right.'

'You didn't mention Carling's name to Maguire?'

'No. I didn't even mention it after the meeting and when they were throwing me out.'

'And Maguire's boss had OK'd your contact with Henney.'

'That's what Maguire told me.'

'But when you raised the subject of Carling with Hank Henney he seemed suspicious. Asked if we were trying to pin something on him, or words to that effect?'

'Yeah.'

'In the café before Maguire got the phone call he was normal and co-operative, yes?'

'He was just his usual self. I wouldn't say he was co-operative because there was no co-operation asked for.'

'Then they didn't even let you go back to the hotel. Said you were already booked by them on a flight and that if you didn't co-operate they'd hand you over to Immigration to cancel your visa and make you an undesirable.'

'They didn't mention making me an undesirable but that's what it would have meant. I'd have been barred from any future visit to the States.'

Kennedy sighed and leaned back in his chair. 'So what do you think it was all about?'

'The only thought I had was that they thought I'd gone behind their backs in contacting Henney.'

'Rubbish. You'd contacted Maguire. No objection from him about protocol. The blessing of Maguire's boss, yes?'

'So he said.'

'So the only problem was raising the subject of Carling?'

'Seems like it.'

'There's something very odd here, Tim. I've looked up his record and at the time he was in Washington he was responsible for smoothing out routine problems between SIS and the CIA. Their assessments always gave him the highest rating and when he was brought back to London they made strong representations that he be left there for another tour of duty.'

'It's really crazy, isn't it? What did they say when they phoned you that I was on my way back?'

'That's what worries me. The man who spoke to me wasn't CIA and all he said was that they objected to our clandestine approach.'

'What rubbish.' Mathews paused. 'If he wasn't CIA I suppose he must have been some goon from Foreign Affairs.'

'I wish he had been that.'

'What was he then?'

'I asked him who he was speaking for and he refused to answer. He just hung up. That in itself made me very suspicious and I asked Cheltenham to trace the origin of the call.' He looked at Mathews. 'Guess where it was from?'

'Washington? New York?'

'Neither. It was a Maryland number. Fort George Meade, the National Security Agency. It was the direct line to the NSA's chief of security.'

'My God. What's going on? Was Carling ever at NSA?'

'No. Neither did he have anything to do with Cheltenham and GCHQ.'

'It's crazy. It doesn't make sense. What interest can NSA have in Carling?'

'That's gonna be for you to find out, my friend.'

'What do you want me to do?'

'Go on exactly as you have been doing. Don't, whatever you do, confront him. But just bear in mind that there's more to George Carling than we thought.'

'He's been so open and friendly.'

'Fine. Keep it that way. But keep a small doubt at the back of your mind.'

'Maybe the Yanks have warned him about me contacting Henney.'

Kennedy shrugged. 'Who knows? See what you think. D'you want me to take you to lunch?'

'No thanks. I want to be back at his place before he gets back himself.'

'He's due back Monday. I'll let you see a copy of our chap's report on his visit.'

'Could be interesting now.'

'I doubt it. Whatever he's up to he's been in the business a long time.' As Mathews turned to leave, Kennedy said, 'It surprised me that GCHQ didn't try and conceal the source of the call. They just treated it as a routine SIS enquiry.'

'Why's that significant?'

'Because it means that GCHQ aren't covering up anything for the benefit of NSA. They normally work hand in glove with one another.' He went on as he saw that Mathews hadn't grasped the point he was making. 'It means that whatever Carling's connection was with NSA, Cheltenham didn't know about it.'

'But what could Carling do for NSA? They're only concerned with telephone and radio surveillance.'

'Those guys in Fort George Meade cover everything that moves. They can listen to a Soviet tank commander giving orders to his men as they head up the main highway to Smolensk or Kiev. They can record every telephone conversation in the world. Military, espionage, civilian, political and economical. They know more about what's going on in the world than the President of the USA himself, and the heads of every government that exists, plus anyone who's trying to overthrow them.'

'I still can't see the Carling connection.'

'Neither can I, but it means that there's more to Carling than his connection with Philby and his mates.' He paused and shrugged. 'Just bear it in mind, Tim. That's all I'm saying.'

CHAPTER 15

Swanson was talking on the phone when Newman walked into his office. He nodded to his visitor and pointed to a chair. When he put down the phone he said, 'I thought we'd better have a word together about this cock-up by Hasset.'

'Has any damage been done?'

'From what I've been told so far, no. But it's far too important to take any risks at all.'

'Why did Hasset give the OK to his guy Maguire in the first place?'

Swanson sighed. 'Ignorance. The standard problem of too much security, I guess. There are only three people who know about the operation. You, me, and our friend at Fort George Meade. And as far as I know it's worked. We're completely watertight. Even if it had been a normal top-secret operation Hasset would not have been in the picture.' He shrugged. 'Why should he be? It's not his area. Maguire is a trusted officer and the request for Hasset's approval for the Brit to meet Hank Henney was more a courtesy request than asking for official approval.

'Hank's long out of the business. A Brit from SIS wants to meet a retired operator. So why not? If the Brit hadn't been a pal of Maguire he could have ferreted out Henney's location independently with very little trouble. The SIS offices in New York and Washington could have trawled around for Henney without us even knowing.' He shrugged. 'Let's face it, if it wasn't for Henney's suspicions we would never have known what the Brit was after.'

'Who did Henney speak to here at Langley?'

'He contacted Delaney, who hit the panic button and set the Brit on his way home.'

'Why was Delaney so hasty?'

'Treated it as the Brit and Maguire and Hasset going behind his back. More a status thing than anything to do with security.'

'The Brit didn't protest – threaten to ring London or call the SIS office in New York?'

'No. I gather from Maguire that the poor bastard's feet didn't touch. He was on a plane two hours after Henney called in.' He smiled. 'Cost us his hotel bill and plane fare.'

'Any complaints from London?'

'That's the main problem, Vic. The call was made to Kennedy who's a pretty laid-back guy. Said he thought we had been over-reacting. Mountains out of molehills, et cetera. Said we owed him one and I agree.'

'So how's that the main problem?'

'When it all blew up somebody here at Langley had done a quick check on Carling and saw that he had been liaison between SIS London and the NSA at Fort George Meade. So they contacted NSA Security and Bauer took the whole thing over. It was Bauer who phoned Kennedy in London. He didn't say who he was, his name or his status and Kennedy wasn't hunting bear and just accepted the call as being from Langley.'

'Bauer's an arrogant bastard. A pity he had to be brought into the operation in the first place. But again, what's the problem?'

'The problem is, did Kennedy really accept the call as a routine apology for precipitate action by juniors in our setup? Or did he check where the call came from and start wondering what was going on?'

'Who would he have checked with?'

'He will have tried British Telecom, who would have referred it lock, stock and barrel to GCHQ.'

'Could they have traced it?'

'No problem at all.'

'And they wouldn't have protected the security of our operation because they don't know anything about it?'

'Exactly. There's no way I can find out what Kennedy thinks without stirring the pot and raising even more suspicions in London. We'll just have to ride with it. But I thought you ought to know.'

'What exactly did the Brit ask Henney about Carling?'

'I didn't want to show too much interest but what alerted Henney was two things. First, why was a Brit from SIS checking up on another SIS man who was long out of the business? And secondly, why, when challenged, did the Brit insist that it was just a routine check? Apart from all that, it seems that old Hank was a great buddy of Carling's,' he smiled, 'and thought the Brits might be trying to do him out of his pension.'

'Where do we go from here?'

'I feel that unless it blows up in London it's best to let it go. Do nothing, unless we're forced to.'

'Any back-up plans in case it all falls apart?'

'No.' He looked very serious as he said, 'I'd be prepared to break a lot of rules to keep this on the road.'

Chapter 16

A phone call from the embassy in Prague had been a message from His Lordship, who would be most grateful if someone could pick him up from Gatwick. Monday evening from Berlin. The scheduled British Airways flight.

Mathews drove the ancient Rover 3-litre and had an hour to wait before the delayed flight was due in. He cashed in on his passenger's title and used the VIP lounge. He took the opportunity to phone Kennedy. It was an insecure line so they talked in the limited but translatable jargon of intelligence and Kennedy said that he already had the report from their colleagues in Prague and Kennedy was sending a copy to him care of the Central Post Office in Tunbridge Wells. No names were mentioned, nor was there any reference to the shambles in New York.

As he sat sipping coffee and barely aware of the garbled announcements of landings, takeoffs and delays, his mind was sorting the pros and cons of raising his abortive New York trip with Carling. It was either confrontation or saying nothing. He decided that silence was truly golden in the circumstances. Confrontation would ruin his established good relationship with Carling and could even offend him enough for Carling to send him packing.

His Lordship was escorted to the VIP lounge by a senior airport official and a BA stewardess. He was all smiles and bonhomie and all Mathews's instincts told him that Carling had not heard of his furtive trip to New York.

They all sat around with sandwiches and Napa Valley wine discussing the possibilities of Gatwick setting aside the space for a gallery of British paintings and photographs. The Tate and Kodak had already promised co-operation and hinted at a possible subsidy if the Arts Council matched it. It seemed amazing that a seventy-year-old man could always create such an atmosphere of enthusiasm and new thinking no matter what was being discussed, whether it was young girls with babies or a commemorative concert for some previously unappreciated composer.

'And what have you chaps been up to?' Carling said as he headed them back down the M25.

'I was away for a couple of days and yesterday I took the girls and the baby down to Bexhill.' He laughed. 'We actually paddled, and made sandcastles.'

'Now there was a nice thought.' He paused and, as if he had been considering it, he said, 'Well done, my boy, well done.' He paused. 'You know. That's the only way we can save the world. Take care of one another. What we ought to do is each one of us take responsibility for one other human being.' He waved a hand from the wheel. 'We hear of thousands of people somewhere killed by floods or famine or war and it's too much to absorb. But see one small Colombian baby on TV yelling its head off as they stick in a syringe, we can't wait to send off a fiver. We're very soft-hearted you know, we Brits. Good people.' He said, 'Nice people underneath.'

His Lordship's dialectic wandered over the Samaritans, the Salvation Army, Barnardos, Oxfam, Save the Children and finally Mother Theresa. Not the slightest sign that anything had changed in their relationship.

Carling had finished his breakfast and was reading *The Times* as Mathews poured himself another coffee.

'This is interesting, Tim.' He looked across at Mathews. 'Your ex-wife's solicitor. What did you say his name was?'

'Thomas. Roger Thomas.'

'Where's he live?'

'In Esher. Lives in a flat over his offices. Why do you ask?'

Carling folded back the unwieldy pages of the newspaper, and folded it again, handing it to Mathews.

'Read that. Top right-hand corner.'

It was only three column inches but the headline was enough – 'Surrey solicitor arrested by Fraud Squad.' Mr Roger Thomas, a solicitor in the commuter suburb of Esher, Surrey, had been arrested late the previous evening and charged with offences related to the fraudulent misuse of clients' funds and of making false returns to both the Inland Revenue and Customs and Excise. He had denied all charges and would come before local magistrates in two days' time.

Mathews put the paper to one side. 'It was only a question of time.'

'You think it's true?'

'I'm sure it is. From what I gathered he's been at it for years.'

'You must be delighted.'

Mathews shrugged. 'I'd like to have seen her face when she heard the news. We all have our lessons to learn.'

'And what lessons have you learned out of this, my boy?'

Mathews thought for a moment. Then, with a quizzical look on his face he said, 'I guess I spend too much time looking at other people and fail to look at myself. I thought – and still think – I was a reasonable husband and father.' He shrugged. 'But I obviously wasn't.'

'Will it make any difference with this chap out of the way?'

'I've no idea.'

'Have you ever seen a trout farm?'

'No.'

'There's one about a mile up the road. Let's take a walk and have a look at it.'

There were two large lakes and on the hill behind them was the big house that had been converted into apartments that all had magnificent views across the valley. There were half a dozen anglers around the larger lake, and a clubhouse with several expensive cars parked alongside it.

Carling led Mathews along a narrow pathway at the edge of the lake to what had once been a boathouse with a wooden jetty. They sat in the sunshine watching the anglers on the far bank casting their flies on to the smooth surface of the water. After a few minutes Carling said, 'What do you want to talk about next?'

'What did you do in SIS after the war was over?'

'Because of my German and the experience I had on the denazification programme I was posted to Berlin.'

'When was this?'

'About 1957.'

'Was George Blake in Berlin then?'

'He was there about a year before me.'

'Did you know that he was a KGB agent?'

'No. I knew from hints from my Russian contacts that

there was somebody in SIS Berlin who was passing them information but they were always very careful not to break an agent's security.'

'What was your role with the Russians?'

Carling smiled. 'It wasn't a role. But we were well into the Cold War by then and I did what I could to calm them down.' He paused and shrugged. 'And to calm our people too.'

'What was your SIS job at that time?'

'I was responsible for getting information on what they called the Russian Zone, which became East Germany.'

'What sort of information?'

'The influence of German communists, their relationship with Moscow and the general population's attitude to the Russian occupying forces.'

'And what did you give the Russians?'

'Mainly my opinion on the various moves they were making. At the time they were sure that the West was going to invade the Russian Zone and they built up huge forces on the borders between the zones. And that made our people sure that the Soviets were going to come over the border and smash through to the Channel.' He sighed. 'It was typical of the whole Cold War period. Suspicion, rumour, false information and neither side understanding the other side. It was a nightmare, believe me.' He shrugged. 'I did my best for them and us to sort out the rumours from the facts. I can remember when our staff in border cities like Brunswick, Göttingen and Hamburg were issued orders to destroy all their records in twenty-four hours as a Soviet invasion was imminent.

'The Russians had moved in troops around Magdeburg. Mainly to make the local population pay for their keep. When I warned them how it was seen in our camp they were amazed and reluctantly dispersed half their divisions to other parts of their zone. It was like keeping two wild animals from one another's throats. The intelligence on both sides was appalling. Inaccurate, misconstrued and looking for trouble. I'm not sure how my situation assessments to either side made any difference but I did my best.'

'How long were you in Berlin?'

'Eight or nine years with a two-month break when London called me back for a temporary assignment.'

'What was the assignment?'

'When they closed down Bletchley they kept on some of the cryptographers who were breaking down top security codes, especially those used by the Russians. It was the group who first gave the clues that eventually identified Maclean as "Homer", the Russian codename of a British diplomat working for the KGB. They were all experts at their jobs and like most experts they were bad administrators, politically naïve and resentful of any civil service attempt to organise them. I had got to know them well at Bletchley when they were working on Enigma and Ultra; SIS suggested me as a co-ordinator and everybody was surprised when they agreed.'

'Where did they work after Bletchley?'

'They had a place in a London suburb, Eastcote, and I had a couple of rooms on the top floor of the building.' He smiled. 'It worked quite well. They got on with their work, which was all they cared about, and I kept SIS, the Foreign Office and the Civil Services at bay.' He smiled. 'In the end they all finished up as a special section of GCHQ.'

'Were you ever at GCHQ?'

'No. I had quite a lot to do with them but I was always SIS, or Foreign Office on secondment from SIS.'

'Were you ever PV'd at some later stage in SIS?'

'Like I told you, there was no such thing as positive vetting when I first joined, but I was PV'd before I was sent to Berlin as a matter of routine. And I was PV'd again in the late sixties.' He smiled. 'I think that was because somebody had suggested way back that I was gay because I wasn't married.'

'But being gay wouldn't have automatically affected your career.'

'Agreed. But that's not what matters. If you have never disguised or hidden that you're gay, that's one thing. But if you are revealed or exposed as being gay, it means that you told lies when you were recruited and in subsequent checks. And under those circumstances you'll certainly be sacked.' Carling stood up. 'Time we were getting back.'

As they walked back together Carling, seemingly apropos of nothing obvious, said, 'Never, never, trust politicians or bureaucrats. They live on lies.'

When Mathews woke in the night he switched on the bedside lamp and looked at his watch. It was 2.30 a.m. and he knew there was something that he should be thinking about. The little warning bells in his mind had rung as they walked back together from the trout farm. It was something that Carling had said. But he couldn't isolate it.

CHAPTER 17

There was a brown envelope for him at the post office in Tunbridge Wells and Mathews went for a coffee at Importers.

The contents were mostly junk mail but there was one envelope with a red wax seal. In it was the report from the SIS in Prague.

Surveillance: 1096
Subject: Earlybird
Operator: Cooper

Subject arrived at RUZYNE airport Thursday noon. Was driven with other members of the delegation to ADRIA HOTEL at VACLAVSKE NAMESTI 26. Subject allotted suite. Others to rooms, some sharing.

Ascertained that subject was not part of ARTS COUNCIL party but guest of CZ government.

Thursday evening subject attended PART ONE of Young Musician of Year Competition at NATIONAL THEATRE. Later attended buffet at BRITISH CULTURAL CENTRE at NARODNI 10.

Friday. Subject spent whole day and evening with Czech cultural officials at MINISTRY OF CULTURE. Ate in evening at SHALOM, MAISELOVA 18, in Jewish quarter. Was with six others. All nationals, two were senior members of former Czech Comm. Party now in govt employ as diplomats.

Saturday. Subject had visitors in his suite all day. Mainly actors, musicians and artists. In evening attended PART TWO of competition and was on judging panel. Later with mixed party from competition at CAFE SAVOY, VITEZNA 1.

Sunday. Walked in old town with unidentified young woman approx mid-twenties. Seen with subject and others on other occasions. Evening was interviewed on TV on subject of 'Acting as a Visual Art'. Ate with same young woman at SHALOM in evening.

Monday. Subject paid courtesy call to BRIT EMBASSY. Mid-day accompanied delegation to airport but did not board booked flight back to Gatwick. Lost contact at airport with subject but was able to ascertain that subject took LUFTHANSA flight to BERLIN, TEGEL. Arrived BERLIN approx 14.00 hours. Left TEGEL on BRITISH AIRWAYS late evening flight to GATWICK but have no information on subject's movements in BERLIN. Flight details solely from bookings clerk.
ENDS

Mathews read it through a second time and then slid the two pages back into the envelope. He knew Cooper, an ex-policeman who had been recruited into SIS from Special Branch much to MI5's annoyance. The codename Earlybird for Carling was typical schoolboy humour and words like 'ascertain' were giveaway echoes of long ago police statements. He wondered who the young woman was. Mid-twenties was a bit young as a seventy-year-old's companion.

The rest of the mail was junk except for a couple of letters, one from his mother and the other a postscript to the surveillance report.

Subject: Earlybird
Operator: Cooper
Subsequent to my report I have been able to ascertain that the previously unidentified young woman seen with subject was

not local. Her name was given to me as RACHEL MARIA AARONS and her nationality as GERMAN. Other background unknown but speaks fluent ENGLISH, GERMAN and RUSSIAN.
ENDS

Back at Lake Cottage, Julie gave Mathews a cup of tea in the kitchen and as he helped himself to sugar he said, 'Where is he?'

'He said he was going away for a couple of days.' She hesitated, then said, 'He seemed upset, I heard him moving around in the night. Have you two had a row about anything?'

'Not that I know of, Julie.' He smiled. 'We don't go in for rows. Anyway, there's nothing for us to have rows about.'

'What do you talk about with him?'

He shrugged. 'Just old times. The way things were a long time ago. Long before you were born. Long before I was born for that matter.' He paused. 'What made you think he was upset?'

'He didn't talk at all. It was as if his mind was far away. He didn't hear what I said when I spoke to him, tried to jolly him along. He always chats away at breakfast.'

'Did he ask where I was?'

'No. He didn't mention you.'

'Any idea where he was going?'

'No. Just gave me a list of people to phone to cancel things and say he was indisposed.'

'If he phones I'd like to talk to him. Maybe I could cheer him up.'

'I don't think so, Tim. I'll tell him but I think he wants to get away from all of us.'

'How much luggage did he take?'

'A travel bag and a holdall.'

'Don't worry, Julie. He's a very wise man. He'll be OK.'

'I hope you're right.'

Carling avoided all the VIP stuff at Gatwick but nevertheless travelled Business Class. He read a paperback version of Cyril Connelly's *The Unquiet Grave* and refused the offered tray of food and courtesy drinks. At Tegel he took a taxi into the city and signed in at The Savoy in Fasanenstrasse. The city was full of conventions but his title got him a suite on the first floor.

He sat in the comfortable armchair, his case and holdall on one of the single beds. He needed time to think. Talking day after day to Mathews had brought back memories that he hoped had long been buried. For them it was a matter of possible treason. For him it was a reminder of what had been the happiest days of his life. Maybe the only happy days of his life.

As he walked down the Kurfürstendamm later that evening it seemed strange that the burnt out Tiger tank was no longer half buried in the huge shell hole in front of Kempinski's.

TWO

CHAPTER 18

Even after the ruins of Hamburg, Berlin had been a shock.
The Soviet tanks and artillery had systematically reduced
every street, every building, to mountains of rubble, which
were still there fifteen years after the war ended.

They'd allocated him a small apartment, two rooms, a
kitchen and bathroom in one of the side streets of Savigny
Platz, over what had been a fruit shop. The building
had been saved from the blast by the taller buildings on
either side that were now just a shell. There was electricity
for Allied services four hours a day. Unfortunately there
was no way of discovering which four hours it would be
but the offices at the Olympiad had a permanent supply
of both electricity and water and the officers' mess had
reasonable supplies of food, but it was forbidden to buy
locally produced food. There was little enough for the
surviving Germans.

It was 1960 and nearly five years after he left Hamburg
when Carling first saw Yuri again. There was still a pre-
tence of co-operation between the occupying forces. It had
been at a cocktail party given by the French. Yuri was
wearing a well-cut olive-brown uniform with black riding
boots and the three gold stars of a full colonel.

They avoided each other until they were in a group

of people waiting to claim their hats and coats from the tables that were serving as a cloakroom. As they stood shoulder to shoulder Yuri smiled and said softly, ' "*Zur letzten Instanz*" in an hour. Yes?' Carling nodded but didn't speak. The meeting place was a beer-house that had escaped the shells and the bombs. It was just inside the Russian Zone.

Yuri had changed into a civilian shirt and was waiting for him at a table in the garden at the side of the pub. He smiled as Carling sat down at the table.

'Nice to see you again, Georgi. How are you?'

'I'm OK. Congratulations on the double promotion.'

Yuri smiled. 'Just dressing up for the occasion. I'm still a major.'

'And still KGB?'

'Yes,' he smiled.

'What are you doing in Berlin?'

Yuri shrugged. 'I'm posted here in the hope that you'll go on helping us.'

'Helping you do what?'

'Helping us survive.'

'You won the war, Yuri.'

'But our cities all look like this.' He waved a hand at the city around them. 'The Americans want to break us economically and our old allies are wondering if it isn't a good time to wipe us off the map.' He paused. 'Twenty million Soviet people killed, our money spent on the war. It's a grim time. Believe me.'

'But how could I help you?'

'Just keep us informed.'

'About what?'

'Anything you learn about Western moves that are aggressive towards us. Economically, politically or militarily.'

Carling shook his head slowly. 'The war's over, Yuri. Without the war as the background I can't help you.'

'The war's not over. It's a cold war now.' He paused. 'The Soviet Union is the target of the most powerful government in the world. Not that long ago the American public were raising funds to support us, and Western governments were sending us guns and tanks. Today an American can be hounded out of his job – not for being a communist, but just for being suspected of being a member of the Party. Even knowing a communist can cause you to be ostracised by your friends or fellow workers. Nobody is free from suspicion. We were heroes and now, a few months' later, we are criminals. The American government took a long time before they put down McCarthy.'

'You haven't convinced me, Yuri.'

'We've always had a two-way deal, Georgi. You helped me and I helped you. I can still help you.'

'How do you know you can help me?'

Yuri smiled. 'We know that you are responsible for intelligence about the so-called Russian Zone. We don't have any love for our East German colleagues.'

For long moments Carling looked at Yuri. It was not just a handsome face but gentle, with smile creases at the eyes and an incipient dimple when he laughed.

'Ask me one thing that's really important to your people. Not to you but to your members.'

'No problem, Georgi. Are the West intending to invade our zone or our homeland?'

Carling looked surprised and shocked. 'Absolutely not. I've never heard even the most tentative suggestion of any aggressive action.' He smiled. 'But I have heard our people wondering why you have so many Red Army divisions around Magdeburg. There are those who wonder if your people might be thinking of coming over the border.'

It was Yuri's turn to look shocked. 'That's crazy. We moved troops from Leipzig and Dresden because the Magdeburg area is mainly farming. The big cities couldn't support our troops with food and accommodation. We didn't even send their tactical units with them.'

'Where are those units?'

'Still back in Leipzig and Dresden.' He paused. 'Maybe this is going too far but if you check carefully you'll find that there are no tanks or armoured cars with our troops. They are all in a vehicle park at Halle.' He paused. 'How did your people react?'

'They made contingency plans for if you came over the border.'

'Did you move troops?'

'No. We don't have enough fighting units to move around.' He shrugged. 'We demobilised most of our troops years ago. Our soldiers had had enough of the war.'

'Can I use what you've told me?'

'I guess so. Maybe you're right. Maybe we *should* keep in touch.'

Yuri leaned back, seemingly relieved. 'I won't go too far, Georgi. And it'll be a fair exchange, I promise you.' He waved his hand around at the tables. 'We can meet here or at my place, any time.' He reached in his pocket for a pen and scribbled two numbers on a piece torn off the bar menu. 'The top phone number's for my place, the bottom number will contact me twenty-four hours a day.' He paused and pushed forward his pen. 'Write down where I can contact you.'

Carling smiled. 'Let's leave it that I contact you.'

Yuri shrugged. 'Doesn't have to be business, Georgi. I always enjoyed your company.' He paused. 'I've just realised. Music, you're fond of music. I've got a few musician friends coming to eat with me tomorrow.' He smiled. 'Two local Germans, and two Czechs.' He laughed. 'All glad of a meal. Why don't you come?'

Carling shrugged. 'Why not? Where and when?'

'Seven o'clock.' He reached for the piece of paper with his telephone numbers and wrote his address and pushed it back across the table. Carling didn't recognise the street. 'Where is it?'

'It's off Alexanderplatz. The north-east corner. It was a block of flats. Mostly ruined but better than nothing.' He smiled. 'I'll look forward to that.'

Carling relaxed. 'So will I.'

The others were already there when Carling arrived. They were all a little younger than both he and Yuri. But from the moment he was introduced to Rachel Aarons he could barely speak. It took a glass of vodka to loosen his tongue. She wasn't just pretty, she was beautiful. Jet-black hair below her shoulders, heavy-lidded dark eyes, a neat nose and a full soft mouth. She was wearing a black silk dress that she said one of her aunts had given her. And she played the violin in a quartet that sometimes had to be a trio when the viola player was on duty as a policeman.

They ate sausages and bread, on plates on their laps, and Carling had brought a jar of coffee. Yuri had 'liberated' a banana each for the two girls. The talk was all of music and performers and they listened intently to Carling's picture of the music scene in London. None of them had either a radio or a gramophone; all they had was the usual musicians' gossip and the music they made themselves, even if it was no more than a piano transcription of some symphony. There was much talk of Wagner and Furtwängler.

It was Jan, one of the Czechs, who turned to Rachel Aarons. 'You're a Jew, Rachel. Should former Nazi musicians be allowed to perform in public now?'

'Of course. They're musicians first, and if they hadn't joined the Party Hitler or Goebbels would have probably had them thrown in jail.' She smiled. 'Being a musician is what matters, not whether you are a Party member . . .' she laughed '. . . or a Jew.'

Yuri joined in. 'The Furtwängler row is nothing to do with him or his membership of the Party. It's a public contest between the Soviet Kommandatura in Berlin, who want him to be the conductor of the Berlin Philharmonic which is now "ours" and the British and American Control Commissions, who insist on sticking by the rules. Furtwängler accepted the title of Prussian State Counsellor way back and that means it is mandatory that he has to go before the Denazification Commission.'

Carling said, 'Does that mean that you agree with our attitude, Yuri?'

'Of course. So do most Soviets in Berlin except for the bureaucrats.'

'And bureaucrats in the British and American sectors who want to apply the rules to annoy the Soviet authorities.' Rachel Aarons was at least smiling as she said it, but Yuri avoided looking at Carling, whom he had introduced just as a British officer.

Back in his apartment Carling tried to recall what Yuri's place was like, but all he could remember was the girl. It was almost midnight but he phoned Yuri's home number and arranged to see him at his rooms the next day.

Yuri's place was in a narrow alleyway not far from

the police station. The buildings on either side had been completely destroyed and Yuri's building was held up by massive wooden struts at an angle, cemented into the ground. In daylight it looked totally unsafe. Yuri's rooms were on the ground floor and the other rooms in the house were also occupied by Soviet officers of middle rank. In the bombed area at the side, a wooden hut had been constructed to house a diesel generator that supplied electricity for the whole house.

Carling could see the setting sun through the skeleton of a ruined building. It was big and glowing against the pale, misty blue of the sky. It reminded him of sunsets at the family home in Scotland. Sunsets that others saw as beautiful but for him always looked ominous and angry.

Yuri was at the open door, leaning, relaxed and smiling, his shoulder against the door frame. When they were in Yuri's room the Russian poured them both a fruit drink, passing a glass to Carling and raising his own, smiling as he said, '*Na zdrovia*.'

Carling smiled and said, '*Slaintye*.' When Yuri frowned, Carling laughed and said, 'It's Irish.' He paused. 'Who is she, Yuri?'

Yuri frowned. 'Who is who?'

'The girl who looks like Audrey Hepburn – Rachel Aarons.'

'You mean you've risked coming into our zone just to find out about a girl?'

'Not just a girl. A special girl.'

Yuri shook his head, smiling. 'I can't believe it. You had girlfriends in London and even more in Hamburg. I'm sure you slept with many of them but I can't think of one of them you'd have done this for.'

'So tell me about her.'

'Sit down, for God's sake, while I collect my thoughts.' As he sat down himself, Yuri said, 'Can I take it that your interest in the girl is personal, not professional?'

'Entirely personal.'

'You won't use her or involve her in any way in your work?'

'No. Never.'

'Well. Let's see. She's nineteen or twenty, I'm not sure which. Her father was German, her mother was Russian. She's now a resident of East Berlin. Speaks fluent German, Russian, English and French. Can get by in Czech and Hungarian.' He paused, thinking, and then he said, 'If she didn't live here she'd be playing violin for some major orchestra. She's had offers from America and England already.'

'Why didn't she take them?'

'Our East German colleagues wouldn't allow her to leave, even for one concert.' He smiled. 'They prefer athletes and gymnasts to musicians.'

'Tell me about her parents.'

Yuri sighed. 'A great example of the stupidity of politics. Her German father died from the effects of being in a concentration camp because he was a Jew. Her Russian mother died way back, worn out by worry and ill health. She gave music lessons to disabled people, Germans, here in Berlin. Rachel's father had been deputy chief of the main Berlin library. Neither of them belonged to or were interested in any political party. Educated and talented, they lived for their only child – your Rachel.'

'Why *my* Rachel?'

Yuri laughed softly. 'She asked me about you, so I guess I'll be right in the end.'

'What did she want to know about me?'

'Just background.'

'What did you tell her?'

'Nothing much. Son of an earl. British officer. Intelligent. Well off. Liked girls and music and all the other arts. Not formally political but had views on how the world should be run. Hopelessly sentimental views that would not work.' He smiled. 'Do you want to see her again?'

'Yes. Of course. Will she meet me?'

'I'm sure she will. But you'd have to use this place. She lives in a hostel and it's controlled by the local Party officials. Mean, puritanical bastards.' He shrugged. 'So when do you want to see her?'

'Tomorrow OK?'

'Sure. Let's make it early. Say six and then you can take her back into your zone and give her a meal somewhere.'

'That's great.' He paused. 'There's something I want to ask you, Yuri. Why did Moscow refuse Marshall Aid from the Americans? It was a generous gesture by the Americans and it looks aggressive to the rest of the world to refuse it.'

Yuri smiled. 'A condition of receiving payouts under Marshall Aid was that the country concerned would not claim reparations from the Germans. We are determined to make them pay for what they did to us. The conditions for Marshall Aid were insulting to the Soviet people.'

Carling shook his head slowly. 'Good old Virgil. "I fear the Greeks even when they bring gifts." '

Yuri laughed. 'An American said it better.'

'Who?'

'Tennessee Williams. "We have to distrust each other. It is our only defence against betrayal".'

'Sounds like Camino Real.'

'It is.'

'Are you sure she'll let me see her?'

Yuri shrugged. 'Pretty sure. It was obvious that she liked you from the way she asked about you and talked about you last night after you had gone.'

'Do I have any rivals?'

'She's very attractive so she has lots of men friends. But none of them is more than that.' He paused. 'So far as I know.'

'Thanks for letting me use your place.'

'You're welcome.'

CHAPTER 19

She was there, alone, when he got to Yuri's place. He had bought a small Blaupunkt radio for her on the black market; it had cost him two packets of Woodbines.

'Just so that you can hear some music,' he said as he gave it to her.

She looked at it carefully, turning it on and tuning it to different stations. Then she looked up at him, obviously delighted.

'What a wonderful gift. I'll be the envy of everyone at the hostel.' She smiled. 'I'll think of you when I'm listening to music.'

Despite the many ruined buildings still acting as grim reminders of the war, by 1960 Berliners had begun to build both industry and commerce. In the Western Zones there were reasonably well-stocked shops and several cinemas were showing American films. In the basements of ruined buildings there were dance-halls and a wide variety of restaurants and cafés. It was to one of these that Carling took Rachel Aarons that first evening. It was run by a Viennese couple and Carling was a favourite, not only as a regular customer who sometimes provided luxuries like real coffee, and sugar for their cakes, but because he could slip naturally into a Viennese accent and vocabulary. Earlier that day he had brought in candles for their table.

He had asked her about her family and she had told him of the pleasant civilised life they had recounted to her of before the war, and the turmoil of the war and after, when she was growing up. And Carling had told her about his parents, especially his mother from whom he had absorbed his love and knowledge of music. It had been an extraordinary evening. It was as if they had known each other for years. He tried not to use his training to probe about possible relationships with other men and he had been ridiculously pleased when she challenged him.

She laughed as she said, 'You're trying to find out if I have a steady boyfriend, aren't you?'

He smiled back. 'Yes. Was it so obvious?'

'Yes.' She laughed. 'I'm flattered.'

'Can I see you again tomorrow?'

'The quartet are playing at a local hall. You could come and hear us.'

'And I can see you afterwards?'

She smiled. 'Of course.' She paused. 'By the way, I expect you guessed from my name that I'm Jewish.'

He shrugged. 'I didn't, actually.' He smiled. 'It makes me wish I was Jewish.'

She laughed. 'I'm not religious. My father was, but my mother was a lapsed Catholic. Music was their religion. Jewish music sometimes affected my father, especially when I played Max Bruch's *Kol Nidrei*.' She smiled. 'It made him cry but he loved it.' She paused. 'With your Scottish connections I'll have to play you Bruch's *Scottish Fantasia*. That's quite sad music too.'

'Where were you when the war started?'

She laughed. 'I wasn't born when the war started. I came along in 1940. It was 1947 before we were together as a family again. My father was still in bad health when he was released from being in a concentration camp. My mother had moved from Dresden to Berlin a few months after the surrender so that she could be near where the camp prisoners were released. He was already in a hospital. When Mama died, father's sister came to look after us both. And father died last year.'

'Do you miss them?'

'Yes. But conditions have been so bad and there were always so many problems that there hasn't really been time to think about anything much except just surviving.'

He reached out to touch her hand. 'I'll try and make it better for you from now on.'

'You have already. This is the first time I've ever eaten at a restaurant.' She smiled across at him. 'I'm glad you asked me out. And I'm glad you want to see me again.'

'I'm a very lucky man starting tonight. No . . .' he said '. . . starting last night.'

He walked her back to her hostel and made arrangements for the next evening. He kissed her cheek and she was standing on the steps when he turned back to see if she was there. They waved to each other and he was the happiest man in Berlin.

The old man facing Carling across the small table had once been a member of the SPD, the left-wing party that had been taken over by the Communists in the Russian Zone but still functioned in West Germany. He was seventy-two years old, one of Carling's most useful informants. In 1953 the Russians had opened fire on workers protesting against the conditions in East Berlin and so far as Kurt Lang was concerned it was unforgivable. He had no family that could be used as hostages for pressure on him. Carling had persuaded him to join the Communist Party and act as an informant, and the old man was a shrewd observer of what was going on.

'They've created a new committee. They call it the Committee for Conserving Labour. It's run by a chap from Moscow but the rest are locals.' The old man looked at Carling. 'You need to watch that committee, my friend.'

'Why?'

'The Party's worried about all the skilled people who are slipping over to the West. It's getting to be a real embarrassment politically and economically. There's companies ready to pay a fortune to get hold of a skilled electrician, and toolmakers can get a flat thrown in. There's a lot of real criticism from Moscow. Threats of dismissals and worse. I was told there had been hints of jail sentences – enemies of the State and all that stuff.'

'Is it likely to affect us?'

'Who knows? I just wanted to warn you that they'll do something sooner or later to stop the flow of people into the West.'

Carling nodded in acknowledgement. 'My people have asked me for an opinion on what the ordinary people feel about the Berlin communists, and what they feel about their standard of living.'

The old man smiled. 'You got all day?'

They talked for three hours and Carling asked his man to come back with all the detail he could uncover about acts of nepotism and corruption by Party administrators. The Foreign Office information section was planning to mount a radio series on abuses by the Party in East Berlin.

Carling had informants in all walks of life in East Berlin and although he realised that he was witnessing and recording the skirmishes of the Cold War, he found it grindingly boring. He longed for someone, even someone on the other side, to show a spark of imagination, a gesture of faith in human beings. But as always in politics every day was given to moves and countermoves in the struggle to command people's minds and lives. If it had not been for Rachel he would have pressed for a posting to some more rewarding area. Not that he knew where that could be. Maybe he should consider resigning from SIS altogether. But what would he do for a living? He had not been raised or trained to oversee the family's assets.

All his free time was spent with Rachel Aarons and his work for SIS gave him every excuse and opportunity to spend his time in East Berlin. She knew now what his work was, but by a kind of osmosis rather than being told by him. He had never used her as a source of information. Amongst her circle of friends they were seen now as a couple. A few wondered why they didn't marry despite the administrative difficulties that would be raised by both sides' bureaucracies. But Carling was cautious about disturbing her life by what would amount to open defiance of both sides' tensions in the uneasy city. He believed that the Good Lord would send a sign when it was right to take that step. That they would marry was never in doubt for either of them. Life went on and they were happy enough.

At the year-end meeting in London to summarise the year 1960, it was agreed that it was not a good year for Western intelligence. Both in political terms and espionage, the Soviet's shooting down of the American U-2 plane well inside Soviet territories was the significant feature of the year. The sequence of events left both the White House and the CIA exposed to the world as both liars and inept fumblers in the intelligence business. There was no doubt that 1960 was Khrushchev's year.

Carling's report on personalities and conditions in East Berlin was praised for its information but criticised for not indicating what would happen in the next twelve months. They agreed with his view that Moscow was angry and frustrated that all their attempts to make the Western Allies withdraw from Berlin had failed. But what would Moscow's next move be? There had been long and indecisive discussions about using Carling's contacts for counterpropaganda but he had refused to allow his informants to be involved in any kind of direct espionage. They were informants, not agents, and most of his sources would dry up if they were asked to do anything even bordering on espionage. Their dislike or even hatred of the system didn't go as far as treason.

CHAPTER 20

On New Year's Day 1961 Rachel, thanks to some string-pulling by Yuri, moved into the luxury of a two-roomed apartment near St Nicholas' church. The Nikolaiviertel had been rebuilt to reflect, as near as the authorities could afford, the beautiful old buildings that had been ruined in just one half-hour midday raid by American Flying Fortresses. The new buildings housed shops and cafés as well as people, but in a harmony that satisfied those locals who could remember the historic quarter before the war.

With Rachel now independently accommodated they spent even more time together and on Easter Sunday he asked her to marry him. She had laughed, kissed him and said – 'When?'

'We'll have to do a bit of investigating.' He looked at her. 'It will mean you moving to our zone. Is that OK?'

She smiled. 'Like it says in the Bible – "Whither thou goest, I will go; and where thou lodgest, I will lodge." '

'Have you got any kind of passport?'

'No. Just my birth certificate.'

'I'll have to do some trading with Yuri. You'll need to have an identity card at least. And it will mean getting married in the British Zone.'

'Do your people know about me?'

He shook his head. 'No. So far as they are concerned, I just come over here to do research.'

She looked up at his face and said softly, 'Are you a spy?'

He sighed. 'There are no such things as spies. I'm an intelligence officer.'

'And Yuri?'

'He's the same as me. But he's KGB.'

'So why are you such good friends?'

He shrugged. 'We've known each other a long time. From the war. The Russians were our allies then. We helped each other.' He smiled. 'We kid ourselves that we can help keep the Cold War cold and not hot.'

She put up her lips and they kissed and then she said softly, 'I'll always remember today, Georgi. It's the best day of my life.'

'So far. There will be better days.' He smiled. 'Where shall we go to eat? How about our old friends at Mutter Hoppe?'

She slid her arms around his neck, looking up at him, smiling and happy. 'I love you so much, Georgi.'

He smiled and kissed her nose. 'I love you too, my dear.'

Her face looked solemn as she said, 'Shall we have children, Georgi?'

'Of course.' He hesitated. 'I mean if you want to.'

'Would you want to?'

He laughed. 'It would be great. I can't wait.'

'I'm two months' pregnant. I wasn't going to tell you.'

'Why not?'

'In case it was not what you wanted.'

'Don't be silly. Of course I want us to have a child. Are you OK? Have you been checked over properly?'

'Yes. I'm having another check in two weeks' time. Are you sure it's OK with you?'

His arms went round her and she knew that he meant what he said as he kissed her avidly.

CHAPTER 21

The meeting was in a room at Karlshorst, the Russians' command HQ in East Berlin and when Yuri was shown into the room he didn't recognise either of the officers sitting at the table.

They were both colonels, one with infantry insignia and one an artillery officer. Yuri guessed that the insignia were probably spurious. Just used to conceal their real status.

The older man introduced himself as Litvak and the other man as Panov.

'Tell me about this man Carling.'

'I've been working with him since our days in Hamburg. He has always been reliable.'

'How much do you pay him?'

'He's never been paid.'

'So what is it? Girls, young boys or what? Don't tell me he's a communist.'

'He first contacted our London embassy during the war to express his appreciation of our struggle against the Germans. Since I took him over we have just exchanged general information.'

'About what?'

'My reports are all on file, comrade colonel.'

'About what? You tell me. I don't ever trust reports. For

me reports are there to cover the writer's arse if anything goes wrong, meantime a bit of publicity in the hope of promotion.'

Yuri was tempted to point out that they were not KGB officers and he wasn't ready to accept casual insults from unknown men. But he held his tongue.

'We discuss the reality of things in the media that are attempts to stir up tensions between our two countries.'

'You mean all you do is no more than gossip about gossip?'

'No, comrade. I mean exactly what I said.'

'Can you tell him what you want him to find out for you?'

'No.'

'Why not?'

'Because that's not the way we work. He is not my agent and I am a contact not his controller. And the same applies to me.'

'Is he worth the time you spend on him?'

'I leave that to my senior officers to decide. I've been under instructions to keep a close relationship with him.'

'Does he make critical comments on our regime?'

'About the same as I do about his government. We aren't political.' He half smiled. 'No dialectic from me and no *Daily Telegraph* from him.'

He saw a quick smile on Panov's face and then Litvak said, 'I'll contact Belinkov. It's up to him but I like to get my own impression face-to-face of what's going on.'

Yuri drove back slowly to KGB HQ in Normannenallee where Belinkov was waiting for him.

Pointing to a chair, Belinkov said, 'I've just had Litvak on the phone, shitting his pants about Carling's problems.'

'Did he oppose my proposals?'

Belinkov shrugged. 'Just putting down a marker to protect himself if anything went wrong.'

'He controls the police and the local politicians. Could be a nuisance if he chose to be.'

Belinkov shook his head dismissively. 'I'll deal with him.' He paused. 'It's too good an opportunity for us to miss, Yuri. He'd *have* to co-operate.'

'I still don't like it. It seems a poor reward for his help and goodwill towards us.'

'D'you want somebody else to handle it?'

'He wouldn't go along with any of it if it was somebody else.' He paused and hesitated before he said quietly, 'We are good friends with years of proven trustworthiness behind us. It's more than just an informer contact. Are we ready to lose that?'

'Of course not, but Moscow are involved now. They see this as an incredible opportunity.'

'Opportunity for what?'

'To have our own man right inside SIS.'

'Even hint at that and we'll lose him for good.'

'It's a risk worth taking, Yuri. And the success will all be down to you.'

'And if it fails? Who carries the can then?'

'You won't fail, Yuri. You won't fail.'

'I shall need co-operation from a lot of officials.'

'You'd get it but you must string him along for at least three months.' He shrugged. 'After that we'll see.'

By the end of May Yuri was telling Carling that he was having no success with the East German authorities. They were raising difficulties about issuing Rachel with an identity card and they had said that any application to be allowed to leave their zone would have to go before a commission that met very infrequently.

As they moved into June, Carling decided that he would have to try alternative ways of arranging their marriage. It was at that point that he started listing Rachel Aarons as an informant on his official list. He had told none of his colleagues of his love affair and because he operated virtually independently of the SIS setup in Berlin there was little on the record of any of his informants. But there might soon be a time when he would need to use his official status to get things done. Helping an informant could be seen as a reasonable reward for past co-operation.

He was uncertain too about the wisdom of letting it be known that he was proposing to marry a German. Especially a German from the Russian Zone. And who could he get to officiate at their marriage? There were padres attached to several British units but they would probably want to check that his marriage to a German was authorised, especially as he was an SIS officer. He would have to check if a marriage performed by a German pastor was equally valid in the UK.

What worried him most was his feeling that Yuri's attitude was changing. He seemed uneasy about something. They still met regularly and exchanged information but he sensed that Yuri was now looking for information that he must know Carling was not going to reveal.

Carling had past favours he could cash in on in both zones and he reluctantly decided that he should go ahead and deal with his problems with his own resources.

It was the end of June when he received notification of his promotion to the SIS grade equivalent to a lieutenant-colonel in recognition of the work he was doing in the Russian Zone.

* * *

Pastor Franks was in his sixties. He had been cleared by a denazification panel. He had been a padre to a Wehrmacht artillery unit but had never, despite a lot of pressure, become a member of the Nazi Party. At the end of his second meeting with Pastor Franks, Carling's instinct was that the priest was both sympathetic and unconventional enough to be told most of the truth. On the third visit the pastor listened in silence to Carling's story.

When he had finished Pastor Franks said, 'Why go to all this trouble when you could tell your superiors exactly what you have just told me?'

Carling shrugged. 'Because I know they would never give me permission to marry a German because of my job. Especially a girl from the other side.'

'How could they stop you?'

'First of all I would be posted to some other country. Probably South America or an Arab country.' He sighed. 'They are powerful people, there are a lot of other things that they could do.'

'Like what?'

Carling shrugged. 'Harassment of the girl maybe.'

'Sounds like the Gestapo.'

Carling shook his head. 'These are the means that all intelligence organisations have at their disposal. They don't always do anything. The threat or the expectation is usually enough.'

Pastor Franks nodded. 'You must love this girl a lot. Does she love you as much herself?'

'Yes. Absolutely.'

'Well, let's look at some of the facts. First of all, a marriage in Berlin or anywhere else by a genuine priest is valid anywhere in Europe. I have married several British soldiers to German girls because that was what the girls' parents wished. But, of course, the soldiers concerned have had permission from their commanding officers to both marry and to marry here in Germany. It's over fifteen years since the war ended.' He smiled. 'We Germans are being allowed to be part of Europe again. So the ceremony itself is no problem.

'However, there are other problems. I should need some official identification for your girl and a permit for her leaving the Russian Zone. And, of course, a permit from the British for her to be a resident of the British Zone for seven days before the marriage.'

Carling was silent for long moments and then he said, 'One way or another I could fix all those things.' He paused. 'Would the marriage still be valid if it were found at some later date that some document was not genuine?'

Pastor Franks smiled. 'I thought you might ask me that. Let us say that provided the documents concerned looked genuine to me when I was shown them, that would be enough. And once you two are married not even the joint efforts of the Kremlin and Whitehall could invalidate it. You will be married in the eyes of the Good Lord and that is all that matters, even in these ungodly times.'

'Will you marry us then?'

'Yes. Of course.'

They had talked for over an hour and Kurt Lang had said it again and again.

'They're up to something. I don't know what it is but they're having secret meetings. Some of them seem scared of whatever it is. But mark my words, my friend, they're going to do something that scares them, and that scares me too.'

'Is it going to mean another Berlin airlift, d'you think?' asked Carling.

Kurt Lang shrugged. 'I just don't know.'

'There's something I wanted to ask you, Kurt. Can you get me a blank identity card and a permit to leave the Russian Zone?'

'The ID card I can get you for cash.'

'How much?'

'Forty dollars last time I heard.'

'And the permit?'

'I've never ever seen one but I'll ask around. Would a photocopy do?'

'Better than nothing. How long would it take?'

'The ID I could get you in a week. The other I just don't know.'

'I've got a Leica IIIb, if that would help.'

'I'll come back to you on that.'

The French had their usual party for 14 July and Carling had used it to talk to Yuri. They stood in the evening sunshine of the garden identifying the guests one by one.

Yuri frowned. 'Who's the girl with Barrault?'

'She's his mistress. I can't remember her name. She's a nurse at their military hospital.'

'But I thought that young German girl, Ursula, was his mistress.'

'Yuri, you bring your French mistress to Bastille Day parties, not your German one – even if she is prettier.'

'Are you going back to Rachel's place after this?'

'Yeah.'

'I can give you a lift if you want.'

'OK. About half an hour after the speeches, yes?'

'Suits me, comrade.'

Carling laughed. 'Don't comrade me. I'm not a bloody comrade and never will be.'

'Aren't we heroes any more, Georgi?'

Carling smiled. 'Just people, Yuri. Same as the rest of us.'

On their way back in Yuri's battered BMW, Carling said, 'You know that Rachel's pregnant, don't you?'

'I guessed she was. She didn't tell me. When's it due?'

'Round about October.'

'I still haven't had any luck with the Identity Card.'

Carling shrugged and said nothing. But he knew then that something was wrong. It wouldn't have taken even a day for Yuri to arrange for an ID card for Rachel. But it didn't matter any longer. Kurt Lang had come up with one, and Hermann Stahl who used to forge documents for the *Sicherheitsdienst* was completing it for him including the official stamp and a beautiful forgery of the correct signature. It was back-dated a month and valid for two years. But why wasn't Yuri co-operating? Maybe Yuri was out of favour and didn't want to take even small risks. Or maybe their contact was no longer considered useful by Moscow.

As he walked back later that night through the Brandenburg Gate to his place after seeing Rachel, he decided to put in for some of his overdue leave. When they had fixed the date for her to come over to the British Zone he'd claim leave from two days before. He'd been given two dates by the pastor for the wedding. Saturdays, 19 and 26 August. He would book a flight for them for the same night and they would spend a few days in London. When a specialist had checked her over they'd rent an apartment and she would stay there until the baby was due. And he would stay as long as he could. If he had to go back to Berlin before the baby arrived, he would claim more leave and get back to her.

Kurt Lang had not only got a genuine blank exit permit but also a photocopy of a cancelled copy that Hermann Stahl could use as a reference. Carling looked at the old man. 'I'm very grateful, Kurt. Will the Leica be enough?'

The old man smiled. 'You can keep your Leica, my friend. It cost nothing.'

'I don't understand.'

He rolled up his sleeve and pointed. 'There are still people who count this as something that matters.' He was pointing at the tattooed numbers on the inside of his thin, pale wrist.

There were tears in Carling's eyes as he looked back to the old man's face.

'I don't know how to thank you, Kurt. I really don't.' He paused. 'There must be something.'

The old man smiled. 'You remember Kurt Schumacher, ex-Reichstag deputy for the SPD, ex-concentration camp victim and now head of the West German SPD?'

'Yes, of course. I met him once. He was living near Hanover then.'

'He still does.' He nodded. 'So get me a signed photo of him.'

'That's dangerous for you to have, Kurt. You know that.'

'I'm too old to care about those bastards. I just want to have it. I won't put it up on the wall.'

'OK. I'll get it for you. It may take a couple of weeks to make contact.'

'No problem.' He shrugged. 'Time is what I've got.'

'I'm in your debt, Kurt. I won't forget it.'

CHAPTER 22

Carling began to wonder if he was becoming slightly paranoid. He had seen the man on the motorcycle so many times in the last few days. Always in East Berlin. But the man and the girl he had seen only in the British Zone. The number on the motorcycle had been changed several times but Carling knew enough about motorcycles to be sure that it was always the same 350 cc BMW. A model made just before the war, when BMW held the world's motorcycle speed record. The rider was a man in his late twenties and whoever had instructed him on how to carry out surveillance from a motorcycle had been singularly inexpert.

The couple were about his own age. The man was well-built, balding at the front, with red hair. The shoes he wore weren't German, neither were his clothes. The jacket was a good tweed and the chinos looked new. The girl wasn't pretty but she wore quite modish clothes and what looked like an expensive wristwatch. Carling tried dodging them on a couple of occasions and although he lost them he saw them again ten minutes or so later. They spent too much time looking in the windows of shops that were closed.

Yuri and he had always had an unwritten deal. Neither of them would put the other under surveillance. And if their colleagues arranged a surveillance the other man would be warned. There had been no such warning from Yuri.

Perhaps it was just a coincidence. The sightings weren't all that frequent but from the instincts that came from his training Carling sensed that something was wrong. Or different. Even Yuri's rather distant attitude seemed like a warning.

But none of it really mattered. He saw Rachel every day and he had never been so happy. He had bought her a ring from an old Polish woman who dealt in fine jewellery from the back of a junk shop near the zoo. It was a single diamond with a beautiful claw setting.

All the occupiers of the city of Berlin insisted on exercising their free rights of access to all zones including the Russian Zone. Mainly these rights were exercised formally and without deliberate provocation. Allied officers in uniform were seldom challenged and then only by the Russians. German civilians frequently lived in the Russian Zone and worked in one of the Western zones. Carling seldom wore uniform.

Twice he had phoned both of Yuri's numbers but there was no response and he decided to go to his place to see if there was some problem.

The main door at the top of the steps was open and he rang the bell on Yuri's door, the first inside the hallway. But there were no sounds from inside. Almost without thinking he put his hand on the door-knob and turned it. The door opened and he called out, 'You there, Yuri?'

There was no reply and he walked into the room, closing the door behind him. As he looked around he saw that the room was not only empty but it had been stripped. Even the single naked lightbulb had gone. He could hear the sounds of children playing in the street and he knew something was wrong. Very wrong.

It seemed a long walk to Rachel's place and he decided not to tell her about what had happened. Why worry her? In another week she would be with him on the other side. Everything was arranged. On 19 August they would be married and that was all that mattered. He took her across to the British Zone for a meal and then to a showing of Antonioni's *La Notte*. He had half a mind to take her to his place for the night but decided against it. Keep to the routine. Take no risks. His leave had been agreed and left open for him to decide when to take it. In two days' time he would warn his main informants that he would not be around for a week or more.

He used an official car from the pool to take her home and on the way back he told the driver to drop him at the Brandenburg Gate and, despite the rain, he walked the rest of the way.

As Carling opened the door of his flat he saw an envelope on the mat inside. It was addressed to 'C'. He opened it slowly and took out the slip of paper inside. It just said, '*Sonntag – Mauer*': 'Sunday – wall'. He didn't understand it and he crumpled it in his hand and tossed it into the metal basket by his desk as he reached for the phone and dialled Yuri's numbers. There was still no answer at either of them. He took the crumpled paper from the basket and smoothed it as flat as it would go. It was handwritten in ink, in old-fashioned German script. For long minutes he looked at it, even slanting it against the light to check if there was a microdot. But there was nothing. And it meant nothing to him. It must have been delivered by hand, there was no stamp and no postmark. It reminded him of a note written by a suspect KGB line-crosser caught in Göttingen. He'd said he had information that he was afraid to talk about. He'd offered to write it down. The message said,

'*Die Russen sind im besitz ein halbes Litre von schweres Wasser*': 'The Russians are in possession of half a litre of heavy water.' He had assumed the man was mentally ill until a month later when he had heard on the BBC news that heavy water was used in making atom bombs. It was revealed that the German plant for manufacturing heavy water had been the target of a commando raid in Norway. The suspect line-crosser had long been released. But the possibilities that he had let go by still haunted him.

The next day, Saturday, he had picked up Rachel from her place mid-morning and they had spent the afternoon at Grunewald on the banks of the Havel river. An enterprising woman had set up a stall selling coffee and sandwiches near the Kaiser Wilhelm Tower and they had stayed until late afternoon. In the evening the quartet were playing at a student concert at the university building. Schubert and Beethoven.

After the concert, which was a great success, Carling took Rachel for dinner at the Austrian place where she was now as welcome a customer as he. It was a day of sunshine and music and when they kissed goodbye he said, 'It's going to be like this every day of our lives.' They were to be married the following Saturday.

At midnight on Saturday, 12 August 1961 all the S-Bahn trains travelling from East to West Berlin stopped running. East German police and Stasi men were checking the papers of all passengers. West Berliners were allowed to continue their journey on foot and East Berliners were told to go back home. The confused passengers, as they walked out of the various stations, were alarmed when they saw the streets full of troop carriers and armoured cars along the sector boundary. And behind the armoured vehicles were Soviet tanks.

There were workmen working under floodlights tearing up cobblestones and paving slabs and manoeuvring tank traps to block off the streets. Those who ventured as far as the Brandenburg Gate watched jackhammers digging holes for concrete posts to carry barbed wire. It was obviously a well-planned operation being implemented with military precision.

When the phone rang he switched on the bedside light and glanced at his watch, 02.50 hours. He picked up the phone.

'Carling.'

'It's MacIntyre, George. You'd better get down to the Brandenburg Gate. Your people over the other side have gone amuck.'

'What are you on about, Mac. What people?'

'The East Germans. They've closed the Gate. They're building a bloody great wall. Tanks, guns, the lot. They say they're closing the whole border of their zone.'

'Have we got anyone there?'

'Who knows? It's chaotic here. London are raising hell. I'm just manning the phones.'

There were lights everywhere and it was as bright as day. There were Russian tanks lined up with guns levelled and pointing straight down Strasse des 17 Juni, the former Charlottenburg Chaussee renamed as a memorial to the East German workers killed by Soviet troops when they protested against conditions in East Berlin. There were other tanks fanning out to cover the Tiergarten, and hundreds of men and dozens of cranes laying huge concrete blocks along Ebert Strasse as far as the eye could see.

He could see Soviet officers moving from group to group and long lines of lorries all the way down Unter den Linden to beyond the university block. The noise of generators, the engines of lorries and the building machinery was deafening but beyond the lights West Berlin police and British military police were pushing back the crowds of civilians who were beginning to arrive as the word spread of what was happening.

As Carling pushed aside one of the metal barriers that had been put up, he was stopped by a Military Police major who asked for his ID. As he handed it back the major said, 'They've told me they have orders to fire on anyone who goes beyond the barriers.'

'What's the idea of closing the Gate?'

'Their liaison chap told me they're doing this along the whole of their zone border with us. No movement is going to be allowed in or out either way.'

'You mean permanently?'

'Seems like it. The wall here could take anything we could throw at it except for artillery.'

'What are we doing about it?'

'They've called a meeting of the Control Commission later today but from the way they're talking over the other side they won't budge an inch. The Red Army officers I talked to said if we attacked the wall in any way it would be treated as an attack on the Soviet Union.'

'D'you think they mean it?'

'I'm bloody sure they do. They were shit-scared, I tell you. They think the East Germans might turn on them if there was any fighting.' He shrugged. 'Anyway, don't go near them.'

By then the crowd numbered thousands. Shouting, jeering and booing the men working on the wall. From time to time a Russian officer used a loud-hailer, speaking in rough German, warning that anyone coming beyond the barriers would be shot. And whenever he spoke the gunners on the machine-guns that were now in place under the Tower would fan the barrels of their weapons in arcs across the crowds.

And as he stood there Carling remembered Kurt Lang's constant warning that the Russians and their East German stooges were going to do something to stop the flow of workers to the West. And he knew now what the note meant. It must have been a last-minute attempt by old Kurt to warn him.

There was no point in waiting around. He needed to find out what was going to happen. It was a deliberate provocation by the Russians and it wasn't going to be easy to ignore it. The Western allies could lose face with the Germans if they backed down. But nobody in the West would relish starting World War Three. Sunday, 13 August 1961 was going to be a milestone in many people's lives. For Carling only one person mattered and no matter how he would do it he was going to get her into West Berlin.

At SIS's offices at the Olympiad Stadium Carling had been congratulated for the warnings he had given about some impending action by the East Germans to stop the flow of skilled people to the West, but his mind was on what to do about Rachel.

In the evening he went again to the Brandenburg Gate. There were groups of people still watching the work going on but the big crowds had gone, afraid of what they saw and afraid of what might be about to happen.

There were tanks and armoured vehicles on both sides now and there was a group of senior officers, British, American, French and Soviet talking at a spot where one of the barriers had been removed. Both the War Office and

Whitehall had decided to take no retaliatory action. Let the West Germans see what the Soviets were really like, with their East German puppets ready to turn East Berlin into a prison camp for their citizens.

At a meeting of the Occupying Powers in the afternoon, an agreement had been reached by threats and counterthreats from both sides on a rough and ready *modus vivendi*. The memorial to the Red Army soldiers who had lost their lives in the battle for Berlin was in the British Zone. A Soviet honour guard, changed twice daily, would be allowed to mount guard on the memorial. Two Soviet Jeeps would be allowed access to the Western Zone daily on a prescribed route and after a formal check at a checkpoint to be erected that night. Soldiers of the three Western occupiers would be given unchecked access to East Berlin in uniform but only in vehicles, without stopping, and with no contact with civilians. This protocol would be observed until further meetings at top level could decide on future access and restrictions. For two weeks no civilians from either side would be allowed access to the other zone. After that time, access would be by certain agreed checkpoints, with identities and reasons for movement subject to a check and interrogation. Civilian access would be strictly limited.

For no particular reason Carling walked back to the Olympiad, just because the activity there gave him a feeling of security. There were things that could be done but he would have to think about it carefully.

The phone was ringing as he opened the door of his place and when he lifted it there was silence at the other end. He hung up and seconds later it rang again. When he picked it up the voice was familiar.

'If you recognise my voice don't mention my name.'

'Go on.'

It was Yuri Porenski.

'We should meet.'

'Where? And when?'

'At the barrier at the Gate. In an hour. But in civilian clothes.'

'OK.'

He hung up without waiting for an answer. He knew then why Porenski had been avoiding him. He would have known about the wall that was going up. And that meant he was no longer to be trusted. But maybe he could be used.

Carling saw Yuri straightaway. He was standing on the fringe of a TV camera crew right up against one of the metal barriers. As he approached Yuri he heard the Russian say softly, 'Where in your zone? Say it quickly.'

'Back entrance to Kempinski's. When?'

'About half an hour. Move away. Now.'

There were two taxis parked on the rank outside the rear entrance to Kempinski's and Carling stood between the two cabs watching for Yuri. He came five minutes later, hurrying round the corner from the Kudamm and walking through the open doors to the reception area in the hotel. Carling waited for another five minutes to make sure that Yuri was alone.

Inside, Yuri was sitting in an armchair, half rising as he saw Carling come in and walk over to him. Carling sat on a leather couch facing the Russian.

'What is it you want, Porenski?'

'Can we talk somewhere else? Somewhere less public.'

'About what?'

'About you and me. And the girl.'

'You knew about the barbed wire and the wall, didn't you?'

'Yes. But there was no way I could warn you.'

'Don't give me that bullshit. You phoned me tonight. You could have phoned me days ago.'

'I've been a virtual prisoner.'

'Did you put me under surveillance?'

'Not me. That was people above me. I had no part in it.'

'Did you tell them about our deal? No shadowing on either side?'

'Yes. I told them.'

'And?'

Yuri shrugged and looked at him. 'They don't care about such things.'

'Was it the young couple?'

'I don't understand?'

'The surveillance team. Was it a young couple?'

'No. Our man was on a BMW motorcycle.'

'So how did you get to be a prisoner?'

'Because of my relationship with you.'

'Tell me more.'

'They see you as a great catch. They want you to go much further with them.'

'Further? What's that mean?'

'They want you committed to us. Hard information.'

'They must be crazy. Didn't you tell them I'd never go along with that?'

Yuri looked away for several moments and then looked back at Carling. 'Yes. I told them. But they said you would have no choice.'

'Go on.'

'First they could threaten that if you didn't co-operate they would make an anonymous call to your people at the Olympiad and tell them you were spying for us and had been for years.'

Carling shook his head. 'The information you gave to me and the opinions I passed on to you are all in my reports. It was my job to talk to you. I told you nothing you couldn't have worked out for yourselves if your people only bothered to learn about the West.' He paused. 'You said first – let's hear secondly.'

Yuri shook his head. 'I couldn't bring myself to say it, my friend. I'd rather you met them and heard it for yourself.'

'Who is "them"?'

'The head of the KGB in East Berlin.'

'Why should it make any difference who says whatever it is you people want to say to me?'

'Because you probably won't believe it if it's just me telling you.' He looked at Carling. 'Don't you understand? They're not playing games. They mean what they say and they'll do it, believe me, they'll do it.'

Yuri's voice was shrill and he put his hands to his face, his head bent, his body rocking backwards and forwards as if he were in pain.

There were passing people, waiters and guests, who looked at the strange figure in the armchair. Carling leaned forward and said, 'You'd better come back to my place. Come on.'

He stood up, lifting Yuri by his arm, to his feet, then leading him out into Fasanenstrasse heading back towards Savigny Platz. As they walked through the almost empty streets, Carling tried to put aside in his mind the thoughts that were gathering there. Thoughts that didn't bear thinking about but wouldn't go away.

Yuri had never been to Carling's place before and he looked uncomfortable as he sat at the kitchen table facing Carling.

'Did your people order you to contact me?'

'Yes.'

'To do what?'

Yuri sighed. 'To give you a message.'

'From whom?'

'From the KGB in East Berlin.'

'But who? What's his name?'

'Does that really matter?'

'Yes.'

'He's my boss. His name's Belinkov. Nikolai. He's a full colonel.'

Carling nodded. 'And you're going to make things difficult for me and Rachel if I don't co-operate the way you want. Yes?'

'Something like that.'

'Go on.'

'They've put her under protective custody.' As he saw the anger on Carling's face he said hurriedly. 'She's not in jail. They've moved her to a house under guard.'

'You won't leave here, Yuri, until she's been released.'

'Georgi, if you arrest me and shove me in jail they wouldn't give a damn. I'm expendable. And it would mean that they'd just apply more pressure to you through the girl.' He paused. 'Remember she's pregnant. Due to have the child in late October. She'll be well cared for if you co-operate.'

'And if I don't?'

Yuri shrugged helplessly. 'You know what they're like. The only way they can get at you is through the girl. They'll give her a hard time. She'd be in prison. Enemy of the State and all that stuff. And they'd put the child in a State orphanage.'

For long moments Carling was silent and then he said, 'When can I see Belinkov?'

Yuri fumbled at the inside pocket of his jacket and pulled out a card, checking it before he handed it to Carling.

'You can contact me twenty-four hours a day on that number. He'll see you any time you want. It's that important.'

'How do I get past all the barbed wire?'

'From tomorrow morning there'll be a checkpoint at Friedrichstrasse. It won't be in use for a week but it will be manned. You'll have to come in civilian clothes and on foot. I'd be there every day with a car.'

Carling stood up. 'I'll think about it.'

Yuri looked relieved. 'I hate all this, Georgi, I really do.'

'You don't hate it enough, my friend. You can always refuse to go along with it.'

'And then they'd shoot me.'

'Yuri, they'll shoot you in the end when they've got no more use for you. Just so you can't talk about what they've been up to.' He paused. 'Can you make your own way back to the barbed wire?'

'I guess so.'

Willy Brandt, the mayor of Berlin, was on a train between Nuremberg and Kiel when he got the news of what had happened and he flew back to Berlin immediately. He was angered by the complete confusion of the Allied military authorities and even more angered that the Federal Government in Bonn was just avoiding any reaction. All his calls to Adenauer went unanswered. His public statements were forceful and emotional, but only he spoke up. It was as if those responsible were paralysed into inaction. Meantime the Wall was growing higher and longer by the hour.

One of Carling's most valuable talents in his work with SIS had always been his ability to get to the heart of any problem. Cutting away the inessentials to identify what really mattered. Then deciding what had to be done. But faced with this personal problem it was not so easy. He knew from the start that he'd have to go along with their demands until he could find a better solution, but he also knew that he would demand certain conditions no matter how hard they pressured him. He spent all of one day deciding what those conditions would be and they gradually became clear.

Twice he was called to meetings at the Olympiad about the situation concerning the Wall. He had given his comments on both long-term and short-term reactions to the Soviet moves. He emphasised, and his was a lone voice, that the Wall must have been approved by Moscow and that Khrushchev himself must have given his own approval. It was East German thinking but done with Soviet blessing. He stressed that in his opinion Moscow would certainly not back down and that all Allied retaliation should be aimed at the East Germans.

CHAPTER 23

The checkpoint was a builder's asbestos cabin and there were steel rods sticking up from the road to prevent any vehicle short of a tank from forcing its way through.

Yuri was there as arranged but the car was parked a couple of hundred yards away. It was a Russian Zil with no number plates and a civilian driver. After a few minutes Carling realised that they were headed for the Soviet military HQ in Karlshorst.

When they arrived Carling was checked at two guard boxes and it was obvious that he was expected. He was treated politely but the body searches were efficient.

A pleasant young woman in uniform escorted them to Belinkov's office. It was a large room with a long table with seven chairs each side. Belinkov was waiting at the door. He smiled amiably as he led them to where several chairs were placed around a low, circular coffee table.

Carling had been in the intelligence game too long to imagine that all KGB officers looked like the villains in American gangster films. They were just men. Some good, some bad. But you shouldn't trust even the good ones.

Belinkov waited until they were all seated and then smiled as he said, 'You must forgive me, I looked you up in *Who's Who* but I don't know whether I should address you as Lord, Earl or Viscount. Which should it be?'

Carling shrugged. 'My name is Carling and I'm a lieutenant-colonel in the Intelligence Corps.'

Belinkov nodded, still smiling. 'OK. Let's get down to business. As you can imagine, Yuri Porenski has kept me informed about your mutual chats. They have been useful, I think, to both sides.' He waved his arms. 'Preventing unnecessary friction, explaining another point of view. And I've been much impressed by your basic thinking. I know you are not an admirer of our Soviet system but you seem to have a balanced eye.' He paused. 'And we don't forget that kind letter you sent to our Ambassador in London way back in the war. It was a generous gesture. Much appreciated. As I think Yuri has explained, we want to ask you to go just a step further with us.' He smiled. 'To help us avoid making silly mistakes—'

Carling interrupted. 'Colonel, we don't need to go into motives and justification. We are both in the same business. We all do things that make us ashamed of the business we're in. We all do things that would make us look like criminals to a normal person. What you are doing so far as I am concerned is blackmail. Let us not pretend otherwise. If I don't do what you want you will make the life of my fiancée a misery. Harassment, prison, who knows what depths you would sink to? So let us cut out the bullshit and find out what is left.'

Belinkov nodded. Not smiling now. 'Agreed. So how do we go about it?'

'I've made a list of my demands but there is one thing that you have to understand right from the start.' He paused. 'I will not – repeat not – ever supply information that could cost one of our men his life. Do you accept that?'

'Who would be the judge of that?'

'Me.'

'OK. I understand your attitude. Please go on.'

Carling reached into his jacket pocket and pulled out a sheet of paper and handed it to Belinkov.

'My typing is not very good but please ask me if there is anything you don't understand.'

Belinkov nodded as he unfolded the typed sheet. The room was silent for several minutes before he looked up at Carling.

'Tell me. What would you do if I said that these conditions were not acceptable?'

'Nothing?'

'Really? But we could just hold you here as a prisoner. You could be in the Lubyanka in Moscow by this time tomorrow.'

Carling smiled, shaking his head. 'That would be very stupid, Colonel. Before I went to the checkpoint I posted a letter to my home, addressed to me. To await my arrival. In it I have given details of all my dealings with Yuri and the details of this meeting. If I was absent from my room in West Berlin and my office for two days they would start looking for me. As the days went by they would widen the search to my home and they would find the letter.' He paused. 'You might end up in the Lubyanka with me.'

Belinkov raised his eyebrows. 'I don't think so, my friend. But you have a point.' He paused and then said briskly, tapping the typed paper he was still holding, 'I accept your conditions.'

'All of them?'

'Yes. I'm not sure about the marriage but I'll check on it.'

'It has to be before the child is born.'

'Of course.'

'So tell me your first enquiry of me.'

'I would like details of all people serving SIS in West Berlin. Names and responsibilities.'

'That will take about a week.' He paused. 'When do I see my girl?'

Belinkov looked quizzically at Yuri who shrugged. Belinkov said, 'How about you arrange an afternoon meeting here next week? You bring the details and Yuri takes you to see the girl.'

'No. That won't do.'

'Why not?'

'I have asked for a weekly meeting with my girl. It's one of the conditions you agreed to. I don't want my meetings to be related to when I provide information. It may take weeks sometimes to get you what you want.'

The Russian shrugged. 'OK. When do you want to see her?'

'Tomorrow.'

'OK. Fix it with Yuri on your way back in the car.' He stood up. 'We have both been in this business for a long time. I think we can have a friendly relationship.'

Carling nodded. 'Let's see how it goes.' He paused. 'When can you let me know about the marriage?'

Again Belinkov looked at Yuri.

Yuri said, 'It'll only take a few days. Some time next week.'

Carling nodded at Belinkov and then followed Yuri out of the office.

As they walked together down the corridor Carling made the arrangements with Yuri to see Rachel the next day. They were to meet at the checkpoint at 6 p.m. It had been one of Carling's conditions that he saw her once a week for a minimum of two hours, and alone.

There was a TV crew taking shots of the temporary checkpoint and Carling had stood in the checkpoint cabin with Yuri until they had packed up their gear and gone. As he waited his mind was on the information that Belinkov wanted. The names and status of the SIS detachment in West Berlin could have been put together in a week by any intelligence organisation that knew its business. Just the gossip at diplomatic cocktail parties would do it. He knew who all his opposite numbers were in the CIA, French intelligence and the German station of the BND in Berlin. The KGB problem was that most of them were such obvious thugs that nobody ever invited them to semi-official parties. They didn't understand the West. They didn't even understand their own East Germans.

It was dark when Carling finally strolled through the gate avoiding the tangle of barbed wire on each side. He thought about having coffee and a sandwich at the Austrian place on the way back, but decided not to. They would ask why Rachel wasn't with him and he didn't want to be reminded of that. He looked up at the sky. It was dark blue with no clouds and the moon was full, gentle, glowing and peaceful. It made him think of Puccini's aria, 'O Silver Moon'. And that too made him think of Rachel.

CHAPTER 24

———————

'She's got a small house actually in the Tierpark. It used to be the head keeper's house. It's quite pleasant and I think she likes it.'

'It doesn't worry you, that, Yuri? Making a prisoner out of a friend?'

Yuri shrugged. 'I carry out my orders just like anyone else.' He paused. 'What did you think of Belinkov?'

'No comment.'

'Just off the record.'

'Nothing's off the record from now on.'

'When had you planned to marry her?'

'This Saturday or the following Saturday.'

'I can arrange it for the second Saturday if you want.'

'Well done. Tell me more.'

'You don't mind it being at a Catholic church?'

'It can be at a Muslim mosque just so long as it's a legal marriage, recognised in any country.'

'It's at St Hedwig's.'

'The Cathedral?'

'Yes.' Yuri smiled. 'Even an organist.' He could see that Carling was impressed by what he had done in less than a day.

'Have you told Rachel?'

'I've told her about your visit but not about the wedding.'

The gates of the small zoo were open and Yuri drove the car along a narrow drive to a small house with a garden.

She was standing at the open door, smiling and waving to him.

Yuri said, 'I'll come back for you about ten. OK?'

'Yeah.'

They had talked for half an hour. She seemed to have been treated quite well but obviously didn't understand what it was all about. He told her everything. About his work and what he had agreed with the KGB.

When she said, 'Do you trust them?' he put his hand to his mouth and shook his head. He winked as he said, 'I'm sure they'll stick to our bargain.' He paused. 'Let's walk in the garden while there's still some sunshine.'

In the garden he said, 'They'll have the whole place bugged. Never say anything that really matters.

Then he told her about the wedding. At first she couldn't believe it.

'But it's a Catholic cathedral. The most important in Berlin. And I'm Jewish.'

'Do you mind?'

'No.'

'So no problem. And it's a proper marriage. Recognised everywhere.' He laughed and kissed her, then drew back his head to look at her. 'And an organist too.' He paused. 'With the deal I've done I can be with you every Saturday. I'll try and persuade them to increase that.'

'I'm so happy now I've seen you.'

When they opened the double gates of the park as he and Yuri left, Carling noticed that the two guards were in Red Army infantry uniforms. A sergeant and a private.

When they were parked away from the checkpoint, Carling handed Yuri an envelope.

'That's the stuff Belinkov wanted. I wasn't intending to hand it over until you'd fixed the marriage arrangements.'

'He pulled a lot of strings with the Bishop.'

'Good for him.'

'Do you want another visit on Saturday?'

'You bet. Can you arrange it?'

'Yes. Same time as today.'

That Saturday was a busy day for Allied personnel in West Berlin. Vice-President Lyndon Johnson flew in accompanied by General Lucius Clay, who had once been US military commander in Germany. The hero of the airlift that had saved Berliners from starving and had broken the Soviet's attempt at blockading the city and forcing the Western allies to withdraw from Berlin.

It had poured with rain most of the day but despite that, thousands of Berliners had assembled to hear the speeches by the Americans and Willy Brandt. In a cosmetic gesture to the locals there had been a march past of the newly arrived US Army reinforcements.

Late on the Friday evening he had a phone call from Yuri saying that their 'mutual friend' would like to see him, so could he make it an hour earlier for their meeting the next day? Wondering what it was all about, Carling agreed.

On the way to Karlshorst Yuri had said that Belinkov had been much impressed by Carling's report.

They had gone through the usual rituals at the Soviet HQ and Belinkov had taken them to a small room near his office. It was more a room for socialising than an office, and Belinkov had asked Yuri to leave them alone.

When Yuri had gone Belinkov said, 'That first request was a test, Colonel Carling.' He smiled. 'We already had the information concerned. Although your report was more up to date.' He shrugged. 'People move on in our business. The co-operation I really wanted from you lies in another direction. I hope you'll forgive my little test but you'll understand why it was necessary when I say that you might find my actual requirements more acceptable than our previous arrangements.' He shrugged and smiled. 'Let me jump in feet first.' He paused. 'We lack information on our most important target – the CIA. You will not be offended, I hope, if I say that the Americans are more important to us than the British.' He sighed. 'We know almost nothing of our adversaries in the CIA in West Berlin. We hope that you will help us to rectify that.' He leaned back in his chair, his eyes intent on trying to read the reaction on Carling's face.

After a few moments of silence Carling said, 'I must say, you people never fail to surprise me.'

'I don't believe that, my friend. Maybe in this case you are surprised.'

'The idea of asking an SIS officer to act as your mole inside the CIA is certainly novel.'

'I have to confess that it was a brain in Moscow that designed this scenario. How do you feel about it?' He leaned forward. 'Just a quick reaction.'

Carling smiled. 'My first reaction is that you're crazy. Why not use a Soviet national?'

'Very simple. We don't have a Soviet national capable of getting alongside an American.' He smiled. 'We're beginning to realise that. We are looking at the young men and women of the Bolshoi for training. You must know very well that we don't fit in to a sophisticated Western background. Some day it will be better but that will be too late for the likes of me.'

'What do you want to know about them?'

Belinkov spread his arms wide. 'Anything. Who they are, what they are doing and what they are planning against us.'

'Let's give it a try. But I shall want better conditions with my girl.'

'We'll find a way of living together.' He looked at Carling, pointing his finger to emphasise the point. 'Remember, these CIA people spy on your country too. It's not just us.'

Carling laughed softly, recognising the truth in the thinking of that cunning mind.

Belinkov said, 'Contact me through Yuri but from now on it's you and me. Yuri's just a messenger.'

CHAPTER 25

St Hedwig's Cathedral behind the newly renamed Französische Strasse had been heavily damaged during the war but had since been lovingly restored, combining the classical features of the old church with creative innovations. Like a theatre-in-the-round, the congregation faced the altar on three sides. Even the East German government had provided substantial finance for the restoration.

The Cathedral was normally open to the public every day, but on that Saturday it was closed for an hour to accommodate an unusual marriage ceremony.

The bride, Rachel Aarons, in a white silk dress, was formally made the wife of a man in a dark blue suit whose name appeared on the marriage certificate as George Carling, occupation: civil servant. The best man was wearing the uniform of the Volkspolizei although his witness signature said 'musician'. The bride's supporter was the organist's wife. The music played was the traditional 'Wedding March' by Mendelssohn and a piece by Dr Thalben Ball called simply 'Elegy'. This latter at the request of the bridegroom, who had previously played it on a piano to the organist who had never heard it before although it had been specially written for church organs.

The party enjoyed a lunch at the Metropol Hotel in Friedrichstrasse and the bridal couple spent the early evening together on one of the Weisse Flotte excursion boat-trips on the river. They spent the night and the following day at the house in the zoo park at Friedrichsfelde.

It was midday on the following Monday when Carling got the phone call. It was a voice he didn't recognise.

'Hello.'

'Carling? George Carling?'

'Who's speaking?'

'Maybe you won't remember me but I'd like to meet you.' It was an American accent.

'What's it all about?'

'Let's say it's about your current situation. I think I could help you.'

'I don't know what you mean.'

There was a brief laugh at the other end and then the voice said, 'I think you do, Colonel. I think you do.'

'Tell me more.'

'Not on the phone. That wouldn't be wise. Could be tapped.' A pause. 'I know you know Kempinski's. We could meet there in about half an hour.'

'How will I know you?'

Carling could hear the smile in the man's voice as he said, 'I know you, Colonel. I'll wait for you near the reception area. Yes?'

'If that's what you want, OK.'

There were several people sitting around in the small lounge space between the reception desk and the rear entrance but Carling knew who the man was as soon as he saw him. He was reading a book – Salinger's *Franny and Zooey*. It was the male half of the pair he had thought were watching him for the KGB. The man looked up, smiling as he patted the space beside him on the leather sofa. As Carling sat down the man closed the book and put it beside him. He said quietly, 'Hi. You're Hank Henney. I've got a room upstairs. Shall we go?'

'Where's your girlfriend?'

'I don't understand.'

'The girl you were with when you were tailing me around Berlin.'

The man smiled. 'You just made me ten bucks. She swore you hadn't spotted us.'

'D'you stay here at the hotel permanently?'

'No. The room's just so you and I can talk and not be seen together in public. Right now we're just casual strangers chatting in a hotel lounge. I'll go first. It's on the second floor. Room 390.' He stood up, smiling, and said quite loudly. 'Glad to have met you.'

Carling waited for five minutes before he headed for the elevator. The man was younger than he had seemed in the streets and the accent was unmistakably American. Almost certainly New York.

It was a bright, pleasant room with modern furniture and the man who called himself Henney was standing at a small bar checking over the bottles. He half turned.

'What d'you fancy? There's everything here.'

'A tomato juice if you've got one. No angostura and no Worcester sauce.'

'My, my. A guy who knows exactly what he wants.' He lifted a bottle, eased off the cap and poured the contents into a long glass. Picking up a glass already filled he walked across to where Carling was sitting and put both drinks on a glass coffee table between them.

'There you are.' He held up his glass. *'Na zdrovia.'*

'Cheers.'

'I guess everybody asks you this but what do I call you – Lord, Viscount, Earl or what?'

Carling sighed. 'They do. Just call me Carling.'

'OK. Carling. Let's face it. You got problems, pal. Lots of problems. I think you need some help.' He paused. 'Am I right?'

'I don't know. Maybe you should tell me what problems I've got.'

Henney grinned. 'You wanna list?'

'Anyway you like, Mr Henney.'

'Hank.' He sighed. 'Brooklyn, New York.' He paused and looked at Carling over the top of his raised glass. 'So. Back to your problems. I guess the root of your problems is that little gal of yours. She's a honey but she's a problem all the same. Am I right?'

'Who are you, Henney?'

Henney smiled. 'You've guessed already who I am, haven't you?' He paused. 'I'm CIA. The new boys.'

'Is this an official contact?'

'Let's just say it ain't an official contact between CIA and SIS. My contact's only with you.'

'Do others in CIA know you're contacting me?'

'Only two, and only one of them knows why.'

'Why was I being followed?'

'Like I said, we're the new boys. We haven't had your people's experience in operating in Europe, especially into an area controlled by the Soviets. We wanted to know what was going on over the other side. So we checked on who was doing it for the French.' He shrugged. 'We weren't impressed. So we had a look at what the Brits were doing about it. And we came up with your name.'

'We thought maybe it would be good to – what shall

I call it? – follow in your footsteps. That was quite an
eye-opener. Your friend Yuri and all that. We did a bit
of research on him too. And in the course of all this
we discovered that the mighty dollar worked even more
wonders over the other side. We made a bit of a run
at them, just a small team of us. And,' he shrugged,
'cutting a long story short, we have access to both the
KGB places and the Stasi offices.' He smiled. 'Very low
level but high-technology, and beyond the dreams of even
J. Edgar Hoover looking for commies in Hollywood.

'We finally judged you as non-political. Neither left wing
nor right wing. Thought we might be able to get you to
help us, but as you got more involved and they started
to use the girl against you we thought you were heading
for trouble.' He shrugged. 'And of course you were. Not
just heading. You were in it. In deep, deep shit. When
we learned about Belinkov's latest proposition to you I
thought I should get together with you.' He smiled. 'What
d'you think?'

For a few moments Carling said nothing, and then he
said, 'What is it you're after?'

Henney shifted in his chair and when he was more
comfortable he said, 'I'd like to join the game.'

'Go on.'

'All off the record. Just you and me. A combined operation. You and me versus the KGB.'

'How did you get all this background information?'

'You mean about you?'

'Yes.'

Henney hesitated, then said, 'Let's say, a bit of experience and a lot of luck. I used to do this job in the Middle
East. I found dealing with East Germans was very like
dealing with Arabs.' He smiled. 'Greed and corruption are

international. Maybe some day I can tell you the sordid details.'

'This sounds crazy to me. What, exactly, have you got in mind?'

'Our friends over the border want information about the CIA. They want you to provide it. I could give you information that will keep them very happy. And more important, that will do no harm to either American or British interests. We could work it out together.'

Carling shook his head slowly in disbelief. 'This *is* crazy.'

Henney smiled. 'You know as well as I do that half of what we do in this business is crazy. But I'd reckon what I've suggested isn't all that crazy. You're committed because of your girl to provide information about the CIA. Just think of what that involves compared with what I'm suggesting. It ain't gonna be all that easy getting an inside track on my lot. And if you got caught you'd be in deep, deep shit. Nobody would want to touch you. Diplomatic incident and all that jazz. Washington after your head and London wishing they could give it to them. My way, the most your people could hold against you would be doing something without an official OK.'

Carling nodded. 'I realise all that. What worries me is that it all fits in so well. Almost too well.'

Henney shrugged. 'So count yourself lucky and grab the chance. It's better than your way. Your way you don't just risk being caught playing games with the CIA but of playing ball solo with the KGB.' He paused. 'If I were you I'd be very glad to solve a tricky problem like yours in a way that keeps me totally clean.'

'What if I decline the offer?'

Henney shook his head. 'Forget it. You won't. You've got more sense than that.'

'Tell me about the other two who you said know of your contact with me today.'

'I'll tell you anything you want to know about 'em. But only after you've agreed to let me in on your game with the Russians.'

'Tell me about you then.'

'Fine. Same age as you, give or take a year. Born in Wichita Falls, Texas. Grew up in New York. My old man was a plumber and my ma sewed dresses in a sweatshop. We lived in Brighton Beach, couple of miles from Coney. I did well in school. Got a football scholarship to Boston U. Took law and when we got into the war I was recruited into OSS. When OSS folded and CIA started up I was transferred to them. Served in OSS in Italy and in CIA I've worked in Cairo, Beirut, and a stint in Damascus. Grade?' He smiled. 'I guess about the same as yours. Married, one child, a daughter. Hobbies . . .?' He shrugged. 'radio ham and playing low-grade jazz.'

Carling smiled. 'What kind of jazz?'

'Piano. Anything from Joplin to Fats Waller.'

Carling was silent for a few moments and then he said quietly, 'When do we get started? We've got a lot of planning to do.'

'I'm real glad.' The American stood up. 'Can you stay for a meal and talk?'

'Sure.'

'I'll ring room service.'

They had talked about Hank Henney's family and about Rachel and the wedding while they ate, but when the waiter had cleared away the debris of their meal and brought them coffee, Henney reached inside his jacket and brought out an envelope.

'Take a look at that. It's our first move but we don't hand it over for a couple of weeks. Don't wanna make it look too easy. Have a look. See what you think.'

It was twelve pages of an internal telephone directory of the CIA unit in West Berlin. Carling looked through it slowly and then looked at Henney.

'Real or doctored?'

'Absolutely genuine.'

'Tell me about the other two people who know about our operation.'

'The guy who knows but doesn't know the background – your background, Rachel and the rest of it – his name's Morgan. Glenn Morgan. In his fifties. Rock solid. Knows how the machinery works. The other guy is my immediate boss. It was he who agreed to having a watch put on you. His name's Kaufman. Albert Kaufman. Ex-OSS but concerned with desk operations. He's in charge of case-officers – what I guess you'd call agents. Agents for us are foreigners who work for us. The CIA guys who control them are never called agents but case-officers.' He smiled. 'All same as the KGB. Kaufman's about five years younger than us. A very cool cookie. He can clear anything we want to do.'

'What about Washington?'

'They're not in the picture. But when we've been going for a few months we'll inform them provided you agree. OK?'

'Yeah.' Carling pointed at the directory. 'That's too good for the first thing I pass them.'

'It ain't even classified as secret, George. Back home our telephone numbers are in the telephone directory.'

Carling shook his head. 'It's still too good, believe me.'

'What else can we give 'em?'

'How about a grainy photograph of your building?'

'It's just a house, for Chrissake.'

'That's fine. That's enough for a start.'

'OK. You know best.'

'When can I have the photo?'

'Tomorrow.'

'Not a real estate shot. The kind of picture an agent would take.' He smiled. 'And next time we can make it a rough sketch of the ground-floor offices.'

Hank Henney laughed. 'Anything you say, old buddy. Anything you say.'

They exchanged telephone numbers where they could be contacted at any time. They arranged codenames for places to meet and codenames for people's names they may need to refer to.

As Carling walked back to his flat it was raining heavily. He sat in the kitchen in his bathrobe with a mug of coffee. It seemed to be too good to be true. He had been well aware of the risks he had been taking in doing the deal with Belinkov, but for him he had had no choice. SIS wouldn't see it that way, for them it would be treason no matter how unimportant the information he passed to Belinkov was. They would dismiss the information he got back from Belinkov as being 'planted'. But the joint operation with Henney could only be criticised because it was not disclosed. No information on SIS was involved and the CIA material was their own choosing. What he got back from Belinkov would benefit both the CIA and SIS. Operationally he would be no more than a combined messenger and listening post. The deal with Hank Henney was the best insurance he could have.

Two days after their first meeting Henney had provided

the photograph and Carling had passed it on to Belinkov, who was delighted with the first fruits of the new arrangement. It was at that meeting that Carling raised the possibility of getting the CIA's internal telephone directory.

'There would be names and job titles. Would that interest you?'

'You mean you might be able to get a copy of an original?'

'No. I'm negotiating for an actual original.'

'And all the staff names and status?'

'Exactly.'

'That would be fantastic. Moscow would be delighted.'

'It won't be easy and if I get it I want something in return.'

Belinkov's face went from smiles to neutral. 'What is it you want?'

'I want a pass in German and Russian that means I can come and go into and out of East Berlin unhindered and no time or date limitation. And signed by your top brass.'

Belinkov looked relieved. 'No problem. I'll get it arranged by tomorrow.' He paused. 'When are you likely to get the directory?'

He shrugged. 'Two or three days' time if all goes to plan.'

'OK. I'll get the special pass done for you.'

Belinkov made no effort to conceal his excitement as he read through the directory. He had already handed over the pass that Carling had asked for. It was in German and Russian and signed by the Soviet commander of both the Russian Zone and the rest of East Germany.

It required all authorities, both civilian and military, German or Soviet, to allow the bearer to pass 'without let or hindrance' and without questioning at any time. And such authorities must render any services or assistance required by the bearer. There was a photograph of Carling's face taken by an army photographer in the open air so that there was no background.

Putting aside the directory, Belinkov said, 'We are concentrating all our efforts against the Americans now. Not only here but in the United States. We have sustained many losses of our people in America because we have not made the necessary arrangements to protect them. Too many had their controllers based at our embassy and consulates. We need people who can operate independently. Here in Europe we know what to do but the Americans are from another planet. We need to learn how to beat them.'

'What are your people hoping to get in the United States?'

Belinkov pursed his lips, thinking. 'Above all we want information on the atom bomb but we also need to know what their government is planning against us. New weapons, new devices, communications. Troop deployment. Signs of aggressive moves before they happen.'

'And what do you want from the CIA in Berlin?'

Belinkov shrugged. 'Almost anything. They will have agents over here. Who are they, what are their objectives, who controls them?'

Carling nodded. 'I'll see what I can do.'

Their daughter, Rachel, was born in a private nursing home that was solely for the use of wives of senior Soviet officers and officials. Mother and child were well looked after and Carling was able to take them home after only three days in the hospital. A nurse came to visit the new mother and baby every day for the first month.

By this time Carling was living a strange life that would have seemed bizarre to almost anyone. The house at the Tierpark he treated as his home. His rooms of Savigny Platz were just 'his place'. He spent three or four nights a week with Rachel, rather as if he were some travelling salesman who couldn't always make it home.

Despite Belinkov's dismissal of Yuri as just a messenger, Carling kept up his contact with him. Yuri was too shrewd to ask what Carling was doing for his boss. Carling kept up all his old contacts in what, since the building of the Wall, was now officially East Berlin. His work for SIS gave him virtually complete independence and at the weekly joint briefing meetings he was highly respected for his insight into what was happening on the other side of the Wall. Hank Henney too was obviously impressed by what Carling knew about the other side, but he valued most Carling's reports on his contacts with Belinkov. The Americans seemed fascinated by the Russians despite the fact that Berlin itself was living proof that ordinary people were eager to escape from communism. With both the British and the Americans Carling did his best to get over to them the fact that despite the material attractions of the West there were many people, particularly older people, who found comfort and comradeship in the atmosphere of East Berlin. East Berlin was like Berlin in the old days. Lace curtains moving gently in the summer breeze, old values maintained, a¹most no major crime, and old ladies could walk alone in the streets at night without being robbed or molested. East Berlin was Berlin in the thirties, Thomas

Mann and *Buddenbrooks*. Oddly enough, the Americans seemed to understand this better than the Brits did. It was like the front covers of the *Saturday Evening Post* by Norman Rockwell that used to make them feel that all was right with the world.

CHAPTER 26

Hank Henney had an apartment near the Europa Centre. They had met there just after the Christmas holidays and Carling wondered how the American would react to what he had to say.

'Tell me, Hank, if I told you an American was passing information to Belinkov's people what would your reaction be?'

'A civilian or a serviceman?'

'Serviceman.'

'Officer or enlisted man?'

'Sergeant.'

'How valuable is the information?'

'Some secret, some top-secret.'

'How long's he been doing it?'

'Three, four months.'

'For money?'

'Money and sex. His controller is a young woman.'

'What you really want to know is would I put him straight in the slammer?'

'Would you?'

'We'd have to work it out, you and me. If we just jump on him they'd realise you could have told us. We'd do better just to ease him away from wherever he gets the information he passes to them.'

Carling nodded. 'That's what I wanted to hear, Hank.' He paused. 'The chap's name is Carmichael. Randolph Carmichael. Randy to his friends. He works in your signals group responsible for all US service communications in Berlin with a feed back to your HQ in Frankfurt.'

'That means he knows the status of all our units, troop movements, responsibilities and operational orders. Not good, old friend. Not good.'

'Think about it, Hank, and we'll talk again.'

'You got any ideas?'

'If he was one of ours we'd probably promote him to make him feel safe and then post him to another command. Maybe back home. Depends on his background. We'd keep him under close surveillance and wait until he was contacted in his new place. Photographs and meetings and so on. Then move in on him. After interrogation we could decide whether we'd turn him back on them or put him on trial. There would be no connection with his job here in Berlin.' He paused. 'Our experience is never to be in a hurry. Jump in right away and you've generally exposed your informant, and you'll almost certainly be faced with indignant denials and you can't prove a thing that would stand up in court.'

Henney smiled. 'All that Brit experience based on a hundred years of being in the business. But you're right. Our instinct would be to grab him and put him away. Not very subtle.'

Carling smiled. 'I've got the feeling you're learning fast, you guys.' He looked at Henney. 'I need a tit bit for our friends. Have you got anything?'

'Our head of mission is going back to Washington in three months' time. I could give you a bit of background on the new guy.' He smiled. 'Nothing that hasn't appeared in the papers back home.'

'They'd love that, Hank. Tell me more.'

Carling was amused at the obvious irritation of the Stasi and plain-clothes KGB officers at Checkpoint Charlie. They sometimes tried asking him what was the purpose of his visit and he would point out that they were defying the orders of their highest official in East Berlin. Sometimes one of them would make a phone call and Carling could see him reading from his document. Then the hurried return of the pass, sometimes graced by a salute.

Carling had been working with Hank Henney for nine months and the two-way traffic seemed to be satisfying both parties. The information Carling passed to the CIA man covered the organisation and personnel of the KGB in East Berlin and the major cities in East Germany. What he passed on to Belinkov was information that a competent investigative journalist could have picked up from the usual gossip of the intelligence community in West Berlin.

They had arranged a meeting that day by the bridge over the canal and as they leaned over the railing watching small boys jumping into the canal from the bridge, Carling said, 'I've got a bit of a problem, Hank.'

'Anything I can do to help?'

'I've been notified that I'm to be posted to London in three months' time. They don't know that I'm married.'

'How do you claim your marriage allowances?'

'I don't. I don't need the money.'

'So what's the problem?'

'I don't think the Russians will let Rachel and the baby

leave East Berlin. They would feel they've no hold on me.'

Henney looked at him. 'So. We put something together and get her out.'

'That would still leave the problem of concealing the fact that I'm married. My people can't check on us in East Berlin but once she was over here I couldn't cover up for long.'

'So we get her and the baby out and then you tell your people.'

'Hank, she was an East German. I'd end up in the Tower of London. You know what our people and yours can be like. It wouldn't be just a case of throwing me out. They can be real bastards. Just a word in somebody's ear. The Inland Revenue checking me out like I was a Mafia *capo*. Never park a car without you get a ticket.' He shrugged. 'I've seen it done. I know what it does to even the toughest men.'

'What's your new job?'

Carling shrugged and grimaced. 'I'd be in charge of advising the Foreign Office on policy concerning the Soviets and the Warsaw Pact countries.'

For long moments Henney seemed to be just looking down at the kids playing around in the canal, then he turned to look at Carling.

'If you'd married an American girl without telling them what would they do?'

'They wouldn't be best pleased that I'd not informed them. But they'd just accept it.'

'Would you have had to get their permission to marry?'

'Only if the girl was from the Soviet Union or a Warsaw Pact country. And they wouldn't have given permission.'

'But if it was a French girl, for instance.'

Carling shrugged. 'They'd go along with it. They'd probably check up on her background on the quiet.'

'If she had been English would they check her background?'

'Yeah. But it would just be a routine check. Politics, if any, associates and central records.'

'How about . . .' Henney half smiled '. . . you said way back that our little arrangement was crazy – so you'll say this is even crazier – how about we arrange to make your girl an American?'

'How the hell can we do that?'

Hank Henney shrugged. 'It's been done before. We get her over here, I get my fellas to create documentation for her, she takes the oath with our Consul.' He shrugged. 'And that's it. You can even go through another marriage ceremony in our zone. We've got army padres who could do it.'

Carling turned round, leaning on the railings, looking at the little boys in the canal but not seeing them. Without turning to look at Henney he said, 'Would your people really do this, Hank?'

'Of course. Just say the word and I'll get things moving.'

Carling turned his head to look at the American. 'You realise that my new job would be very different. I wouldn't be much use to your people in Berlin. I wouldn't be down amongst the day to day details. I'd just be a broad oversight of a pretty big map.'

Henney sighed. 'You're a very modest chap, George. We set great store by your opinions.' He paused. 'Anyway, we'd like to pay our debts to you for helping us so far.'

'But I won't be so useful in my new position.'

Henney shrugged. 'Who knows? We'll see.'

*　　*　　*

He had notified SIS of his impending marriage and people who knew him seemed surprised but pleased. There were the inevitable jokes about him marrying an American girl and the unit had presented them with a huge casket of Solingen cutlery as a wedding present. There had been some surprise that nobody from the unit was invited to the wedding but it was reckoned to be typical of Carling who had always been a loner. It was stressed by Carling that not even his father or his fiancée's parents would be at the ceremony.

A USA Army Jeep had exercised its right to go through Checkpoint Charlie unchallenged and the driver and his armed escort had been joined by a third uniformed officer, a woman, at a brief stop in the Nikolaiviertel. She was wearing a standard issue cape against the rain and put a small bundle on the floor of the Jeep between her feet. They were back in the American Zone fifteen minutes later.

Hank Henney had a quick meal with them after the baby had been settled in her cot. Carling had bought his young wife a white silk dress with large red poppies around the skirt to celebrate the occasion. The house they were using was one of the CIA's safe houses.

The citizenship formalities for Rachel Carling had been accomplished the next morning and in the afternoon they were married in a chapel by a USAF padre.

In the evening she read through the documents that had been created to give her a background. She was amused that because of her German accent it had been decided that she had been born in Pittsburg. Her father a teacher, her mother a musician. There was a lengthy exposition of her childhood and upbringing. She had done well at school and had become a professional musician in her teens.

* * *

The day after their second wedding Carling phoned Belinkov. When the Russian answered the phone he sounded tense.

'Who is that?'

'It's your friend. We need to meet.'

'What the hell's going on? Where's the woman and the child?'

'Come to Checkpoint Charlie in civilian clothes in two hours. I'll be waiting for you and I'll see you through the checkpoint. We need to talk.'

'I can't risk coming through to your side, you know that.'

'I did it daily for you, my friend. See you in a couple of hours.'

He watched the Russian walking towards the checkpoint. He had never seen him in civilian clothes before. He looked uneasy in an ill-fitting suit and a short coat that was unbuttoned and flapping in the wind.

Carling had already used his SIS card to instruct the military police guards on the West side of the Wall and he took the Russian's arm and led him to his car.

'Where are we going?'

'The Europa Centre. There's a café there where we can talk. Don't worry.'

Ten minutes later they were at a table in one of the Europa Centre cafés, but Belinkov was still on edge.

'What's going on?'

'I'm going back to London in a few weeks' time. That means I can no longer co-operate with you. I arranged for my wife and daughter to move to this side of the Wall.' He smiled amiably. 'Just a precaution, of course.

Apart from the fact that I won't be in a position to help you there need be no problem. Our little arrangement was useful to us both. There is no need for any recriminations on either side.'

'What are you going to be doing in London?'

'That I can't tell you.'

'I can soon find out. We have experienced people in London.'

'I'm sure you have, Nikolai.' He paused. 'I hope we can remain on good terms and I hope that any guidance I have given you has done a little to help keep our two countries maintain a little respect for one another.' He smiled. 'I'll take you back to the checkpoint, Nikolai.'

As they got out of Carling's vehicle, Carling put out his hand and Belinkov took it reluctantly. He looked up at Carling's face. 'You are a strange man, comrade. I don't understand you.'

'Don't worry, Nikolai, we should both forget we ever met. It's better that way.'

The Russian shook his head in amazement, turned his back and walked off down the road towards the museum.

THREE

CHAPTER 27

———————

Carling sat in the sun on the bench by the lion enclosures. She had been wearing the white silk dress with the poppies and she'd taken the baby to look at the lions. He had sometimes wondered what she saw in him. He still wondered. She was so incredibly beautiful and so loving. Their time in Berlin had been the happiest days of his life. Being together without subterfuge was like being let out of prison. He would never forget the Americans' willingness to help them, and their generosity that had made it all possible. Overnight Berlin had changed from a grim city, a backdrop to the Cold War, to a city with places to walk, restaurants to eat at, shops and concerts and small dinner parties at their rented house. There had been other good days away from Berlin but it was here that it started and it was this now prosperous, bustling city that represented for him the real start of his happiness with Rachel.

He had visited all their old places. The house at the Tierpark, the apartment in the Nikolaiviertel and the rented house in the American Zone. He had even gone back to find Yuri's old place but it was now a twenty-five-storey office block.

He sighed and stood up. He had to go back to the hotel

and check out. His flight was already booked in the name of Aarons. And he'd have dinner with young Rachel at the airport. He liked to be in a busy place with lots of people when he had to say goodbye.

She looked so like her mother that he was never sure whether this made him happy or sad. The same mane of black hair, the big dark eyes, the neat nose and the full sensual mouth.

'It's funny,' she said, 'I don't remember Berlin from when I was a baby but when I come here I always feel at home, even when they had the Wall I seemed to know the place.' She reached over and touched his hand on the table. 'Are you happy?'

He smiled. 'Always happy when I'm with you.'

She laughed softly. 'Now you're giving me that famous Carling charm.' She paused. 'I mean are you happy in general? When you're not with me.'

'I miss her terribly. Every day.'

'Of course you do. I miss her too. But you've got to go on with your life.' She paused. 'You always seem so busy with one thing or another. I'm always seeing pictures of you in the papers. I'm not sure it's a good idea for you to come back here. It's a bit like picking at a scab on a wound that's beginning to heal.'

He shook his head. 'It's not like that. This place was special for both of us. I'll tell you about it one of these days.' He smiled. 'How's that man of yours?'

She laughed. 'Still pressing me to marry him but I like my freedom.'

'Where are you heading for next?'

'I've got a concert in Barcelona and then back to New York and LA.'

'Are *you* happy?'

She smiled. 'I think I'm a lot like you. I'm happy but I'm always holding my breath, hoping the Good Lord isn't about to strike me down.'

'What do you most remember of your mother?'

She frowned, thinking, then smiling. 'I remember that whenever she looked at you she was always smiling. I remember her wearing a white silk dress with big red poppies on the skirt.'

He sighed. 'I can hear them calling my flight. I'd better get on my way.' As he stood up he put his hands on her shoulders and she looked up at him, smiling. 'When shall I see you again, little girl?'

'I'm not sure. Maybe at Christmas or New Year.'

He kissed her and she walked with him to the boarding channel and he turned and waved to her as he went through the checkpoint.

She went back to the restaurant and ordered herself a coffee. She wished that she could find a man like him. He seemed to have been born knowing about all the arts. Especially music. And he was so generous. Not just with money but with himself. He didn't just care about people but he did something about it if it was in his power. And if you're an earl and quite rich and charming you have a lot of power. Her mother had told her quite a lot about him but none of it fitted in with the man she knew now. Even from what her mother had told her it sounded as if he'd treated his intelligence work as if it were just a background to his real life. When her mother had died he had seemed to come to a stop. He had sold up the mansion and the estate in Scotland and she had gone back to England with him, looking at places where he could start living again. The country house in Kent had something that seemed to appeal to him as soon as he saw it. When she asked him what it was he had smiled and said that it was the big red poppies in the garden.

CHAPTER 28

Carling stayed for the night at the Spa Hotel in Tunbridge Wells and drove up to Lake Cottage in time for breakfast. Julie and Gabby were all smiles, obviously delighted to have him back. They had already eaten but he made them sit with him as he drank his tea and went quickly through his accumulated mail.

'Any excitements while I was away?'

Julie smiled. 'Carlotta's got four teeth now.'

'That's great.' He smiled at Gabriella. 'She's going to be nearly as beautiful as her mum.' He paused. 'Where's Tim?'

'He had to go to London to see his solicitor.'

Carling nodded. 'I must do something about that.' He frowned. 'What day is it?'

'Thursday.'

Carling stood up. 'I've got to make a phone call. I'll be right back.'

As he dialled 192 he wondered if, perhaps, the number was ex-directory because of the SIS connection, but there was no problem. It was still under Mathews, Timothy. He wrote the number the operator gave him on his pad.

He turned to Julie. 'There's the number, sweetie. When

she answers you say your piece. A little bit formal but very
friendly. OK?'

'OK.'

Julie dialled the number. It rang only three times before
a rather breathless voice said, 'Hello.'

'This is Lord Carling's secretary speaking. Lord Carling
would like to speak to Pamela Bailey, please.'

'Pamela Bailey speaking. Is this some trick for selling
something?'

'It certainly is not, Ms Bailey. I'll put you through to
His Lordship.'

She put her hand over the receiver, counted to ten and
handed it to Carling.

'Carling speaking, Ms Bailey. I hope I'm not calling at
an inconvenient time.'

'I think you've got the wrong person.' She paused.
'Are you really Lord Carling?'

'If it really worries you, you could get my number from
Enquiries. It's in the book. And ring me back when you're
satisfied.'

'Are you the man who talks about the arts on chat
shows?'

'Yes. I'm afraid that's me. There's something I wanted
to talk to you about. Could I come across to see you
– or better still could you have a bite with me at the
House tomorrow lunch time?'

'Where is your house?' The voice was interested but
cautious.

'I'm sorry. I meant the House of Lords. We've got a
debate on the film industry in the afternoon or I'd have
suggested somewhere a bit more glamorous.'

A few moments of silence. 'Are you sure I'm the right
person? I'm not important or anything.'

'I'm quite, quite sure, dear lady. How about you come along about noon? Say twelve-fifteen?'

'All right. I hope it isn't all a ghastly mistake.'

'Of course not. See you tomorrow.'

'Yes. Goodbye.'

He pulled a face at Julie. 'Only a *white* lie, my dear. And it's in a very good cause.'

'What did she sound like?'

'Pleasant. Matching accessories. But I'm used to all that. My committee ladies are all like that.'

'Is this so that Tim can see his son?'

'Yes.'

'What will you say to her?'

He shrugged. 'I haven't the foggiest idea. I'll have to play it by ear.'

Pamela Bailey was prettier than Carling had imagined, and livelier too. Dressed rather primly. He escorted her to the table he had booked, and as she sipped a glass of wine he discreetly pointed out the lords she might recognise.

'I feel a little bit guilty about inviting you to lunch but I felt we could, perhaps, help each other.'

She smiled nervously. 'I don't see how I could help you. Or you me.'

'Tell me about yourself. Your life and the things that interest you.'

'It's a very simple life. I'm just an ordinary housewife and my main interest in life is my son.'

'That's Tony, isn't it?'

She looked shocked. 'How on earth do you know that?'

'We both have children. I have a daughter, she's about your age. Maybe a year or two younger. She's a musician. A violinist. I don't see much of her. She's based in New York but she gives concerts all over the world.' He paused. 'So I don't see much of her. I miss her a lot.' He paused again. 'Would you miss Tony if you didn't see him much?'

'Of course I would.'

'Can I ask you something very personal?'

She shrugged. 'I suppose so.'

'Do you miss your husband – I mean your ex-husband? Tim.'

'Why do you ask?'

'Because he misses his son and I suspect he misses you a little too.'

She laughed sharply. 'He's kidding if he says that.'

'He didn't say that about either you or Tony but I know him well enough to be quite certain that he misses you both.' He paused. 'In his kind of work it tends to make men conceal their inner feelings.' He smiled. 'I was in the same business myself but a long time ago.'

'How did you come across my . . . across Tim?'

'He's been staying with me for some months.' He smiled. 'Let's say we've been exchanging notes on things that happened way back.' He paused. 'He's very good at his job, you know.'

She shrugged dismissively. 'He never told me anything about his work. He'd be away for days, even weeks, and then he'd come back without any excuse or apology. Our home was just a place to change his clothes.'

'People doing his job are trained not to talk and they go along with it so that their families don't get involved. To keep them away from any possible danger. A wife, a child, a girlfriend are always pressure points. It may not seem like it at your pleasant home in Esher where you keep things calm and sensible and your young husband seems much the same as other husbands who work in the

City or in a local business, but Tim will have been aware of the penalties for talking about his work.'

'You seem to have learned an awful lot about him, so he obviously talks with you.'

Carling shook his head. 'No. Not really. I just read between the lines and fill in the silences.'

'And I don't?'

'How could you, my dear?' He smiled. 'They ought to have short courses for officers' wives at the start. Make them part of the club.'

She nodded. 'That would have helped a lot. It really would.'

'Are you happy with your new life?'

She looked away at other tables and then back at Carling. 'You said my *new* life. I don't really have a new life. I thought I was going to make a new start but that's fallen through.' She sighed and smiled. 'I don't really have a life.'

'Was there anything you liked about Tim?'

'Of course. He didn't mess around with other women. He wasn't mean about money.' She shrugged. 'But he just didn't seem to belong to me.' She paused. 'How is he?'

'He's getting by, but he's a man who's lost his anchor. You may not have felt it was so but I suspect that you were his anchor.'

'I can't believe that. He was so independent.'

'My dear, I'm heading for my seventy-first birthday so I've been around a long time, and I can tell you that I wondered if you could have been what gave him a base. And now I've met you I know I was right.' He smiled. 'When you're as young as you two it's easy to expect too much from your partner. You're not old enough yet to value the quiet, solid virtues. But you will some day.'

He paused. 'Could be with that young man you once were in love with.' He shrugged. 'Or maybe somebody else.' He sighed. 'A pity to throw away the chances without even trying.' He paused. 'And if you both sacked your solicitors it would be a good start.' He looked at her, smiling. 'Why not come over to my place for the day on Saturday? Bring the boy, have a lazy day and do a bit of shopping at Fenwicks.'

She laughed. 'Get thee behind me, Satan.'

'Will you come?'

She looked away and then back at him. 'Yes. I'll come.'

'Good girl. Let's none of us expect too much. Just a few old friends getting together.'

She leaned back in her chair, slowly shaking her head. 'I wish my father had been like you.' She leaned forward again. 'You've made everything seem suddenly brighter.'

It had been a good day. Carling had taken Tony up to the trout farm and borrowed a couple of rods. He had shown the small boy how to recognise where the fish were and taught him how to cast his fly well out on to the pond. They had fished all afternoon. Tony had caught a two-pounder and Carling had shown him how to play the fish away from the reeds and ease it gently into the net.

When they got back to the house Carling was aware of laughter, mainly female laughter, coming from the direction of the bench beside the pond. He occupied Tony with helping him to start up the barbecue and half an hour later they were all eating sausages, frankfurters, lamb chops and burgers. With Julie, Gabby and the baby, and the others, Carling found a strange peace, despite the chatter and laughter. They were all enjoying a brief spell of happiness. All was right with their worlds. Aware that in large part it was his doing that had made it so, he wondered fleetingly if it was a good idea to intrude, even interfere, in other people's lives. Maybe the road to hell was paved with barbecued sausages, fishing rods and a young woman looking at a young man as if she'd never seen him before.

He had sent the gardener in the Rover 3-litre to pick up his two guests from Esher but he registered no surprise when Tim said that he would drive them back himself in his car.

As Carling leaned against the car's open window he smiled at them all and then said, as if it were an afterthought, 'By the way, I've got two box tickets for the Last Night of the Proms. I can't use them, maybe you two could enjoy an outing.'

He stood, hands on hips, watching them drive off into the darkness and then walked back into the house. He sat at the kitchen table drinking a glass of red wine with Delius on the hi-fi coming through the open door to the living room. He was showing Julie and Gabby the movements of the pieces on a chessboard. An hour later he did his regular late-night walk to his shack, then the pond and back to the patio. He stood there for a few minutes looking up at the sky but the moon was obscured by clouds.

Inside the house he looked at his watch. It would be late afternoon in New York and he dialled Rachel's number. But there was no response and Rachel detested answering machines.

He lay in bed reading Len Deighton's latest paperback with the BBC's World Service chatting away almost inaudibly on his bedside radio. It was still on long after he was asleep.

CHAPTER 29

When Carling came down for breakfast Julie, barely concealing a knowing smile, told him that Tim Mathews had phoned and said that he'd be back midday.

Carling was in his shack when Mathews returned. He heard the car and switched on the mains switch before leaving and locking the two locks on the door.

He didn't ask Mathews how things had gone and Mathews didn't volunteer anything.

'I'm going to Tunbridge Wells, Tim. D'you fancy coming with me?'

'Sure.'

Carling put in a cartridge of Fujicolor for processing at Camera Gear in Camden Road and then they walked down to KAC and Carling bought two dozen TDK audio tapes.

As so often when they visited Tunbridge Wells, Carling stopped for coffee at Fenwicks' restaurant. When Mathews said, 'Tell me about your time in Berlin.' Carling was taken aback. How did he know he had been in Berlin? He was quite sure that he hadn't been followed. And then he relaxed, realising that Mathews was asking him about when he was with SIS in Berlin.

'I was responsible for reporting on conditions in East Berlin. Both the military and the general population.'

'How did you get in with the Wall and the checkpoints?'

Carling smiled. 'The Wall didn't exist until later and even when the Wall went up we still had the right of free passage in uniform and in an army vehicle.'

'Did you keep up your contact with the Russians?'

Carling shrugged. 'That was part of my job. I had contact with East Germans and Russians.' He smiled. 'If you look in my file you'll see that SIS were quite pleased with my efforts.' Carling looked around at the people in the restaurant and then back at Mathews. 'Doesn't it seem crazy to you to be talking about these things in a place like this? Couples drinking coffee, families with their children. Shopping in the plastic bags alongside their chairs. People whose only worry is paying the mortgage and the milk bill?'

'It's still going on, George. Behind the scenes.'

'But doesn't it seem crazy to go so far back? Everything was different then. That was then, this is now.'

'What happened after Berlin?'

'I came back to London and was in charge of the Warsaw Pact desk.'

'Did that mean you ran active operations into the Warsaw Pact countries?'

'No. I was responsible for reporting on the politicians, the economics, the civilian population, morale and that sort of thing.'

'But you were informed about our operations in those countries?'

'Of course. Some of the operations were specifically to provide information that I needed.'

'Did your old Soviet contacts keep in touch with you when you were back in London?'

Carling smiled. 'Let's just say that they wanted to.'

'But you didn't co-operate with them?'

'No. We were in the middle of the Cold War. They were no longer our allies in a war.' He shrugged. 'It was a different scenario, a different game.'

'What did you feel about communism by then?'

'Have you ever read the Soviet constitution?'

'No.'

'That's part of the problem. It's like people criticising religion who have never been in a church.'

Mathews smiled. 'I don't see the connection.'

'OK. Let me explain. The Cold War's over, we're into glasnost and perestroika now. Agreed?'

'Yeah.'

'So what lesson do we learn from that?'

'That communism doesn't work.'

'Ah, my boy, that's the rub. Maybe all it proves is that the Soviets weren't communists.'

Mathews laughed. 'How do you make that out? That's crazy.'

'Is it? Let's go back to the Soviet constitution. When you've read it you're left with two, maybe three thoughts. First – that it is very much the same as the constitution of the United States. Secondly, you realise that both constitutions are essentially democratic and creative. And thirdly, that although the Soviets had an excellent constitution based on communism, they didn't practise what they preached. The law was abused, power-hungry men ignored all those well-thought-out intentions.' He paused and smiled. 'So why didn't communism work? It didn't work because of people. *We're* the problem. There isn't too much difference between communism and Christianity. They're both great ideas. And neither of them works. They don't work because we are a selfish, aggressive, greedy species. Wave a flag, promise victory and rewards and it's easy to start a war.

It's no longer a case of wars between great nations, but wars between tribes. You can see it in Africa, in Indonesia and Palestine . . .' he smiled '. . . and you can see it at a football match on a Saturday afternoon. Heroes in claret and blue jerseys and villains in blue and white stripes.'

'It's an interesting theory.'

'It's not a theory, my friend. I wish it was. It's fact.'

'So when did you realise that communism didn't work?'

'I never believed that it worked. No more than I believed that Christianity or Islam or any other religion worked. I helped the Russians because they were our allies and they were dying in their thousands fighting the Germans, our mutual enemies.' He paused. 'I sometimes send money to one or other of the South American countries where people are starving and abused, that doesn't imply that I approve their politics.' He stopped to sip his coffee and then put down the cup and looked at Mathews. 'You know, the problem you young chaps have is that you don't understand the people you're operating against. The latest technology and lots of dull and irrelevant facts – but no humanity.'

Mathews winced. 'Isn't that a bit sweeping?'

'Tell me, how many KGB men have you known personally?'

Mathews laughed. 'None. That's called consorting with the enemy.'

'So how do you find out what motivates them?'

'We don't need to. Like you said, we're only interested in what they do.'

Carling shook his head slowly. 'We had a poster in our offices during the war. The headline said – "Know your enemy". And it showed men in various uniforms. And somebody had put an arrow against one of the figures and scrawled in pencil – "And he likes screwing blondes". The chap who wrote those words was the most successful interrogator we ever had.'

'In what way was he successful?'

'He didn't interrogate suspects. He chatted to them. Got into their minds. Enabled us to understand what motivated them.' He smiled. 'Ask your boss. Ask Freddie Kennedy. The man I'm talking about was Kennedy's father.' He paused. 'And that's why he sent you down here to chat with me because he knew full well that if he called me into Century House he wouldn't learn a thing. He's a very shrewd man is Freddie, but I was in this business before either of you were born.'

'What did you learn by being friendly with some KGB man?'

Carling thought for a moment and then said, 'I suppose the most important thing you learned was that a KGB man didn't have his eyes close together or horns growing out of his head. He was just a man. A man who was often berated by his wife for not being around when he was needed, or not getting the heating fixed. A man who liked sitting on his small daughter's bed at night and reading her a story before she went to sleep.' He sighed. 'What you learned all too often, my friend, was that you had more in common with the KGB man than you did with the kind of people who gave you both your orders. He was recruited in much the same way as you were, the same training and the same kind of work. It slowly dawns on you that despite the propaganda and the media there isn't all that much difference between you and your opposite number in the KGB.' He smiled. 'Or in the CIA for that matter.' He looked at his watch. 'We'd better get back.'

'Does it worry you that one of the tabloids seems to be taking an interest in you?'

'No way. They know that I've got just as much money as they have when we get to the High Court. Whatever they printed I'd have a writ on their editor's desk in an hour.' He stood up. 'Come on.'

Kennedy had listened intently as Mathews gave him an outline of his conversations with Carling, and when he had finished Kennedy said, 'Tell me again what he said about his time in Berlin.'

'He just told me that he was responsible for general intelligence from East Berlin.'

'No details of his contacts over there?'

'No.'

'I was hoping you'd get more. If there's any chance of nailing him it would be from that time in Berlin.'

'Was a report done when he finished his time there?'

'Yes. But it was useless.' He paused. 'D'you want to see it?'

'Yes. It might give me a lead.'

He had sat in Kennedy's outer office with a photocopy of the Berlin report.

SUMMARY OF ROUTINE CHECK ON SERVICE PERIOD IN BERLIN OF LIEUT.-COLONEL CARLING

Given brief (see routine task file 7042)
Subject was to gain information from East Berlin and adjacent *Länder* on the following:

1. Morale of Soviet and East German armed services.
2. Morale of civil population.
3. Relationship of Soviet authorities, military and civilian, with East German equivalents.

4. Economics and production.
5. KGB and Stasi personnel and organisation.
6. Operations of item 5.
7. Media attitudes.
8. Troop movements (Soviet and E. German).
9. Student opinion.
10. Building construction (public and private).

Distribution

1. SIS Berlin
2. SIS Düsseldorf
3. SIS London
4. Foreign Office (Extracts through SIS London)

Classification: Top-Secret. Certain edited items down to 'Secret'.

Local evaluation

Lt.-Colonel Carling's work was highly praised by all concerned in SIS Berlin and the London evaluations were all favourable. It was also noted that when the subject was posted back to London the flow of information from East Berlin was not only substantially reduced but was not much more than uncorroborated gossip.

Security

Subject operated virtually independently but there was no evidence of security breaches. However, I note that there is no record of subject's marriage to an American citizen in his 'P' file nor does he appear to have claimed marriage or accommodation allowances. When I queried this locally and in London I was given no satisfactory reason for this omission. I only learned of his married status by chance from a casual comment made by a local journalist in the Berlin Press Club who asked what had happened to the wife who, it seemed, was particularly attractive.

Signed: J.T. Hooper

Mathews read the report through several times and then said to Kennedy's PA, 'Where is Freddie? I need to talk to him before I go back.'

'He's at the Imperial War Museum but he'll be back in an hour.'

'I'll wait.' He stood up. 'I'll go to the canteen and get a coffee. Could you bleep me there?'

'Of course.'

Twenty minutes later Mathews was back with Kennedy.

'I read the summary.'

'Good. I can't remember what was in it but I seem to recall that it was very favourable.'

'It was.'

'So what's the problem?'

'Why wasn't I told that Carling had been married?'

'Where is the copy of the report?'

'With your PA.'

Kennedy pressed a button on the internal phone and said, 'Bring me the document that you gave to Tim Mathews.'

Kennedy sat without speaking but clearly disturbed or angry, it was hard to tell which. He almost snatched the two pages from his secretary, dismissing her with a wave of his hand as he started reading the report. When he had finished reading it he leaned back, looking up at the ceiling. Slowly he lowered his head to look at Mathews.

'I shouldn't have let you read that report. It should have been shredded way back.' There was a long pause. 'I'll tell you what happened but before I do I want you to listen very carefully to what I say now.' He paused. 'Under no circumstances will you ever raise this . . .' he waved his hand dismissively '. . . this episode with Carling. Neither will you ever mention what I'm about to tell you with anyone but me, either inside SIS or outside.' He paused and pointed a monitory finger. 'Believe me, if you don't stick to what I say your feet won't touch. You'll be out. And you know what that means. You'll get the treatment.' He paused. 'Do you understand?'

'I guess so.'

'And you'll take this as an order?'

'Yes.'

'OK. I'm going to give you just the basics. Mainly because it's only the basics that I know myself. Nobody, apart from Carling, knows what really went on.' He leaned back in his chair, both hands palm down on his desk. 'It seems that Carling fell in love with a German girl. East German, that is. He got her pregnant. He didn't want us to know. Thought we'd disapprove. Too bloody right, of course. So he used some pal of his at the American consulate to get this girl American citizenship. And some bloody US army padre married them. When it was all done he tells us. Not the full story. He told our people that she was an American and her parents wanted her married according to American law by an American priest. Very reluctantly the brass accepted the situation, for two reasons. First, Carling was a valuable and irreplaceable asset and secondly we did our own check-up and found she was in fact East German. And what was worse, her mother was Russian. You can imagine what the media would have made of that if they got hold of it. Top SIS man marries an East German commie. And, of course, puts her in the family way.'

'Was she a communist?'

'No idea. It didn't matter. It was too late to stop it.' He paused and lined up a pencil with his blotter. 'Carling would spill all he knows about everything if the truth got out.'

'Where is she – his wife?'

Kennedy sighed. 'She died. Killed in a street accident in Berlin. Carling was working for us there at the time.'

'What happened to the child?'

'The child? Oh, yes. A daughter. I think she became a musician of some sort. Goes under her mother's name. Seems both she and Carling doted on the mother.' He sighed. 'Very sad story, really.' But there was no sorrow in his eyes nor in his voice. Mathews had seen that kind of face at the funerals of SIS men. Mourners in dark suits and bowler hats, with rolled-up umbrellas even on sunny days.

'Do you still want me to carry on with Carling?'

'Of course.' Kennedy seemed surprised at the question. 'You've really got alongside him but I don't want anything to rock the boat.' He smiled. 'I meant to ask you before – how are things going about your son?'

'The court bit is in abeyance for a couple of months.' He hesitated but went on. 'There's a chance we might get together again. But it is only a chance.'

'Well done. I hope it works out well for you, Tim. Keep me in the picture, won't you?'

'Of course.'

On the train from Charing Cross to Frant Mathews sat in the First-Class carriage with his head back against the rest and his eyes closed. He found his meeting with Kennedy disturbing. He had been suspicious right from the start that they were concealing something, so that he was being used to fish around for something that would get Carling into the High Court. But why should they want to do that when it was all so long ago? Carling hadn't had any connection with SIS or even the Foreign Office for at least ten years. He never spoke in the House of Lords and he was a cross-bencher not controlled by any party's whips. Maybe Pamela was right and he ought to get out of the business right now and find some more routine job. But he had no qualifications for a normal job. And he had seen what happened to others who rebelled and took early retirement and half-pension.

They must have battened down the hatches on Carling's marriage very successfully. There was nothing about it in his *Who's Who* entry, and no mention of a wife in the newspaper cuttings.

CHAPTER 30

As they were going to include the Carling business on the agenda they met at the safe house rather than at Century House.

Kennedy outlined to Farmer and Shelley such details as he thought they needed to know and when he had finished it was Shelley who spoke first.

'Sounds to me, Freddie, that we're wasting our time. What does the DPP say about what you've got so far?'

'I can't consult the DPP in case I could be accused of prejudicing either the case or the fact that he *does* prosecute on evidence that I have already discussed with him.'

Farmer said, 'You said you'd got top legal advice. Who was it?'

'The Solicitor-General, Sir Frank Lewis.'

Shelley frowned. 'Wasn't he in intelligence during the war?'

'After the war actually. He was an I.Corps major.' He smiled. 'Who better?'

'Was it an unofficial chat?'

Kennedy smiled. 'Let's say demi-official.'

'And what did he say?'

'He said he felt we should keep going and that Mathews had established such an unusual and close relationship with our friend that we shouldn't think of throwing it away.'

Shelley was always one for negatives. 'I still think we're wasting our time.'

Kennedy nodded to Farmer. 'What about you, Dickie?'

'We probably are wasting our time but there are several good reasons why we should keep going . . .'

'Such as?' Shelley snapped.

'Calm down, Peter.' Farmer paused to collect his thoughts again. 'First of all, if something does come out eventually we can establish that we did everything legally possible to ascertain the facts. Secondly, we might even come up with enough hard evidence to put him on trial and use the rest as substantiation. And finally, what are we wasting – one guy's salary and some expenses and a few months of time.' He smiled. 'It's better odds than Premium Bonds give you.'

Shelley wasn't appeased. 'You know, Freddie, I've got a feeling in my water that you're up to something. Are you?'

Kennedy shrugged. 'Like what?'

'Like some hidden agenda that Farmer and I don't know about.'

'You've got a Machiavellian mind, old pal.'

Shelley was flattered by the comparison as Kennedy knew he would be. 'I've been in the business nearly as long as you have and I can hear the little bells ringing. I just don't recognise the tune.'

Kennedy shrugged dismissively as if mystified by Shelley's suggestion. 'It's your item next, Dickie.'

They discussed the character and life-style of an Iranian whose front was as a buyer of bits and pieces for obsolete aircraft but who was in fact working for Gaddafi gathering intelligence on the intentions of Islamic fundamentalists operating in his neighbouring states.

As Shelley and Farmer strolled towards Victoria Station

Shelley said, 'I'd like to know what that bastard Freddie is really up to.'

Farmer laughed. 'Forget it, for Chrissake. You see problems or disasters everywhere you look.'

'And I've saved us from walking into both in my time. You mark my word, that bastard's up to something.'

Farmer grinned. 'Maybe it's that girl in cyphers.'

Back at the safe house in Ebury Street, Freddie Kennedy was telling Mathews how satisfied the committee was with his work on Carling.

Carling has been asked to open a small exhibition of paintings by a local artist at the Bayham Abbey ruins. It was in a room at the back of the old house where the caretakers now lived and sold tickets to visitors.

The paintings were undistinguished watercolours and charcoal sketches and his audience was a junior reporter and photographer from the *Courier* and seven or eight people sheltering from the sudden rainstorm outside. He found things to praise in the paintings and sketches and emphasised that all people had talents but most people were too modest to try out their latent skills. If a thing is worth doing, he said, it was worth doing badly. A photograph with a lengthy caption made the front page of that week's *Courier*.

When the visitors had left, Carling stood at the open French windows looking towards the ruins of the abbey.

'He was a spiteful man was our Henry.'

'Who?'

'Henry the Eighth. He ordered the destruction that turned the abbey into a heap of stone just to avenge himself on the Pope. Two powerful men who didn't understand each other's motives. The Tudor King who wanted his marriage dissolved because he wanted a male heir, and a Pope who thought that by refusing the dissolution he was defending the Catholic faith.' He sighed. 'But I guess we mustn't complain. Out of that bloody conflict we at least got *The Book of Common Prayer*. Not to mention the first Elizabeth.'

Mathews was looking at Carling's face. His eyes seemed to be on something far away. Carling shook his head as if he were trying to wipe out whatever had been in his mind.

'You ready to walk back, Timothy?'

'Yes.' He paused. 'Can I ask you a question?'

'Go ahead.'

'Where did you live when you came back to London?'

Carling stopped and leaned against the oak gate that led to the road. 'In King's Road, Chelsea. Three floors over the Scotch Wool and Hosiery shop.'

Carling took Mathews' arm. 'We'd better get back, I've got visitors this afternoon.' He grimaced. 'Once a year I have to listen to the bankers telling me what they did with my estate last year. Jolly chaps, and not so dumb as they appear, but talking the jargon of finance that could be Mandarin Chinese so far as I'm concerned. A few bottles of champagne and the promise of tickets for England v. Scotland at Twickenham or Wembley depending on what schools they went to, and Rollses and Bentleys back to London.' He smiled. 'Better than politicians anyway.'

Mathews was with Gabby and the baby in the garden when Julie called out to him.

'Somebody on the phone for you, Tim.'

'Who is it?'

'Wouldn't say. Said he was a friend. Got an American accent.'

Mathews used the receiver in the hall.

'Mathews.'

'Hi Tim. It's Joe.' A long pause. 'Joe Maguire. I'm in London.'

'Have a nice day, Joe.'

Maguire laughed softly. 'I know. I wanted to apologise for what happened. Can we meet?'

'How did you get this number?'

There was silence for a moment and then Maguire said, 'Somebody owed me one and I cashed it in. I'm going back tomorrow so how about we have a meal tonight.'

'Where are you staying?'

'The Hilton. The one in Park Lane.'

'What time?'

'To suit you. Seven, seven thirty?'

'OK. Seven thirty in the coffee shop.'

'Great. Look forward to seeing you.'

Mathews drove the couple of miles to Lamberhurst and used the public phone on the Down. He dialled Kennedy's direct number and it was Kennedy who answered.

'Freddie, it's Tim Mathews. I've just had a phone call at the cottage. It was Joe Maguire, the CIA guy who was my contact to meet Hank Henney.'

'How the hell did he know you were there?'

'No idea. I asked him . . . waffled about collecting on a past favour.'

'What did he want?'

'Said he wanted to apologise. I fixed to have dinner with him at the Hilton. What do you think? Shall I go?'

'Yeah. See if you can find out why they ran you out. And he picks up the tab, not you.'

'I'll contact you tomorrow.'

'Do that.'

* * *

Joe Maguire looked like a man from IBM. Well-cut blue suit, white shirt and decorated tie, with cuff links like silver dollars. He was sitting at a table with all the trappings of tea for two, and half stood as Mathews arrived. As Maguire waved Mathews to the seat facing him he said, 'Good to see you, Tim. D'you take milk and sugar?' he grinned. 'I'm learning how to be the perfect hostess now I'm on my own.'

'Both. Sugar and milk.' He paused. 'How long have you been in London?'

'Got here yesterday morning, go back tomorrow afternoon.'

He handed over the tea and a bowl of wrapped sugar. 'I know it's hygienic but this wrapping drives me crazy.' He looked at Mathews, smiling. 'Apologies from Langley for that cock-up. Won't happen again.'

'What was it all about?'

Maguire shrugged. 'Crossed wires, rivalries, bloody-mindedness and fingers too quick on the trigger.'

'Whose finger, Joe?'

'Hard to tell. By the time Langley had at least traced the gun somebody had wiped it clean.'

'Convenient all round.'

'Not really. We made ourselves look fools to you people and we were grateful for your guy Kennedy not pressing the point too hard.' He stood up. 'I've booked a table upstairs, let's go and eat.'

They had a table by the windows that looked over Hyde Park to the traffic on the Carriage Drive down to Knightsbridge.

After they had given their orders to the waiter Mathews said, 'Now tell me how you found out where I was and how you got an unlisted telephone number.'

'Well, finding out where you were was a process of elimination. We checked your old number in Esher and got a frosty reception from a lady but a new number – your new rooms. No response and answering machine not on. Then we thought about the reason for your trip to New York. We had words with Hank Henney who not only wasn't helpful but was positively obstructive. A bit of pressure was applied and we got the name George Carling. Lord Carling, in fact. Now when you get among the lords our embassy's the place to try.' He paused. 'Seems like your Carling guy is a quite frequent visitor to Grosvenor Square.'

'And how did you get the number?'

'I got back to NSA at Fort George Meade. They cover everything. Seven minutes flat.'

'A lot of hard work just to apologise for a cock-up.'

Maguire shrugged. 'Why not. We value the goodwill of our friends in Century House.'

Mathews snorted. 'You could have fooled me.'

'Hank Henney said you were asking him about this Lord guy. What's so special about him?'

'Why not ask Henney?'

Maguire smiled. 'Henney said he thinks you're trying to frame this guy.'

'A pretty delayed action if we were. He hasn't been in the business for at least fifteen years.'

'That didn't stop you people from putting the skids under Anthony Blunt.'

'It was a book that eventually exposed him, not SIS. They kept their side of the bargain.'

'Our guy at the embassy said he'd heard that one of your tabloids was working on an exposé of Carling.'

'There's always rumours about somebody about to be exposed as a crook or a traitor.'

'So why are you alongside the Lord?'

'You don't expect me to answer that, do you?'

'Why not? He must be important or you wouldn't have flown over to the States to talk with Hank Henney. You could have phoned him and saved the fare.'

Mathews grinned. 'I only paid one way, remember?'

Maguire ignored the crack, seemingly intent on keeping the talk to Carling.

'I think Langley have got a soft spot for your guy Carling.'

'What's that mean?'

'I think they wouldn't want him to get hurt.'

'Who says he's gonna get hurt?'

Maguire shrugged. 'Nobody.' He paused. 'So far.' He looked at Mathews for a moment before he said, 'What are you people trying to pin on him?'

'Joe. You're getting very near thin ice. You'd better back off. Carling's our man – not yours.'

For a moment Mathews thought that Maguire was going to argue and then the American said quietly, 'It's just a word to the wise, old pal. Just a hint.' He paused. 'How are things with your old lady?'

'Calming down. I see my boy now without any hassle.'

'Good – when are you coming to the States again?'

'No idea.'

'If you're coming let me know and I'll pay you back for the cock-up last time.' Maguire stood up smiling and then, his face serious, he said, 'By the way, Hank Henney sends his best wishes to friend Carling.' He held out his hand and Mathews took it without comment. Maguire stayed behind to settle the bill and Mathews took the elevator back to the ground floor.

* * *

Mathews dialled Kennedy's direct office number and the phone was answered immediately.

'Kennedy.'

'It's Tim Mathews. I've just left Maguire. Shall we meet?'

'Sure. I've been waiting in case you called. Where are you? I'll come over.'

'In Park Lane. At the Dorchester. OK, I'll wait for you.'

Kennedy was in white tie and tails and looked quite impressive.

'Forgive the rags, I'm going on to a late do. Tell me what happened.'

Mathews went carefully through his conversation with Maguire and when he was finished Kennedy closed his eyes, thinking. When he opened his eyes he said, 'What was your impression?'

'I got the feeling that Maguire had been sent over officially to find out what the state of the game was with Carling.'

Kennedy nodded. 'I agree. But why are they interested in Carling after all these years?'

'Maybe for the same reason that we are. They want to know something out of his past.'

'Or maybe there's something that they know that they don't want us to know.' He shifted in his chair. 'Has Maguire gone back?'

'He said he was leaving tomorrow.'

'Any idea where he's staying?'

'At the Hilton.'

'Whoever wants to protect Carling over there must be high level. After the balls-up they made when you were over there they wouldn't be letting Maguire pussyfoot around unless some top brass thought it was really necessary.'

'What did Carling do when he was over there?'

'He was our man at the embassy. Third Secretary or something like that as his cover. It was more or less a liaison job. There was so much rivalry between the CIA and the FBI, and the CIA and us that we were constantly getting crossed wires. Nothing serious but they had to be dealt with diplomatically.

'I think they leaned on Carling for information about the Soviets and the Warsaw Pact countries because he knew far more than they did. But we wanted him to keep it low level. Then it was decided to appoint an SIS guy as full-time liaison with CIA. Independent and nothing to do with the embassy who constantly protested to the FO about us having an SIS man using the embassy as his cover.

'We put up several names – at least two. The Americans said no to both and then came back and said that they would accept Carling because they valued his judgement.' Kennedy shrugged. 'So we went along with it. And that's what he did for a few years before he came back here.'

'Did he retire from SIS or was he eased out?'

'Officially he retired but he stayed on our strength because the Foreign Office wanted his advice from time to time.' He looked at his watch. 'I'm sorry, Tim, but I must go.'

Mathews had phoned the cottage to warn Julie that he would be late back but she had given him a key to the main door before he left for London.

It was 2 a.m. as he drove his car over Waterloo Bridge and headed for the A21. There was little traffic on the road after he left the suburbs and he switched on the radio. He listened for a few minutes to LBC. It was a phone-in patronised by all the usual crazies and bigots not yet asleep, and he switched it off.

The strange thing about his time with Carling was that it demonstrated why they had never got Philby into court. Except for the Albanian business they had both done more or less the same things. With all the media crap about Philby it created a background that left no doubt in the public's mind that he was a traitor. But there was no way Mathews could class Carling as a traitor. Misguided maybe, but nothing more. But the media could make him into another Philby. Like Carling said, it isn't possible to make a judgement today on what happened thirty years ago. And as Carling often said – that was then, and this is now. Mathews was glad he wasn't doing his job in those days.

Julie and Gabby had waited up for him, the baby in her carrycot on the table in the kitchen alongside the chessboard. For a few moments he couldn't speak as they made him a mug of tea, he was so moved that they should stay up half the night just to welcome him back. Despite feeling guilty at his reason for being there at all he still felt more cared for than he had ever felt before in his life. It wasn't just politeness, they obviously genuinely cared about him.

CHAPTER 31

Carling was standing at the window of Mathews' bedroom. He was sipping from a large teacup and was wearing a rather worn silk dressing gown.

'You won't believe it but it's starting to snow. Real fat snowflakes coming down in slow motion like feathers. And outside it'll be wonderfully silent. "*Stille Nacht, heilige Nacht.*" Wonderful. Shame it won't last, this time of year.'

He turned to look at Mathews who was still in bed, the tea at his bedside untouched.

'The girls tell me that you were frightfully late getting home last night. A good evening?'

Mathews smiled wanly. 'Not really. But I had a good meal at the Hilton.'

'Which one?'

'The one on Park Lane.'

'Ah, yes. The only real one. The others aren't Hiltons at all. Could be in Red China for all the use they are.' He paused and said casually. 'What do Freddie Kennedy and his pals think about your time with me? Are they happy . . .' he laughed '. . . or disappointed.'

Mathews smiled but not with conviction. 'I don't really know.'

'Somebody at the Travellers' told me that one of the rags, the *Sun* I think it was, was trying to scrape together a piece on me as the Fifth Man.' He laughed. 'Or maybe the Sixth Man. They'll probably try and cross your palm with silver sooner or later.'

'They don't know anything about me.'

'Don't be so sure. Julie says she's certain that some creep has been watching the cottage recently.' He grinned. 'Maybe Kennedy's put a tail on you as well as me.'

'I don't see me as a tail on you. Far from it.'

'And how do you see yourself?'

Mathews sighed, leaned up in the bed, and it was several moments before he responded.

'I see myself as looking from today's perspective at things that happened decades ago.'

'To what purpose?'

'To do justice to all concerned.'

'You're kidding.'

'I'm not, I assure you.'

'What you're actually doing, or supposed to be doing, is trying to establish to the satisfaction of the High Court that the things that Kim Philby and the others did during the war and after were treasonable. They couldn't do it when Philby was around and they can't do it now that he's dead. They wonder if they might do it with me as a substitute. And you're their hunting dog, their bloodhound, quartering the years.' Carling smiled suddenly and said, 'Don't take it to heart, dear boy. The more you learn about those days, the more you'll have your doubts.'

'So why don't Kennedy and the others have doubts?'

'Oh they do, my boy. They do. You've got a double role. First you're just a piece of insurance and secondly, you're on a fishing expedition. Neither you nor they know what you're looking for . . .' he shrugged '. . . but who knows – maybe you could find something.' He smiled again, 'But you have to take care to make sure you land a trout not a shark.'

'I've got a feeling you're telling me something.'

'Maybe Kennedy's trying to tell you something too.'

'Give me a clue.'

Carling opened his mouth to speak and then closed it slowly, shaking his head.

'No. It's not a game. It's people's lives that are involved.'

He turned and walked to the door turning the big brass knob slowly as he looked round at Mathews. Such a young man. What was he – thirty-four maybe thirty-five? He probably understood computers and CD-ROMS but not the human mind. He could drive a high-powered car but he couldn't skin a rabbit, he knew the words of Joan Baez's songs but not what they meant. And his heart? His heart was somewhere between his belly and his head when it should have been halfway between his eyes and heaven. Like the others he had probably read Freud's words but would never understand what he meant – that men's minds were the products of fears and instincts struggling with the cobwebs of emotions and experience.

He waved his hand to the young man and quietly closed the door behind him.

CHAPTER 32

On the drive back from Esher, Mathews realised that he was glad to be returning to the cottage. Pamela was obviously considering taking him back and making a fresh start. But he didn't belong there any more. He was a visitor. Treated with a politeness that he had never had as a husband. And even for young Tony he was an interruption to his normal life. If he asked about their daily lives it sounded as if he were probing, a tourist who didn't speak the language checking on the life-style of the natives. He was seldom there for longer than a couple of hours but it had become just a duty. A duty from which he was glad to escape. Aware that in truth nobody benefited from the time he spent there. They were as relieved to see him go as he was to leave. Everybody could get back to their normal lives for another week or so.

Carling had played the piano for them after the evening meal. Viennese songs, a bit of Fats Waller stride piano and, with a smile at Mathews, one of Chaminade's *Songs Without Words*.

After Julie and Gabby had gone to bed the two men watched an OU programme on robot technology until Carling had switched off the TV in exasperation.

'There are times when I'm in sympathy with the title of the song from the musical – "Stop the World I Want to Get Off".'

Mathews smiled, he was used to Carling's outbursts of indignation. 'Why at this particular moment?'

'We make great play on the dignity and satisfaction of being in work. Unemployment must come down. The top priority. And on the other hand we extol the virtues of technology. One robot doing the work of ten men. So ten men lose their jobs. Maybe we should call a halt to technology and say that men having jobs is more important than the economies of robot production lines.

'The government urges youngsters to study maths and science and engineering – why? Because the nation needs more scientists and engineers. What arrogance. Education is for being alive with not just for getting a job. This is getting to be like Orwell's 1984. And the opposition talk about "the workers". We're all workers now, one way or another, whether we like it or not. Over six hundred idiots calling themselves MPs. A hundred would be more than enough for what they do.'

Seeing the look on Mathews' face Carling laughed. 'I'm at it again. On the soap box.'

'Why don't you say your say in the House of Lords?'

'Waste of time.' He sighed. 'If there's one thing I've learned it's that you can't do anything on a mass basis. All you can do is a bit of good here and there with individuals. Give a chap his weekly rent money and he'll take care of it but hand it out from the state and it's not valued. It's not just doing good that counts, it's how you do it.'

Carling stood up, yawned and stretched his arms. 'I'm off to bed. Lock the back door before you go up.'

* * *

With the battery run down on Julie's elderly Fiesta, Mathews had driven her into Lamberhurst to the village stores. Carling insisted that the village shops should be supported where possible for all their shopping, not just when they ran out of sugar.

There were enquiries in the shops about the wellbeing of His Lordship, and when he would next be on TV, and Mathews could tell that the interest was genuine. It seemed odd that a man with such unorthodox views should be so universally liked. Maybe it would be a good idea for Kennedy to fix for him to meet someone who was not one of Carling's fans.

Back at the cottage he used his mobile phone to contact Kennedy's PA and make an appointment. Kennedy could give him twenty minutes at 4.30 p.m.

Kennedy was in an amiable mood and said, 'You're right. All that bloody casual charm works on everyone.' He paused. 'Including me.' He frowned. 'The only likely critic who comes to mind is Parsons. Sir Peter. One-time Director-General of SIS. I understand that he detested George Carling. He's retired now, of course. Has been for years. Lives somewhere in Hampstead. Great cricket fan. Wants to be near Lords.' He looked at Mathews. 'Would he do?'

'Sounds ideal. Would he see me?'

'If I hint that we're taking a hard look at George Carling he'd see you all right.' He reached for his internal phone. 'Find me Sir Peter Parsons' address and telephone number, will you?'

A few seconds later he was writing on his pad. 'How do you spell that? OK. Yes – thanks.' He hung up, tore off the page of his pad and pushed it across his desk to Mathews, leaning over to read it as he dialled the number. He said to Mathews, 'Get yourself a coffee or something while I talk to . . . ' He paused. '. . . Sir Peter. I hoped I'd get you . . . it's Freddie, Freddie Kennedy.'

Mathews took the hint and left. Half an hour later he came back. Kennedy was still on the phone and he waved Mathews to a chair. He seemed to be finalising the time and place of a meeting '. . . of course . . . ten o'clock . . . at your place, tomorrow . . .' Kennedy nodded as if his listener could see him, '. . . of course . . . yes . . . thanks for your help . . . no, not Jim, Tim . . . Tim Mathews . . . good . . . take care of yourself.' As he hung up he said, 'That OK with you? Ten tomorrow at his place?'

'Where's his place?'

'Hampstead. Wedderburn Road – it's on the piece of paper I gave you.'

'Tell me a bit about Sir Peter.'

Kennedy sniffed and loosened his tie. His hands moved to tidy the papers and files on his desk.

'He was our DG for five years. Brought in from the military, supposedly to tame the wild men of SIS. He had been a major-general on the General Staff. A gunner. Left-wingers always feel that putting a soldier in charge of SIS is a suitable revenge.' Kennedy gave a brief laugh. 'We eat them, of course. In our own peculiar way we speak the same language. Carling wasn't SIS when Parsons was DG. Carling had some mystery relationship with the Foreign Office advising on Soviet affairs. Peter Parsons saw it as going behind his back. Probably was.' He paused and sighed. 'So, back to Parsons. Good army record, sports and all that. Bright.' Kennedy waved his hands around. 'That's about it.'

*   *   *

Major-General Sir Peter Parsons MBE lived in the top flat of one of the Victorian houses in Wedderburn Road that had once been the family homes of bankers and businessmen. Pevsner would have classed them as impressive but without grace or style. You got space and bricks for your money. But they were still highly desirable residences. Not mere houses.

Parsons lived alone and everything was spic and span. A place for everything and everything in its place was his oft repeated watchword. Tall, lean, with a hawk-like face and long quite elegant limbs. His voice was high-pitched but still with the rasp of the sergeant-major he had once been. Dress was casual. Sports jacket, corduroys and Royal Artillery tie. His alert dark eyes took in Mathews and was not impressed, but he ushered him into the high-ceilinged sitting room before he left to make coffee for them both.

The few books on the shelves were mainly the reminiscences of men who went on safaris hunting animals in places like the Northern Frontier District and the Ogaden, with titles like *With Rod and Gun in the Danakil Country*.

The coffee was served on a silver salver that had been awarded to Captain Parsons RA for winning the 30 Corps middle-weight boxing championship, Bad Harzburg 1965.

'Mathews, isn't it?' He said and without waiting for an answer he went on, 'Help yourself to milk and sugar.' He sat back in the leather armchair. 'Kennedy said you wanted my views of Carling, yes?'

'Yes please.'

'Never could understand why everybody saw him as a kind of mixture of Robin Hood and Mother Theresa. Lots of charm, of course, but plenty of rascals can pile on the charm to get what they want. They all said Philby had charm. But I could never put my finger on what

Carling actually wanted. And charm or not he was an arrogant man. Saw things his way and if you didn't agree too bloody bad. He was deep. Always that brain ticking away. Didn't miss a thing. I wouldn't trust him. Not a team man. Too much the loner.'

'Did you think he was good at his job?'

'Couldn't rightly say. Was gone before I took over. Farting around at the Foreign Office when I met him.' He paused. 'The only experience I had of his work was in Germany. Called to a meeting. Some chap – turned out to be Carling – had got wind of those bloody East Germans planning to break through the Wall in fifty places and take over the whole of Berlin. Hoped to catch us with our trousers down and overwhelm us. Carling pontificated about the psychology of the East Germans and said if we moved troops and guns up to the Wall they'd know they wouldn't surprise us. That's what we did – and it worked. Not a peep out of the bastards.' He gave a sharp laugh. 'He was right that time. Got to give him his due.'

'Did you see much of him?'

'No. Just odd meetings at the FO and at Joint Intelligence meetings. Never said much but he took it all in.'

They talked to no great purpose for another half-hour and in the taxi home to Charing Cross Station Mathews came to the conclusion that Parsons' dislike of Carling was mainly because he didn't see Carling as a proper soldier. Not only 'didn't stick to the book, but hadn't even read the bloody thing'. But SIS weren't intended to be soldiers.

CHAPTER 33

Carling stood at the bench in his radio shack looking at the four stacks of typewritten sheets. There were twenty-four pages in each pile and an A4 envelope beside each one.

It had taken him two weeks to compose and type the statement, and the original had been copied at the Camden Road copying shop in Tunbridge Wells. Camden Road was named after Marquess Camden who had left the ruins of Bayham Abbey to the State in 1961. Camden Road was no beauty spot but in its long necklace of pokey shops you could find anything. If you wondered where on earth you could buy something you'd do well to head for Camden Road. He had done the copying himself so that the young lad couldn't read the top page which was entitled: 'A notarised statement by George Carling made at the offices of Buss Stone, Solicitors, Tunbridge Wells, in the county of Kent, dated—' The date had been left blank despite the fact that His Lordship would be swearing his oath in a matter of hours.

He pulled up the folding chair and wrote in long-hand the appropriate words on the three envelopes. One was addressed to his friend, the senior partner of a highly respected Mayfair solicitors, the two others to the editor of *The Times* and the Director-General of the Special

Intelligence Service. His own original was taped to the back of an oil painting of a seascape on the wall over the fireplace in his bedroom.

He tucked the three copies into a Jiffy bag, sealed it and propped it up against the monitor beside the decoding terminal next to the transmitter.

He was tempted to dust the radio equipment. It hadn't been used for so long and nobody else was allowed in his shack. He found stopping people from twiddling knobs as irritating as having people smoke in his car.

He sighed as he stood up slowly and then looked at his watch. It was 4.30 a.m. and tomorrow he'd have to go up to London and hand the package over to Arthur with his instructions.

Arthur Parrish had known him for years but while Carling was sitting on the other side of the partner's desk he must be treated as a client. An important client. He listened intently to what Carling had to say and then said quietly, 'I'll do exactly as you say, my lord.' Then he leaned forward. 'D'you really think this is necessary, George?'

Carling shrugged. 'God knows, Arthur. But I'm not prepared to take the risk. This is my piece of insurance.'

'But it's all over now. When did Philby die? Eighty-eight wasn't it? Surely nobody would rake all that up after this time?'

'There's some I haven't told you, Arthur. And yes – there are those who would dig it all up if they got wind of what was in that statement.'

'You think someone could try to kill you, George? Surely not.'

'They could make at least a million, more if they played their cards right.' He smiled. 'The going rate isn't what it used to be. It's in hundreds these days, not thousands.'

Parrish shook his head slowly. 'What a world we've made, George. All those men who died. It sickens me.'

Red sealing wax and a candle were brought in and the envelopes sealed and impressed with Carling's ring.

They had lunch together at the Inn on the Park and talked only of the pre-Raphaelite collection at Birmingham's Art Gallery. Arthur Parrish was a Birmingham man, proud of its gallery, its symphony orchestra under young Simon Rattle, who was, in his opinion, well overdue for a knighthood. Parrish was also prepared to defend Aston Villa FC from all its detractors who criticised its talented waywardness. However, like a good many alumni of King Edward's, Birmingham, Arthur Parrish went back to the city only when business made it unavoidable.

By the time the train was past Sevenoaks the suburbs had given way to a landscape of woods, sheep, hops and apple orchards. Carling had left his car at Frant Station. As he stepped down on to the platform at Frant he stood and watched the train pulling out, the guard smiling and saluting as he went past.

He was the only passenger who got off the train and he stood there long after it was out of sight. There were only two railway stations he really loved. One was Milano Centrale that made him feel that it was all a wonderful mistake and they'd run a railway line through a cathedral. The other was Frant, the small, old-fashioned country station like the one in the film of *The Railway Children*.

He turned slowly and walked to his car, acutely aware of the incredible difference between his feelings now and what he had been doing in London. He was determined not to end up like that wretched man who had died in Moscow two years ago.

They were still sitting at the table after it had been cleared and Julie had brought in the coffee things and a bottle of wine.

As Carling poured coffee for himself he said casually, 'How are things on the home front?'

Mathews hesitated and then said, 'I don't really know.'

'What's the problem?'

'I think the problem's me. I think Pamela would be willing to have me back and have another go.' He sighed. 'But I don't feel any pleasure in the thought. I don't look forward to it.' He paused. 'In fact I dread the idea. But I'm worried about Tony, and seeing him.'

'Any idea why you don't want to try again?'

'Yes. Now I've had time to think about it without the old pressures, I don't think we made a pair. We just don't fit. She won't change and I wouldn't want her to change. Why should she?' He smiled. 'I know you must have talked to her about me. Pointing out any good points I have. And that makes her see me in a different light. But that isn't love. I realise now that she never did love me, and on my side it was physical attraction and I don't even feel that any longer. I don't want to criticise her. She's OK in her own way. But she's not for me. I'm bored when I'm with her. It's like being in a play. A rather boring play.' He shrugged as he came to a stop.

'And what are you going to do about it?'

'God knows.' He half smiled. 'Any suggestions welcomed.'

'D'you mean that?'

'Yes. I really do.'

'I'm not very surprised by your analysis. I think you're right in your assessment. It would be easy to say that the break-up was her fault because of the stupid affair she had with the solicitor. But bearing in mind her rather subdued personality she must have been very unhappy to see that as a solution. And now it's you who has to make the decisions. You can't make her and Tony and yourself happy but you can leave her her dignity and you can be a useful, helping father to Tony.' He smiled. 'I'm afraid there's no prize for you, dear boy. Maybe in the future but not right now. But despite that, be generous. Generous to the feelings of a rather wounded female. Let it be very gradual, maybe.' He paused. 'I know you'll be generous financially. Let her stay in the house and things like that. Practical things are her idea of affection.'

'Do you think I'm unfair about how I feel?'

'No. Not at all. You too have a life to live.'

There was a short silence and then Mathews said, 'Am I wearing out my welcome here? Would you like me to call it a day?'

'Has Kennedy said you should leave?'

'No, he hasn't said anything.'

'If he ever did suggest you should stop would you let me know?'

'Yes, of course. But I'm sure he'd tell you first or discuss it with you.' He smiled. 'I'm sure you'd be glad to hear that they'd had enough.'

'It's not in Kennedy's hands. It's the others.'

'Which others?'

'Why do you think they put you on to me?'

Mathews shrugged. 'Just to check things over. An independent opinion.'

Carling smiled. 'They know all they need to know. You're just a piece of insurance to see what you can find out. Because if you could find something then somebody else could too.'

'I don't understand, George. I'm out of my depth. Why should they want to do that?'

'To see if they can avoid having to kill me. To stop me talking. You can tell Freddie Kennedy that I've already taken appropriate precautions. They would do better just to sweat it out. It's too late to go back over that ground. And anyway it all ended when Philby died two years ago.'

'Could you tell me what all that was about?'

Carling shook his head. 'No. There's no point in involving you.' He smiled. A grim smile. 'Anyway you're part of my insurance.'

'But what if I stumbled on this thing? I'd feel guilty about talking to you in case I caused you trouble.'

'You won't, my friend.' He smiled. 'And if I told you you wouldn't believe it. There are times when I don't believe it myself.' He stood up. 'Forget all this. Just carry on. I'm off to bed.'

As Mathews undressed slowly he realised that those few sentences from Carling had changed everything. For one thing Carling had cut him off from Kennedy. If it was as Carling had described, Kennedy could easily make some unwise move against Carling. And who were 'the others'? And what did they want to hide? And what did Philby's death in 1988 have to do with it? It had all the indications of an SIS cock-up. But craziest of all – why did Carling think they might kill him? He'd said it so casually, as if it was merely another way to solve some unidentified problem.

He hadn't sounded shocked or surprised or apprehensive when he said it. Just the flat statement of an obvious solution. Maybe the old boy's mind was beginning to wander, roaming down the corridors of time to the days when they did solve problems that way. But that was a long time ago. Like Carling said so often – that was then and this is now. Or maybe it was like Dunne's Theory of Time where memory got out of kilter.

An owl hooted from somewhere in the beech trees as Carling walked in the garden and from far away he heard the bark of a hungry vixen in search of food for her cubs.

There were long shadows on the grass from the apple trees in the orchard and he was pleased to see that there was still a light on in Gabby's place over the garage. He walked slowly up the wooden stairs and knocked on the door.

A voice from inside said, 'Who is it?'

'It's me, Gabby.'

He heard two sets of bolts drawn and then came the light from inside.

'Are you all right? Come on in. You look tired.'

She had made him a pot of tea as he sat in the wicker armchair. With the cup halfway to his mouth he said, 'Are you happy, my dear?'

'Of course I am. I love it here.'

'And how's Lottie?'

She frowned. 'It's Carlotta. I don't like Lottie.' Then she smiled. 'She's fine.' She paused. 'Would you have liked to have a child?'

'I have got a child. A daughter.'

'What's her name?'

'It's Rachel, after her mother. Her mother's dead.'

'What does your daughter do?'

'She's a musician. Plays and teaches violin. She has an apartment in New York but she travels all over the world.'

'Do you ever see her?'

'I do when she's in Europe and I can arrange to be in the same place.'

'Are you lonely without her?'

He sighed. 'I'm lonely without her mother. I loved her a lot.'

'Can I ask you something silly?'

Carling laughed. 'Try me.'

'How do you get to be an earl?'

'Oh that's easy. My father was an earl and when he died I was his only child and I became the earl.'

'Do they pay you for being an earl?'

'No. Some earls are quite poor.'

'I read a piece in the *Daily Mail* about you. It said you were very rich.'

Carling smiled and shrugged. 'I get by, my dear.' He paused. 'What would you like to be when you're older?'

'I just want to be me with the baby.' She smiled, her head tilted endearingly. 'You've made me so happy.'

'You make me happy too. You and Julie.'

'Do you want to play chess?'

'Julie tells me you're very good now.' He stood up, a little clumsily. 'But it's time I was on my way.'

At the door he kissed her on the cheek and she stood holding the door open so that the steps were lit. When he turned to wave to her she waved back and he walked slowly back to the cottage. He realised that he had said too much to Mathews but he was sick of the games they played. He had thought that when Kim died that would be the end of it. With him in his grave they could bury their guilt and their fears. But he'd been wrong. They wanted him out of the way too. And if not out of the way at least subdued by constant pressures. They were scared now that that wretched tabloid might ruin it all.

Lying in bed he tried to remember how it had all started, but his thoughts kept going to the young girl who had a baby because she wanted someone to love her. There was a flicker of summer lightning on the ceiling, and a distant rumble of thunder sent his mind to Beethoven and the fourth movement of the 'Pastoral'. A few minutes later he was asleep.

He woke just after 4 a.m., put on his dressing gown and walked to the window, opening it to the scent of the honeysuckle that he had planted himself when he first came to the cottage.

As he leaned with his elbows on the window-sill his mind went back to Mathews. He ought not have given him advice about his marriage and his domestic arrangements. His advice was only suitable for the impetuous, the desperate, the people who bled from wearing their hearts on their sleeves. And Mathews was not one of those. Neither was his ex-wife. They calculated things, weighed things up and were moved only by the negatives of anger and whether they were getting a square deal. Matching shoes and handbag, and tweeds and brogues. Good people but dangerous for a man like him to advise.

It was beginning to get light when he went back to bed. His last thoughts were that it was time he brought it all to a head.

CHAPTER 34

Carling was breaking off the deadheads of a large pink pelargonium in a terracotta pot, tossing the heads into a wheelbarrow. When Mathews joined him, offering to help, Carling stood up slowly. 'I've had enough, Tim. How about you ask one of the girls to do us some coffee.'

When Mathews came back Carling was sitting on the bench by the pond in the orchard. He put the tray between them on the bench, and Carling pointed at the pond. 'This pond is a permanent reminder of the silly things that amateur gardeners can do. When I had it put here I forgot that in the autumn it would be covered with fallen leaves from the trees.' He laughed. 'I was trying for a Renoir effect.' He sighed. 'Never mind, another lesson learned.' He paused. 'There's a team from Radio 4 coming to interview me this afternoon. A series on "Are you a Christian?" '

Mathews smiled. 'And are you a Christian?'

Carling laughed. 'I can only go along with what Clem Attlee said when asked if he was a Christian. As usual he wasted no words. "Accept the Christian ethic, can't stand the mumbo jumbo." '

'What religion were you brought up with?'

'Well, my father was staunch Church of England. Seldom went to church other than for funerals and weddings and, give him his due, didn't make me anything as my mother was a Roman Catholic.' He smiled. 'And I swear she only went because she loved the singing, and all the mumbo jumbo. I think on reflection I rather liked aspects of it too.'

'What aspects?'

'The theatricality, the visual, the showbiz, the singing, the saying of prayers for sick people in the congregation. The assurance that there was forgiveness for all us sinners. Must be very consoling to have that belief.'

'So what didn't you like about it?'

Carling snorted. 'I'd never want to be part of a faith that maintained that if a baby dies before it's baptised it goes to purgatory. What arrogance. What kind of mind can think up that sort of rubbish?' He paused. 'I've just realised. I hope you're not a Catholic, Tim. I wouldn't want to detract from anyone's faith.'

'No. I'm not anything. But not with your conviction. More indifference and laziness.'

Carling turned his head to look at Mathews. 'Something I meant to ask you. Tell me, just briefly, what your impression was of Philby before you and I talked.'

Mathews thought for a moment. 'That he was a traitor, had cost men their lives, was a drunk, an adulterer.' He shrugged. 'Just a general shit.'

Carling nodded slowly. 'Are you going to be around this evening?'

'Yes. If it's OK with you.'

'Right. I'm going to tell you what Philby was really like.'

The BBC team had stayed for tea and His Lordship was obviously a firm favourite. He had eventually said that if he had to be something he thought he would be a Jew. When pressed for his reasons he had laughed and said that he would have been a more talented pianist and musician with Jewish blood in his veins.

They had dined alone and when they got to the coffee Carling pushed aside a vase of roses so that they could see each other more easily.

'So . . .' said Carling '. . . let's talk of Harold Adrian Russell Philby.' He paused. 'Did you realise that he was awarded the OBE in the 1946 New Year's Honours List?'

'No. I didn't know that.'

'It was his thirty-fourth birthday. I wonder why it's never mentioned. And he got it for his work against the Germans. So that's where we start with the truth.'

'Was it withdrawn when he went to Moscow?'

'No. If they had done that they'd have been stirring up a real hornet's nest. Anyway they had no grounds for doing it.'

'But the media didn't take long to publish the facts.'

Carling smiled. 'They thought they were the facts but they were just part of the game but they didn't know it. They still are, and they still don't know it.' He paused. 'I'd better tell you right now that you're mixed up in something . . . something that happened way back but could still cause far the biggest scandal that SIS have ever been involved in. No matter how skilfully you talked with me you wouldn't ever find out what it's all about. Freddie Kennedy has his suspicions but nothing more. And he's getting very near the line that if he crosses over he's going to be eliminated.' He paused. 'I'm going to suggest that we do a deal, you and me.'

'What kind of deal?'

'A deal that gets Kennedy off the hook that he doesn't know he's on. I'll give you some information that he'll see as valuable enough to call off this investigation but won't do anybody any harm.'

'What if the tabloid carries on its so-called investigation?'

Carling shook his head. 'They won't do a thing. They've been told what will happen to them if they don't back off. They're a big organisation with lots of interests in the UK and the USA, they could be wiped out in a couple of months. No apparent connection with us but they'd know who had pulled the plug on them.'

'They could publish that they'd been blackmailed or pressured.'

'They're in the business of making money. They've already been squeezed a little. They'll back off all right.'

'But why should I do this? Why should I make a deal that my people may not approve?'

'Because the deal is based on you not telling them what I'm prepared to tell you.' He shrugged. 'I'll give you the titbit for Kennedy and he'll be satisfied.' He paused. 'I'm relying on the fact that when you know the real facts you won't want it to go further. You won't want to turn bad into worse.' He paused and leaned forward as if he was looking at his reflection in the polished table. Then he looked back at Mathews. 'You'll learn what only four or five living people know, of something disgraceful. The others who knew, and they were very few, are long dead. It would be a condition that you would make no notes of what I tell you and that you never discuss it with anyone but me and one other person.'

'Who is the other person?'

'Would it make a difference if I told you?'

'I don't know. Depends who it is. Do I know the person?'

'You've met him, only briefly and only once. You met him a few weeks ago in New York. His name's Hank Henney. As you know, he's ex-CIA.'

There was a long pause. Then Mathews said quietly, 'How did you know I'd met him?'

Carling shrugged. 'They keep me informed. They have an interest in what happened too.'

'Am I right in thinking all this has something to do with Philby?'

Carling seemed to be considering his answer and then he said, 'Yes. That's where it started anyway.'

'Can I have time to think about it?'

'So long as you don't consult anyone else. This is between you and me.'

'Will what you tell me make trouble for SIS?'

'No. I'm trying to avoid trouble.'

'What about CIA?'

'The same applies.'

'Can I just go over what I understand you're suggesting? Just so that I don't get any wrong ideas.'

'Sure. Go ahead.'

'You said only four or five people living now know about whatever this is. Does that include you and Hank Henney?'

'Yes. And of the other three, one has been in a coma for several months. He is to have his life-system switched off in two weeks' time. So effectively there are only two others involved.'

'Are they SIS?'

'One *was* SIS and the other is CIA.'

'What does Kennedy know?'

'Nothing. He just has a faint suspicion that I could be what he describes as the Fifth Man.' Carling smiled.

'Or it could be the Sixth Man, depending on his current workload. I'll give you something factual that will keep him happy. Nothing to do with what I propose telling you about.'

'Let me get this straight, George. You're going to tell me something that is so serious it could cause chaos to SIS—'

Carling interrupted. 'And to the CIA.'

'And the CIA. So that I don't carry on with this stuff we've been doing. You'll also give me some other thing that will satisfy Freddie Kennedy that this operation was worthwhile.'

'That's about it.'

'And if I go along with this what happens?'

'Nothing. Kennedy can feel he's done his job. And I can go back to my peace and quiet.' He paused. 'And I expect you'll get a promotion.' He sighed. 'I just want to lay these ghosts once and for all.' He paused. 'I guess you'll just have to trust me – or not, as you decide. I'll have to trust you too, not to tell anyone else what I tell you.' He paused. 'Do you want to think it over for the night?'

Mathews shook his head, sighed and said, 'No. If I ever trusted anyone it would be you.'

'OK. Have a good night's sleep and we'll talk tomorrow. To give you a fair picture of what went on way back it's going to take quite a long time. I've got to try to make you feel what it was like in the early 1960s.'

'Where were you at the time?'

'I was in New York working with Hank Henney on keeping the peace between the CIA and SIS. I was just about to be brought back to London although I didn't know it at the time. Of course . . .' Carling stood up, smiling. 'Don't let me get going. It's a long story. Let's leave it for tomorrow.'

FOUR

CHAPTER 35

In the dog days of summer 1955 when the newspapers and magazines were hard pressed for a titbit, they slipped in a piece here and there about Burgess and Maclean. But the public were not really interested. It was four years since the two spies had fled to Moscow. Questions intended to revive the public interest were tabled in the House from time to time. One of these was asked by George Wigg, a Labour MP who asked – 'Would the Foreign Secretary institute inquiries into the suggestion made in a Sunday newspaper that there is widespread sexual perversion in the Foreign Office?' Herbert Morrison, the Labour Foreign Secretary, was not a man given to witty evasions but maybe he had intended no wit when he commented – 'I can only say that perhaps I have not been long enough at the Foreign Office to express an opinion.'

The first bomb fell when KGB officer Vladimir Petrov defected in Australia and stated that Burgess and Maclean were not just failures on the run, or even merely homosexual lovers, but long-term Soviet agents who had been working for the KGB since they were recruited in their young days at Cambridge University.

A rather bland White Paper was published that admitted a few minor facts but gave very little away. This led to another more pointed question in the House from

Lieutenant-Colonel Marcus Lipton, MP for Brixton. It was the first mention of Philby, and a Third Man.

The question was brief and to the point. 'Has the Prime Minister made up his mind to cover up at all costs the dubious third-man activities of Mr Harold Philby who was First Secretary at the Washington embassy a little time ago, and is he determined to stifle all discussion on the very great matters which were evaded in the wretched White Paper, which is an insult to the intelligence of the country?'

This was a question that could not be evaded. It concerned a named individual's character and by then, the Foreign Secretary was the patrician Harold Macmillan, who dealt with the matter himself. He assured the House that no evidence had been found that Mr Philby, a former temporary First Secretary in the Washington embassy, was responsible for warning Burgess or Maclean. He added that he had no reason to conclude that Mr Philby had at any time betrayed the interests of his country, or to identify him with the 'so-called Third Man, if indeed there was one.'

The next morning Philby gave a press conference at his mother's flat. He claimed that he had been precluded from defending himself because of the Official Secrets Act. He also claimed that although he thought he must have come across Burgess and Maclean at some time he could barely remember them. Most of the journalists were won round. He had been unfairly maligned. They'd leave him in peace in future.

Having once been a foreign correspondent during the Spanish Civil War, Philby didn't hesitate when supporters inside SIS used their influence so that he was offered the job of Middle East correspondent for the *Observer* and *The Economist*, who shared his salary and expenses. What the two editors were not told was that Philby was also commissioned to act on a freelance basis for SIS with his employment as a journalist giving him perfect cover.

CHAPTER 36

Carling had hired a taxi at Gatwick to take him to Marlow. Waring had told him on the phone that he had been booked in at The Compleat Angler. The meeting would be at Waring's house on the other side of the river. At the reception desk there was a note from Waring to say that he would not be needed until mid-afternoon the next day. The envelope also contained five twenty-pound notes and a copy of a letter to the hotel that confirmed that his bill would be paid in cash with no limit on his credit.

The double bedroom was well-furnished and the windows gave a wonderful view across the Thames. He thought it was the big white house on the other side of the river that was Waring's house. The Warings had made their fortune when cotton came into its own. Charles Waring had chosen the diplomatic service and never mentioned the family business which was now into textiles of every kind. He had been a friend of Carling's father. But he wasn't Director-General of SIS in those days. The gardens of Waring's house sloped down to the bank of the river. A rowing skiff and a thirty-foot cruiser were moored alongside a wooden jetty. The late afternoon sun cast long shadows across the lawn from the poplars that lined the tennis court. The meeting was to be at Waring's house but he had been given no hint of what it was about.

*   *   *

It was just Waring, Houghton and Smart. And despite Waring's assurances, Smart had had the whole house checked for bugs. Two Field Security sergeants in plain clothes were wandering around the grounds trying to look like house guests. There were several cars parked on the gravel forecourt. There was Waring's dark red Daimler Sovereign, Houghton's white Rover 105 and Smart's green Ford Prefect that reflected his caution. He was a psychologist and was aware that a car could indicate the character of its owner. The spectrum of Ford Prefect drivers was too wide to provide any clues.

Waring had set the meeting in his book-lined study and a table had been brought up from one of the downstairs rooms. Waring had chosen it himself. It had to be round so that there was no status from where you sat.

'Welcome, gentlemen,' said Waring, as he looked from one to the other. 'Dickie Smart is going to give us his assessment of the man's personality.' He turned to Smart. 'Go ahead, Dickie.'

'OK. I don't propose using the technical jargon of psychology. So this is as much a portrait as an analysis. Understood?' He looked at the other two and Waring nodded and Smart went on. 'Philby wanted out from the pressures that were on him. The questions in Parliament. The press. People in SIS who suspected him and he was aware that MI5 not only had a thick file on him but were just waiting for a chance to nail him . . .

'The offer of working for *The Economist* and the *Observer* seemed like a great solution. He stuck it for a time but he missed the power and the competition that he had in SIS. He missed London. Beirut was just a backwater. He was like those remittance men shipped out to East Africa by wealthy families because of the scandal they caused at home. And like them he passed his time getting drunk and womanising. He was cut off from everything that had been his life. His contacts with us were remote and he wasn't interested in the Middle East. Nobody was interested in him any more. He was a nobody. People avoided him because his behaviour was outrageous. He was desperate to be back in the action. Better the harassment of being a suspected traitor than rotting in Beirut. And even his friends in Moscow weren't interested in him any more. He had nothing to give them. He was out of the game. They kept in touch from time to time but he was no longer useful. He was an old horse put out to grass.

'When his father died he was literally alone; they had shared the house up on the hill. And he realised that his old man was livelier, more used to life in an Arab country than he was. He felt older than his father.' Smart shrugged. 'That's where he'd got to.'

'How up to date is this, Dickie?' It was Houghton who asked.

'That was how it was up to August this year when he got in touch with Henderson at the embassy. And Henderson got in touch with us.' He waved towards Waring. 'It went straight up to the DG.'

For a few moments there was silence and then Waring looked at Houghton and said, 'You'd better relate your bit, Eddie.'

'He didn't exactly get in touch with Henderson. They were at some party, a private party. Kim was very drunk but he said to Henderson that he ought to have stayed with SIS and done a flit to Moscow and worked back to London.'

Smart said, 'Could be just the wandering mind of a

drunk. A fantasy.' He shrugged. 'Even a leg-pull.'

'I said that to Henderson, he doesn't think it was. He thinks Philby was serious. Says he's desperate to be the centre of attention again.'

Waring said quietly, 'Costs nothing to find out. If it worked it would be the most successful blow to the Russians we've ever made.'

Smart sighed. 'And the trickiest. We'd never know where all the mirrors were.'

'We should judge by what he passed to us.'

Houghton nodded. 'And if we turned out to have been out-manoeuvred yet again – so what? He'd be getting nothing from us.'

'So. Do we have a try?'

Houghton smiled. 'You're dying to press the button, aren't you?'

Waring shrugged. 'I don't want to miss out on a wonderful chance.'

'What have you got in mind?'

'I think we should use Carling.'

'Why Carling?' Smart was not a man who took up ideas first time around.

'He's known Philby all through their careers. He's been under suspicion himself from time to time. So he knows what it's like. He always was tolerant towards Philby.' He smiled. 'And before you ask, Eddie, he's not queer and he's not a boozer and he's never been interested in communism or any other political ism.'

'Is that enough to satisfy Philby if he was thinking seriously about such a caper?'

'Well, there's a bit more. Apparently Henderson jokingly went along with Philby's little fantasy and asked him who he'd want as his contact at SIS. Philby thought for quite a time and then said that George Carling was the only man he'd ever trust.'

Houghton reached for the Thermos. 'Anyone want another coffee?' He looked around but nobody responded so he said, 'Would *we* trust Carling?'

Waring smiled. 'More to the point is, would Carling trust us? Would we go along with it?' He looked at Smart. 'What do you think?'

'I've only met him a few times. A strange man. Very aware, very observant. A bit on the emotional side, I'd say.' He shrugged. 'That's about all I can say.'

Houghton said, 'Where is he at the moment?'

Waring avoided the real question and said, 'He's at The Compleat Angler. He doesn't know why he's been called here and I've said I'll talk to him tomorrow.'

'What do you have in mind?'

'I want Carling, if he agrees, to meet Philby, talk this over and decide between the two of them how to handle it. It will need careful planning and even with careful planning it could easily go wrong.'

'How many people will be involved?'

'Directly, only Carling and myself.'

'And indirectly?'

'I shall consult others on what we need to get from Philby. But the people concerned will not know what it's for. And I shall see that Carling formally retires from SIS but that he gets whatever assistance he needs.'

'And if it blows up it will be Carling who carries the can.'

'Let's wait and see.' He smiled. 'Philby may have changed his mind and Carling might not want to play his part, and without him there's no show.'

* * *

As they walked back to their cars half an hour later, Smart said, 'What did you make of all that?'

Houghton laughed. 'You tell me.'

'I think the old boy wants to go out with a bang. He's only got a few years to go before he retires. Having Philby in Moscow and working for us would be a nice act to go out on.'

'Do you think Philby will do it?'

'The state he's in nothing's too crazy if it makes him important again. But what about the Russians? Do you think they'll buy it?'

'Depends on the scenario that Philby and Carling can set up. They'll be suspicious because he's never shown any inclination to head to Moscow and it's at least six years he's been in Beirut. Could have slipped out to Moscow any time he wanted.' He paused. 'What sort of stuff has he been sending back to us?'

'Nothing of any importance. I guess what we get is no more than what *The Economist* gets.'

'Ah well. I guess we won't be kept in the picture.' He laughed softly. 'Not unless it goes down the pan and then it'll be all my idea.'

Smart grinned. 'That's just standard SIS paranoia, my friend.'

The phone call from Waring came as Carling was having breakfast. The meeting was to be at 10 a.m. and Waring sounded unusually friendly. It gave him time for a leisurely walk across the bridge and past the church to the drive that gave access to the half-dozen big houses that spread out along the river bank. Waring's house was the third one along. Not the biggest of the houses but in any other part of the country it would be described as a mansion.

There was a bell on one of the stone pillars that flanked the wrought-iron gates and it was answered immediately by a young man who looked him over and smiled his recognition. 'He's waiting for you, sir. Straight down the drive.'

And sure enough Peter Waring was there at the open door under a porch covered with wisteria and clematis. He was dressed casually, a white cotton shirt and light blue slacks, his hand outstretched.

'Good to see you, George. Come on in. Let's go up to my study.'

In Waring's study there were no shelves of books and no signs of hi-fi equipment and LPs. But the pictures on the walls were surprising. Original black and white prints of photographs by Doisneau, Ansel Adams, and the Westons, father and son, Ernst Haas and Robert Capa. He turned to Waring. 'What a wonderful collection. Are you a keen photographer?'

Waring smiled. 'Keen but not good. And I do mainly portraits and landscapes.' He laughed. 'I think I love cameras as much as the pictures. A bad sign. The apparatus ought not to matter. But the feel of a Leica and a Hasselblad, the workmanship, make them works of art for me.'

'And why not? Like old Doctor Johnson is supposed to have said – "if a thing's worth doing, it's worth doing badly".'

'It makes you appreciate the real thing all the more.' Waring waved Carling to one of the leather armchairs, the kind they have in gentlemen's clubs. When they were both settled Waring said, 'I'm going to ask you to do something for me. Can I ask that whether you agree to do it or not, you never discuss what I'm going to tell you with anyone else. Nobody, absolutely nobody.'

Carling smiled. 'Sounds very serious. Yes. You can have my assurance.'

For fifteen minutes Waring went over what had happened but he didn't mention Philby's comment about Carling.

When he had finished he said, 'What do you think?'

For a few moments Carling didn't reply and then he said, 'If you were talking about anybody but Kim I'd say don't take it seriously. I'd reckon it was just the ravings of a drunk.' He paused. 'But with Kim I'd say he probably means it. He's a driven man, a man who needs to make things happen. If he had been a career soldier he'd have had a chest full of medals. He needs to matter. To be in the inner circle. To be influential and respected as perceptive and far-seeing.'

'Do you think he'd do it? Go back. And work for us?'

'I think it's possible but you'd have to accept that he'd be co-operating with the KGB too.'

'Have you had any contact with him since he went to Beirut?'

'He had a drink with me the day before he left. And I've had a couple of meals with him since. When he was on leave in London. The last time was about six months ago. He was very bitter about the Russians who hadn't been in touch with him for over a year. And the last time he had contact with them he was asked to do a list of all his contacts and movements since he was at university. He was furious about it, and said so quite openly. Said it was an insult. Which it was, of course. But he knew it was because they'd never really trusted him despite all he'd done and risked for them.' Carling smiled. 'Getting his own back on them would be a considerable incentive.'

'What do you think the problems would be?'

Carling leaned back in his chair, thinking. Then he said,

'There would be three problems. Convincing him that we were on his side. That we respected him. All that sort of stuff would be the first problem. Then there'd be the problem of setting up a scenario that would convince the Russians as to why he wanted to go back. And finally there would be the problem of communication. They'd be watching him like hawks.'

'When he was talking to him, Henderson asked Philby who he would want as his control in London and Philby said you were the only man he'd trust.' Waring paused. 'Would you do that? Take over the planning and the continuing contacts?'

'Is that what you want?'

'Yes. Without you nothing will happen.'

'What support would I get?'

'Anything you wanted you'd get.'

'And I could put together a deal with Philby without needing approval from anyone else?'

Waring hesitated for a moment and then said, 'Yes. It would be up to you.'

'What incentives can I offer him apart from the work and money? Could I suggest that if he worked with us efficiently for say four or five years, that he could come back and be publicly praised as a hero rather than a traitor?'

Waring sighed. 'That's OK. I don't want to restrict you in any way.'

'Who else knows about the scheme?'

'Houghton from covert operations and Smart, who's SIS's tame psychologist.'

'What do they know?'

'They know what I've told you, they know that I'm thinking of activating the thoughts. They know that

Philby said that you are the only SIS officer who he trusted. That's it. They won't be told whether you go ahead or not.'

'Why were they in on it so far?'

'Houghton was the one who heard the story from Henderson and Smart could give me a picture of Philby's mental condition and his personality. It was a pretty accurate picture in my opinion.'

'When do you want me to start?'

'As always – soonest.'

'I need to go back to Berlin to clear things up. It'll take a couple of days. Have you got an address for Philby?'

'Yes. He's at what was his father's house in Ajaltoun up in the hills.'

'How much do the two newspapers pay him?'

'About two thousand a year. And much the same from us. He's always pressing both sources to up his pay.'

'Are the newspaper boys satisfied with what he sends them?'

'Far from it. If it wasn't for us helping them in other directions I think they'd sack him.'

'Who's our local contact with Philby?'

'A man named Weston. Do you know him?'

Carling smiled. 'I've met him a couple of times. He gave a lecture on how to recruit and run Arab agents. Absolute rubbish, of course.' He paused. 'It's best we keep it just to you, me and Philby.'

'I agree. Let's do that. And let me say I'm very pleased and relieved that you'll have a go at this rather crazy scheme.' He stood up and walked with Carling to the door. 'I won't interfere, George. But if I can do anything to help just let me know. Any time. Day or night.' He paused. 'Let me give you a lift back to the hotel.'

'I'd rather walk.' He smiled. 'I've got a lot to think about.'

They shook hands and Waring stood, shading his eyes from the sun, as he watched Carling until he disappeared at the bend in the driveway.

Philby was no longer at his father's old house and now lived in a flat in the rue Kantari and it was there that Carling left a note with his room number at the hotel. They met the same evening and Philby was obviously delighted to see him. He was leaving Beirut the following day for a holiday with Eleanor, her daughter Annie and his own son Harry, in Jordan. He'd leave them there after a couple of days and come back alone to Beirut. They could talk about the old days.

There was a paved balcony along one side of the flat and they sat there to get the breeze that came from the sea. They had talked for an hour and Philby had drunk very sparingly. When the light was beginning to go Carling turned from the gossip of SIS and asked the vital question.

'Kim, there was a rumour came back to London that you were not too happy with your present setup. And that you were thinking of making a change. Change of status and change of locale. Was it just a rumour?'

Philby smiled the smile that had charmed a lot of people. 'Was the guy at the embassy the source of the rumour?'

'Yes.'

'Who did he talk to?'

'The DG.'

'Waring?'

'Yes.'

'Who else was told?'

'The full facts – only me. Because you mentioned my name.'

'Is this why you came to see me?'

'Yes.'

'To persuade me to do it or to persuade me not to do it?'

'Neither. Just to talk about the possibility if you really were contemplating such a move.'

Philby smiled. 'Tell me what I'm supposed to have said.'

'That you loathed your present setup. That you wish you were back in SIS. That you were amused at the idea of being in Moscow and working for SIS as well as the KGB. And that if you did it you'd want me to be your contact at SIS.'

'And what did Waring say?'

'That if I agreed to handle it he'd go along with it.'

'And you. What do you say?'

'I'll talk with you about it if you really want to do it.'

Philby shrugged. 'I was half pissed when I said it. But not so pissed I didn't mean it.' He waved his arms around. 'I'm tired of living in this shitty town. Bored with the work. Bored with the people. Bored with my life.'

'There are other ways to relieve boredom. A lot less dangerous too.'

'You've thought about it, have you?'

'I've explored the idea.'

'You know what I would want in return?'

'I think so.'

'I doubt if you do. Tell me what you think I want.'

'I think you'd want to put a limit on your time in Moscow so that you could come back to the UK as an acknowledged hero. Cleared of all past suspicions and all

those who were against you proved spectacularly wrong.'
He smiled. 'Something like that.'

Philby was smiling. 'You look like everybody's favourite
uncle but you're quite a shrewd old bugger really. Anyway,
you're right on target. I'd love to see all those bastards with
their pants down.'

'What about the Russians?'

'You know it's like a sign from God. My KGB handler
hasn't contacted me for a year and he turned up just a
week ago. Very solicitous. What could they do to help? So
I asked him. What if I wanted to move to Moscow? He said
he'd talk to the people in Dzerzhinsky Square and come
back to me. He was back the next day. No problem. They'd
be glad to have me as a kind of consultant. Just one little
thing. After I was settled in there'd be a press conference,
revealing that I had always been a Soviet agent. When did
I want to do it?' Philby smiled. 'I told him I'd think about
it and he said they'd need a week's notice before I went,
to make the necessary arrangements.'

'Do you think they trust you?'

'No. I'm sure they don't. But it would be a media coup.
I would be under close supervision and I could be useful.'
Philby shook his head. 'They'd never trust a foreigner no
matter who he was or what he did for them.' He smiled.
'Do SIS and MI5 trust me? Of course they don't.'

'We'd have to play it very, very carefully, Kim.'

'I'm glad you think so.'

'Why not think about it overnight, and if you still feel
like going ahead we could start planning tomorrow?'

'I don't need to think about it. I didn't say my bit at the
embassy just to shock Henderson. I was just casting bait
in the water to see if anyone took it.' He paused. 'Do you
trust Waring? Do you trust SIS not to play silly games?'

'The whole operation will be in my hands. Nobody else will ever know what we're doing. Just you, Waring and me.' He paused. 'Will you be taking the family with you?'

Philby shook his head. 'No. Just me. I'll send Eleanor back to the States, at least until I've settled in.' He stood up. 'Let's go down town and I'll take you to a real Arab place.' He looked at Carling's face. 'I'm excited, are you?'

'Kind of, but I want to be cautious. Make sure we've covered every angle so that you're safe.'

'There's a balance, George. Only the two of them, SIS and the KGB, working together could bring me down. One protects me from the other.'

'Don't count on that, Kim.'

'What's that mean?'

'If one or the other finds out that they've been fooled – even if it's imaginary – there are other things they can do beyond denouncing you in the media.'

'Like what?'

And Carling realised that Kim Philby thought he was too important to be killed.

'If the Russians decided that you were playing it both ways they could just dispose of you. You know that as well as I do. OK, they don't have to shoot you, food poisoning works just as well.'

'So?'

'So we walk very carefully, both of us.'

'You reckon I can trust them about coming back and having my name cleared?'

'Yes. It might offset all the criticisms that were levelled at them in the past.' He paused. 'If they didn't come clean then I would. They know that.'

'That would be a risk for you too.'

Carling smiled. 'It's not that easy to knock off an earl

without the media looking into it. They'd have to be very desperate to do that. It's up to you and me to see that they don't get desperate.'

'How are we going to communicate once I'm in Moscow? They'll be watching me round the clock.'

'Can you do Morse?'

'No.'

'Can you read Morse?'

'No.'

'Let me think about it. When can you talk to your Russian?'

'In a couple of days.'

'I'll go back to Berlin, then London, and I'll be back at the weekend. I'll contact you here, OK?'

'That's fine.' He paused. 'One other thing to think about. The Russians will be trying to work out why I suddenly want to leave when I've shown no signs of wanting to go before.'

Carling stood up. 'I think I can cover that.'

'Tell me.'

'When I come back I'll tell you. It could mean waiting two or three months before you go but it would be a perfect reason for going.'

Philby sighed. 'Apart from all this it's good to see you again, George. I know you don't agree with some of the things I did but at least you always understood even if you didn't forgive.'

'Take care, Kim.'

'You too.'

CHAPTER 37

The defection of Golitsyn provided a solid reason for Philby's planned defection. Both Philby and Carling knew that Golitsyn would have told both the CIA and SIS all he knew about Philby. And he knew quite a lot. A few weeks later Waring had fetched Carling back from Berlin for a meeting. They had met at a small Italian restaurant in King's Road, Chelsea, and after the meal they had walked up Sloane Street towards Hyde Park.

'I've got a problem, George. There has been a lot of pressure from the old China hands to try and get a confession out of Philby. Nothing has happened because nobody who knew enough was willing to go to Beirut and face him out. There's now a strong possibility that Nick Elliott is ready to go out and tackle him. If I stop him it will create a lot of resentment. But I'm prepared to do that if you feel I should. A confrontation could have all sorts of repercussions. What do you think?'

'Couldn't be better. Let him go but don't let him know about my operation, and see that his visit is leaked so that it gets back to Moscow. But I need another few weeks. I'm still trying to work out our lines of communication with Kim.' He paused. 'Could you drag it out to the turn of the year?'

'No problem.'

'A genuine move against Philby could provide all the urgency for a move to Moscow. That's something the Russians will understand. And the thought of whisking him out from under our noses will be an added incentive.'

'OK. I'll be in touch every day. Sorry to have dragged you away.'

'I've got a few things to clear up here anyway. You realise I'll have to move back to London as soon as he goes to Moscow. But I'm not going to activate him until he's been there for two or three months. Maybe a dry run on whatever system I end up with but nothing more.'

'Do you want Facilities to find a place in London for you?'

'That would help.'

'Where do you want to be?'

'Somewhere in this area would be fine. Sloane Square, King's Road, or somewhere off Sloane Street.'

'I'll get them on to it right away. D'you want furnished?'

'Yes, please.'

When Carling got back to Berlin there was a message for him from Hank Henney, who would like to see him urgently. He arranged to meet him that evening at Henney's place.

It had been snowing for an hour as he drove across from Grunewald to Henney's flat by the Europa Centre. It was the last week in November and Berlin had been lucky to escape the heavy snow that had been sweeping across Poland towards Scandinavia. At least Beirut was warm and sunny.

Henney was fond of bamboo furniture but was wondering if his wife would approve when she arrived in a few weeks' time. When he had ushered Carling into the sitting room, Henney waved Carling to a bamboo armchair stuffed with bright cushions and walked over to a small bar. He swung round to look at Carling.

'What you want, George? Got a bit of everything here.'

'Have you got a malt?'

'Glenlivet or Glenfiddich, which you want?'

'Glenlivet, please.'

Henney poured the whisky and walked over to hand it to Carling. And as Carling took the glass, Henney sat facing him on a bamboo settee.

'Good health, George.'

Carling lifted his glass. 'And to you too, Hank.'

Henney leaned down and put his glass on a small table beside the settee.

'George. The CIA had a problem.'

'*Had* a problem?' Carling smiled. 'What happened to it?'

'They passed the ball to me to run with.'

'And you're about to try and pass it to me, yes?'

Henney sighed. 'I wanna say that the only reason I'm involved is because of my relationship with you. None of it is my doing.'

Carling frowned. 'What's it all about, Hank?'

Henney shifted around on the settee, looking embarrassed and uncomfortable. 'I had a visit from two senior people from Washington. One from Langley and one from NSA. You've heard about NSA and what they do, OK?'

'Is that the outfit at Fort George Meade in Maryland?'

'That's the one.' He paused. 'As you know, they monitor everything on air – telephones, short-wave radio, the whole shooting match.' He sighed. 'And on the side they do a bit of bugging for the CIA. Seems like one of the places they've bugged is a flat in Beirut. Your friend Philby. They showed me a transcript and played me some tapes. The stuff they showed me covered you and Philby talking about a move he was thinking of doing.' Henney looked at Carling and shrugged. 'They want in on it, George, and they've got something to offer you that will solve one of your problems.'

'Let's just slow down a bit, Hank. You say your people bugged Philby's place in Beirut – why?'

'Seems they've always seen Philby as somebody special. When Angleton was head of CIA he always said Philby would end up as Director-General of SIS. But others in the CIA saw him in those days as a bit of a loose cannon. They wanted to know what he was up to.'

'You realise that what they heard me discussing with Philby is only known to our DG, Waring, and to me?'

'Yeah, they realise that and it's treated the same way on our side. Only the top man at NSA and one of my people at Langley know about this plan of yours.' He paused. 'And me, of course. And I was only told because I know you very well and we've always co-operated with one another.'

'And what are they asking for?'

'They just want to be in on it. You in charge and me feeding in some CIA input. And sharing what comes out.'

'But Langley were constantly swearing that Philby was the Third Man or some such thing.'

'That's all water under the bridge, George. Your people in SIS were the same. They still are for that matter, aren't they?'

'And what's this solution to a problem that your people are offering?'

'It provides you with a non-physical contact means of communication from a UK base to Moscow.'

'Why so coy?'

'Because the CIA use it for contact with their agents who can't read Morse and where physical contact is impossible or dangerous. Once other people know how to do it we've lost the advantage.'

'Somebody'll break into it sooner or later.'

Henney shook his head. 'No way could anyone do that. But I'll brief you properly if we can co-operate.'

'Let me think about it overnight, Hank.' He paused. 'I'm inclined to say yes but Waring would never agree. I'd have to do it solo. And I'd want to meet your two guys and be satisfied that they'd keep this operation totally secure.'

'What stops you from saying yes now?'

Carling shrugged. 'I don't know. I guess I just need to get used to the idea that I'm here in Berlin talking about something that happened in Beirut that was supposed to be higher than top-secret. Knowing that somebody in Langley ordered somebody else to bug Philby's place. And it never entered my mind, or Philby's mind for that matter, that somebody in Washington would be listening to tapes of our talk a couple of days later.' He paused. 'Why didn't your people go straight to Waring?'

'Waring would rather call the whole thing off than let the CIA in on it. He'd be scared of all the political rows it would cause if it went wrong. What's OK as a bit of private enterprise isn't so good when it brings in foreigners.'

'Maybe he's right, Hank.'

'You know better than that. We already know what's being planned so you don't take any risk on letting us come in on it.'

'What will your people do if I say no?'

'I only agreed to approach you if they swore that they'd do nothing if you turned me down.' He shook his head slowly. 'They won't play games, George. I'll see to that. And they've no interest in rocking the boat.'

Carling knew that he didn't really have a choice. They knew what he and Philby were planning to do. They could have leaked it to the media if all they had wanted was to expose the machinations of SIS. And the fact that they were active participants gave a kind of extra validity to the whole affair.

He looked across at Henney. 'You swear you've told me the truth.'

'I swear.'

'And you'll accept that my word is final on everything, even if it doesn't suit Langley?'

'On my word, George.'

Carling shrugged. 'OK. Welcome aboard. Now tell me about the communication thing.'

'The CIA has a problem in passing instructions to agents in some foreign countries who don't read Morse. They asked for help from NSA at Fort George Meade and they came up with what we call numbers stations. We use them all over the world but particularly in the Soviet Union, the Warsaw Pact countries, China, and the Arab countries. Places where our agents are under constant surveillance. From several different base stations an operator dictates a series of numbers. Five-number groups. We use German, English, Spanish, Arabic and Russian. They are broadcast on short-wave frequencies and can be copied by the agent concerned. There is an indicator at the start of the transmission that indicates the recipient and the basis of the code. The code is generally related to a book, a novel or reference book, or in some cases a specific programme from a normal broadcast station like *Voice of America*. The message is broadcast on several days on different frequencies and at different times.' He paused and shrugged. 'It works very well.'

'Isn't it easy to monitor?'

'Not easy. But even if a monitor comes across a message he has no way of decoding it because the code is not a logical code. Virtually random.'

'What about Philby's communication back to me, to us?'

'We have a couple of dozen safe dead-letter boxes in Moscow. We'll identify them. Photographs and streets maps you can show him before he leaves. He can use them and his stuff will be passed back to you unopened with a special envelope code.'

'Could I see it in operation if I flew with you to the States?'

Henney smiled. 'We've got a base station already operating in the UK. You can see that. But remember the operator doesn't know where his agent is or who he is. He's a signals expert not an intelligence guy.'

'Where is this place?'

'It's at a small village in Oxfordshire called Barford St John.'

'How long has it been there?'

'Just over a year.'

'You cheeky bastards.' He paused. 'Why can't GCHQ pick up the traffic?'

'They can, but they can't decrypt it because it's a totally unknown and random code-base.'

'When can I see the place?'

'Any time you want.'

'Let's fly over tomorrow.'

Carling drove them from Gatwick and came off the main road at the Service Station at Ardley so that they could check the road map and have a coffee. They had to circle round on to the B4100 up to the B4031. Then it was just a few miles to the two Barford villages of St Michael and St John.

The sign by the five-bar gate said Milton Poultry Farm and a smaller line of text said, 'Wholesale and Trade Only.'

There was a cement driveway that led to what looked like a wooden office building, a fairly large garden shed. Beyond the shed was a path to the doors of a dozen long battery houses. As the men got out of the car they could hear the sound of ventilation fans. As Henney led the way to the office shed, the door was opened by a young man.

'Can I help you, gentlemen?'

'My name's Henney, I've come to see Josh.'

The young man smiled and held out his hand. 'Come right in. I was expecting you. I'm Josh Abramski.'

The small office was immaculately tidy with the usual filing cabinets, desks, chairs and an electric typewriter. There was a Pirelli calendar hung on the wall. It was November but it was showing the picture for October. A very pretty blonde facing the sun on some tropical beach. As Carling stared at it, Josh laughed. 'She's my favourite. I don't go for the November girl.' He stood with his hands on the back of the chair. 'It looks like minimum security, but it ain't. That's just part of the scenario. The back of this shed, through the door, is steel-lined on the inside. No windows, no ventilation shafts. Virtually impregnable. You like to see the works, Mr Henney?'

'Yes, please. Can you give us a rundown on it? The procedures.'

The door took two keys and two coded cards to open and the lights were on inside the room already. The walls and ceiling were painted white and a white Formica-covered shelf at waist level stretched along the whole of the longest wall. On the shelf were various pieces of equipment and above the shelf was an array of a dozen or so three-pin sockets.

Josh stood between them pointing at equipment as he described it to them.

'This, gentlemen, is an ICOM transceiver. It receives signals and can transmit signals. It covers both functions in a variety of modes. You can hear normal broadcast stations from all round the world. In FM, AM and sideband, USB and LSB. It also receives in coded Morse which is called RTTY and various codes like AMTOR and SITOR. So far as this operation here is concerned I use only USB or LSB. Upper and lower sideband.

'This, is a sophisticated tape machine. It uses normal high-grade audiotapes. It records and plays back. For recording I use this microphone. Next is this special tape-player where you can stack up to ten audiotapes. This small device is an a.t.u., an aerial tuner. The computer is used together with this radio-controlled clock. The clock is accurate to within one second in a million years. The computer software controls the time, frequency and rate of transmissions.' He smiled and waved a hand. 'That's about it.' He laughed. 'But to operate it you don't need to understand anything more than switching on or off the switches in a certain order. Any questions?'

Carling said, 'Where do your transmissions end up?'

Josh smiled and shook his head. 'You're not cleared for that, sorry.'

Henney said, 'Who dictates the tapes?'

'I do.'

'In English?'

'English and German.'

'Does it work successfully?'

'I've no idea, Mr Henney. I just carry out my instructions. There's no feedback. It's not necessary.'

'And if you're ill or something?'

'There's always a standby twenty-four hours a day. Two in fact. Either one could be here inside five minutes and our traffic schedules aren't heavy. We're on air not more then sixty minutes a day. Some days nothing at all.'

Josh played them one of the tapes and they listened to the drone of his voice as he read out the numbers of the message. When he switched off the tape he smiled. 'My voice goes through a machine after taping so that it's altered.'

Carling said, 'As a matter of interest do you actually produce eggs here?'

Abramski laughed. 'We've got eighty thousand hybrid in-lay hens and we make a good profit. But what really matters is the realistic cover it gives me.'

They talked for another ten minutes or so and then Carling and Henney went back to the car. It was cold and raining and the weather matched their subdued mood. It was a long, almost silent drive back to Gatwick but they managed to get seats on the late flight to Berlin. At Tegel they arranged to meet the next morning and they shared a taxi, which dropped Henney by the Gedächtniskirche and then took Carling on to Grunewald.

Henney had got a set of operating instructions for the numbers system. Carling had found it simple to operate after a few dry runs, and Waring had arranged for the BBC World Service broadcasts to the Soviet Union to insert a codeword in their main news that would indicate 'no-message' or a message the following day. Waring asked questions as to why it was necessary. The only outstanding item was the choice of a book that Philby could take with him as a code-base. Carling had got hold of a proof copy of a book called *The Spy Who Came In From The Cold* by John le Carré and felt that Philby would be amused by the title and interested in the contents. That would be the code-base book.

At the meeting in Beirut with Philby, Carling was shocked by Philby's state of mind. He was deeply depressed and unhappy about his life in general and seemed relieved that he would be moving to Moscow. Philby had no problem in absorbing the basics of the numbers radio scheme and was highly amused by the choice of book for the code-base.

Henney provided two sets of the details of the dead-letter boxes that were to be used. There were pictures and descriptions and brief comments, indications of nearest Metro stations and public transport. This material was not to be taken with him but would be the basis of the first coded messages he would receive in Moscow. When Carling told him about the Americans wanting to be included, Philby seemed to see it as an additional safety factor for himself. Philby disliked Americans but he obviously felt that the American interest was rather flattering. He was obviously affected by the recent savage sentence of forty-two years imprisonment on George Blake. Philby suspected that the KGB defector who had exposed Blake also knew about him. He was now in regular contact with the KGB men in the Lebanon and the particular officer who would arrange his escape to Moscow. When Carling told him of the proposed visit by Nick Elliott intended to get a confession from him, Philby agreed that the visit could supply authentic evidence to the Russians that it was time for him to get out.

They ate together the following evening in the room Carling had taken at the Mushrek Hotel on rue Makdisi.

Philby seemed to have got back a lot of his usual confidence.

'Do you think your CIA friends have bugged this room too?'

Carling smiled. 'I did a deal that there would be no more bugging here or anywhere else.'

'Will you be full time on this game?'

'Yes.'

'Won't you get bored?'

'Not when somebody's life might depend on me not being bored. Don't worry, Kim. I'll back you every way I can.' He paused. 'How do you feel about going to Moscow?'

Philby sighed and looked at his glass as he slowly swirled the brandy around before he looked up at Carling.

'It's strange. Way back when I was young Moscow was the light at the end of the tunnel. The great hope for mankind. Worth taking risks for, worth all the deception and lying. But that was twenty-five years ago.' He smiled. 'It's a bit like having a blind-date with a girl that you couldn't keep. But you knew she was a real beauty and you kept sending her love letters and bunches of roses and she said she loved you too. And twenty-five years later you're going to meet her. She's forty-five now. And married with two kids.' He shrugged and smiled. 'It'll be an interesting meeting but inevitably disappointing. She's not that girl. Probably never was. And you're not the same guy either.' He shrugged. 'But it'll be interesting.'

'What about your connections back here?'

'I shall do my best to forget them. Time will tell.'

'What about Burgess and Maclean?'

Philby smiled wryly. 'Burgess is driving them crazy. His handlers are changed every two months. Can't stand him. The booze and the young boys. They never expected him to turn up. Neither did I. It was a real shock when I heard he'd gone off with Maclean.'

'How is Maclean?'

'I gather he gets by. They don't like his arrogance but he has his uses.' He paused. 'They'll want to debrief me and that can take months.'

'They'll treat you well, Kim?'

'Maybe.' He grinned. 'Even if it's only to make SIS look like the idiots they are.'

'I always felt you rather enjoyed your time in SIS despite the politics.'

'That's very perceptive of you, George. I did enjoy it. Especially when it hurt the Germans.'

'What will you miss?'

Philby thought for a moment. 'Cricket, the Test matches. Reading *The Times*. Being on the inside. Playing Gershwin and Berlin and Jerome Kern. Pubs.' He shrugged. 'That's about it.' He paused. 'Any idea when Elliott is going to appear?'

'I'd guess sometime in the first week in January.'

'Was it his idea or Dick White's?'

'A bit of both, I think.'

It was nearly midnight when Carling walked down to the street with Philby. The streets were still busy. Beirut was a night town. The Middle-East's Paris.

As Carling waved to a taxi and it pulled up he took Philby's hand. 'I won't wish you a happy New Year but I do wish you a life that maybe you can enjoy. Like your girl in the blind date. You'll be a man with two mistresses who you love almost equally. Best of luck, Kim. I'll be thinking of you all the time.'

Philby smiled but said nothing and walked across to the taxi. Carling watched him bend to give the driver his instructions and then get into the back of the cab. He watched until the tail-lights faded into the darkness.

CHAPTER 38

There had been a time when Nick Elliott was amiably
disposed towards Philby. Nobody, not even Elliott himself,
could define when his attitude changed. He had been head
of SIS's operations in the Lebanon at one time so he knew
his way around Beirut. He rented an apartment to ensure
privacy for his confrontation with Philby and he wasted
no time in contacting him. He phoned Kim Philby on 10
January and arranged a meeting.

Nick Elliott was a shrewd and experienced interrogator
and he posed his questions with considerable skill to the
man he had come to despise. But Kim Philby had spent
a lifetime avoiding and deflecting questions about his life
and work. When Elliott laid out a pattern of accusations
Philby denied nothing. But on the other hand he confirmed
nothing. The pressure was considerable. He knew they
couldn't arrest him in a foreign country but there were
other things that they could do and Elliott was insistent
and obviously determined to get a confession, preferably
in writing. Philby said that he needed a few days to think
about what Elliott was proposing.

When Philby discovered that the man who was head of
Beirut SIS was away for some days on a skiing holiday he
was sure that Elliott would wait until he was back before
making any move against him.

After his meeting with Elliott, Philby contacted his KGB handler, Petukhov, and told him what had been said. Petukhov said that he needed four or five days to make the arrangements for Philby's escape to Moscow.

Through a mistaken piece of antisurveillance trade-craft involving the carrying of a newspaper when it should have been a book, Kim Philby eventually had only an hour hurriedly to pack a small bag for his journey.

There were two Russians with him in the back of the car that took him down to the docks that night and handed him over into the care of the captain of the Soviet ship *Dolmatova*. It sailed an hour later on its long sea journey to Odessa.

Carling first heard the news of Philby's disappearance from Hank Henney and the next day it was in all the newspapers. It was a field day for the media and in the following ten days all the old stories and suspicions about Philby had been aired and embellished and exaggerated. There was no official comment from SIS but it was clear from some of the press stories that some SIS and MI5 people were feeding the media with background information.

It was April before Kim Philby browsed through the boxes of second-hand books at the shop in the Arbat and offered the owner an English shilling to pay for a tattered copy of the Russian translation of Dickens's *Oliver Twist*.

The message was in Berlin two days later. Carling had a week to prepare the first message. By June the system was working. Twice a week the numbers were read out slowly in the flat tones that the voice-analyser produced, and roughly once a month something came back from Moscow. Messages picked up from the toilets in a cinema, from cemeteries, from library books, and taped under the slats of park benches.

CHAPTER 39

Mathews looked at his watch as he sat on the bench at Frant Station waiting for Carling's train from London. It was ten minutes before it was due.

He wondered how Carling would be. He had avoided Mathews the day before and had seemed preoccupied when he drove him to the station that morning.

There were blackberries on the hedges that flanked the station platform and a small border of wilting pansies and chrysanthemums that had been planted to decorate the old-fashioned station. The sun was going down, and he could see rabbits in the field on the other side of the track.

It seemed incongruous sitting there in the quiet of the small station having listened to what Carling had told him. And Carling didn't look like a man who had been involved in such a web of deceit and subterfuge. But people involved in intelligence work never did look like spies or counterspies. Like Carling always said, they were just men. There were a few Harry Palmers and a Smiley or two, but there were no James Bonds.

Maybe Carling had told him all that he was going to tell him. Philby obviously hadn't come back, he had died in Moscow in 1988. Mathews had seen the TV news reports of Philby's burial. Full military honours, they said. Mourned by his comrades in the KGB. So the Russians hadn't rumbled him, or had they just been pretending they hadn't. Nobody from the British Embassy was at the funeral and nobody from the American Embassy either. Carling had said nothing about whether the operation had been successful. From what Carling had said the operation had gone on for some years. What kind of information did they get from the solitary man in Moscow? And what a different picture Carling had painted of Philby himself. A man who lied and deceived his colleagues and his women but who seemed to have been liked or loved or at least admired by all he came in contact with. In the pictures he had seen, Philby had a sad, melancholic face, bags under those eyes that were always half closed as if to defend his innermost thoughts. And there were similarities with Carling. That hatred of powerful people, the generosity of mind towards the downtrodden. Cambridge, the admiration of the Russians, even the piano playing they had in common. But he could sense that there was a difference. Carling was a big man, a big mind and a big heart. But Philby was a small man who believed but didn't practise what he believed. Even his flight to Moscow was to suit himself. The co-operation with Carling was a veneer that gave a patina of self-sacrifice to what was really just one more deception. One more abuse of the people around him.

Mathews saw the lights of the train as it swung round the curve into the small station. Carling was the only person to get off. He was laughing at something the guard was saying, then he waved as the train pulled out, still smiling as he approached.

'It's getting nippy, Tim. Time to wear our thermal vests.'

In the car Carling seemed to be in good spirits.

'What did you do today?'

'Took Gabby and Carlotta to the surgery in Lamberhurst so that the baby could have her inoculations. Took Julie into Tunbridge Wells and bought her a hat for her birthday next week. We remembered you by having a coffee together in Fenwicks in the shopping mall. Helped the gardener sweep up leaves in the orchard for half an hour, signed some statements for my solicitor, posted them and listened to you on *Kaleidoscope*.'

'Oh my. It was all very solemn, wasn't it? All those experts claiming that a heap of coal was a work of art because it was at the Tate. Needed Arthur Scargill there, not me.'

Mathews smiled. 'But you got your own back when you defended Andrew Lloyd Webber and *The Phantom of the Opera*.'

'What crass idiots these pseudointellectuals are. There are theatres packed full every night all round the world to hear his music and the critics hate it. They can't stand anything that so many people enjoy. That song of his – "All I Ask of You" – it's beautiful. He writes like Delius . . .' he laughed '. . . and of course the experts of those days didn't like *him*. Not until he was dead anyway. You'll notice in this country that once some artist is dead there are societies that spring up in his name. J. B. Priestley; Elgar, poor soul; Kipling – you could go on all night. Mind that pheasant,' he said, as a worn-out hen pheasant fluttered across the drive to the cottage.

After their evening meal Carling said, 'I've talked all I want to for the moment. I think you need to see what happened through other eyes than mine. I spoke on the phone yesterday to Hank Henney and asked him to come over. He's arriving tonight and he's going to stay here and I'm having a few days break from all this. I've told him he can tell you anything he knows about those days.'

'Do I really need to know any more? You seem to have covered everything.'

Carling shook his head. 'I haven't even told you half of what matters. But Hank can fill you in.' He stood up slowly and for once the energy and liveliness weren't there. He nodded to Mathews as he turned to leave the room. 'I'll see you when I get back and perhaps we can then decide what to do. If anything.'

When Mathews came down the next morning Carling had already left, taking the ancient Rover 3-litre with him. Mathews was used to the machinations of intelligence work but what Carling had been involved in was extraordinary. He could make a fortune by telling the story to a newspaper or by writing a book. God knows, a lot of people had made money out of writing about Philby without any knowledge of what had really happened. But, of course, Carling wasn't that kind of man and he wasn't interested in making money. He lived extremely modestly despite his great wealth. Even his generosity was modest. Kindness and caring for individuals rather than great causes.

Carling had left him a note asking him to pick up Hank Henney at Tunbridge Wells Station off the train from Charing Cross that arrived at 10.32. Julie, who seemed very subdued, told him that she had prepared one of the spare bedrooms for Henney.

Despite his age Hank Henney looked younger than most of the other passengers getting off the train. His face was tanned and he carried his canvas holdall as if it were empty. He didn't recognise Mathews at first but when

Mathews held out his hand the American grinned. 'Long time no see, my boy. And how are you making out these days?'

'I'm OK, Mr Henney. You look fine.'

'I'm OK. I had one of those hip replacement deals and I don't even need a stick these days.' He stopped as Mathews pointed to his car. 'My, that's a neat little thing. An MG. Looks great.'

As Mathews drove to the cottage Henney was admiring the scenery. The golds and reds of autumn leaves were at their best.

'Reminds me of Vermont. You ever been to Vermont, Timmy?'

'I'm afraid not,' he said a little tetchily. He hated being called Timmy. Made him sound like a cat.

They had a rather stilted conversation on the drive back to the cottage. When they got there it was obvious that Henney already knew Julie. But despite the bear hugs and a small bottle of Chanel No. 19 Mathews had the impression that Julie was not very impressed. She smiled a lot and she was polite, and Julie was only formally polite to people she didn't much like.

Julie had laid out a plate of sandwiches and a pot of tea for them and left them alone to talk. It was Hank Henney who got down to business.

'George Carling told me about his chats with you about the old days and asked me to come over and fill in the gaps.' He paused. 'Have you got any specific questions?'

Mathews shrugged. 'He didn't tell me how it all ended. The thing with Philby.'

'I'll tell you about that later. Have you got any questions on what he's told you so far?'

'What kind of information did Philby send back?'

'It was the basis of the deal that the information he was to pass back was general, not specific, and not likely to lead to the arrest of Soviets in the UK or the US of A.

'He warned us about the breakdown of the Soviet-Chinese talks in Moscow. He warned us in advance that in July '63 they would publicise that Philby was one of theirs and had defected and been granted asylum. He told us that Harvey Oswald had not been used way back by the KGB to assassinate Jack Kennedy. He told us in advance that Moscow would agree to exchange Greville Wynne for Gordon Lonsdale. He gave constant warnings to us, the Americans, not to get involved in Vietnam, and he warned us that Moscow were supplying arms to Hanoi. And he told us early in '67 that the Chinese were going to explode their first H-bomb, which they did the following June.

'I guess the most important thing he warned us about was that the Red Army would put down the rising in Prague in '68 with tanks and artillery.' He sighed. 'Very little of it was acted upon.'

'Why not?'

'Well, there were two problems. First and foremost was that because the operation was way above even top-secret level there was no easy way to insert Philby's material without sourcing it, into the working channels of SIS and CIA. How could you explain where you got it from? And secondly, was the lack of trust. Carling passed on Philby's stuff without comment. Said he wasn't in a position to evaluate it one way or another.'

'When did it stop?'

Henney frowned. 'End of '69, beginning of '70.'

'Why did it stop?'

'What did Carling tell you?'

'Nothing. Like I told you, I don't know the end of the story.'

Henney sighed. 'I can't blame him. It must have been a nightmare for the poor bastard.' He paused and looked across at Mathews. 'What d'you think of Carling? D'you like him?'

'I like him a lot. He's something special. I've never met anyone like him before.'

'You don't know the half of it, my friend. That's why he dragged me over to talk to you.'

'Why didn't he just tell me himself whatever it is.'

Henney said quietly. 'When I've told you you'll know why he didn't want to tell you himself.'

CHAPTER 40

After Philby had been put on show in Moscow it had been July before the system brought a response from there. There had been a couple of transmissions in June but there had been no response from Philby.

They were based in a small cottage in the grounds of the CIA cantonment in Berlin. The official sign on the outer door said simply 'No entry'. Part of the problem in the early stages was to provide a reasonable cover for both Carling and Henney. For Carling it was easier, he had always been a lone operator and cut off from the controls of SIS Berlin. For Henney the word was put around that he was now an Intelligence Co-ordinator. Nobody offered a job description nor an explanation of what it meant.

As the weeks went by there was another problem, filling in the time that used to pass when there was nothing active in their Moscow system. But by the winter of '63 both Waring and whoever it was at Langley, considered the material they got from Philby as so valuable that it justified all the time that was wasted. Waring arranged for Carling to be sent the SIS reports on the Warsaw Pact countries and East Berlin for his evaluation and comments and Henney was used for general advice on the CIA's line-crossing operations into East Germany.

The two men were nothing like each other. Henney grew up in New York. He had been a captain in the US Marines and then transferred into OSS in one of its Jedburgh teams that were dropped into Occupied France. When the CIA was eventually formed they recruited a lot of ex-OSS officers and Hank Henney was one of the first to join the fledgeling organisation. He was not fond of Brits but he not only liked Carling but admired him for his knowledge of intelligence operations and understanding of the Russians and East Germans. When he first knew Carling, the Brit was a viscount and Henney had never really understood how, on the death of his father, he suddenly became an earl. For Hank Henney earls were those arrogant fighting characters in Shakespeare's plays. For or against the King. He had asked Carling how you got to be an earl and Carling had laughed and said, 'You just find you've picked the short straw and behave like you won.' Carling had likened the House of Lords to the US Senate but Henney couldn't grasp the function of a senate where not even one member had been voted into office. Anyway, what did it matter? It was just the Brits being Brits.

By the summer of 1964 both Washington and London were pleased with the results of the Philby operation. Eager to maintain the contact as long as possible but looking forward to the day when they could announce to the world that Philby was their man all the time, not the Russians'. Both Waring and Carling were privately more cautious. Maybe their reading of Philby's character was wrong. Maybe the scenario of Philby's flight to Moscow was more courtesy of the Russians than their own. But it cost so little. Encoding the tapes was simple enough, checking them a dozen times for accuracy took hours rather than days. They relied almost entirely on Philby's judgement as to what would come back to them, and their own messages were as much to build up Philby's morale as to indicate the areas that interested them most.

With more advanced radio technology there was vague talk of moving the operation to London, but Berlin was neutral territory for SIS and the CIA, and provided all the support services they needed.

Henney had gone to see the Admin Officer in the CIA's Berlin unit to argue about non-payment of some allowances he was due when Kaufman stuck his head round the door and said he'd like a word with Henney before he left. Kaufman was in charge of the CIA's penetration operations in East Berlin.

Kaufman's parents had fled to the United States in 1934, taking their two children with them. The old man was far-sighted and could see what was going to happen to the Jews in Germany. He sold his tailoring business for a tenth of what it was worth, to a Party member, and they only had money enough for bare survival in their new country. Kaufman's father and mother had worked for long hours day after day to build up the small business they had started in Queens and when Roosevelt declared war on the Axis powers Albert Kaufman Jun. had joined up. He had served in the infantry in Italy and in France. A major by then in the US 4th Infantry Division, he had landed on Utah beach on 5 June 1944 and been still with them on the day of the German surrender on Luneberg Heath.

He was a bilingual German speaker and was posted to a CIC unit based at Kassel in the American Zone. CIC, the Counter-Intelligence Corps, were largely responsible for the denazification operations in the American Zone.

CIA had head-hunted him away from the army and he had
successfully run line-crossing operations into the Russian
Zone for several years. It was a toss-up as to who he hated
most – the Germans or the Russians.

His office was a plasterboard construction in the main
HQ building.

When he saw Henney come in he said, 'Close the door,
Hank.'

When Henney took the visitors chair he saw Kaufman's
hand on a buff file. It was a thin one but it had the diagonal
red stripe from corner to corner that indicated that it was
'eyes-only'.

Kaufman wiped the back of his hand across his mouth
and put the can of Coke to one side as he leaned forward.

'We've got a problem, Hank. I raised it in our internal
meeting yesterday. They shut me up and said I was to
discuss it with you.'

'What's it about?'

'I gather you're doing something with a Brit named
Carling. Nobody seems to know what it's all about and
I was warned not to ask you about it.' He paused. 'Tell
me about Carling. Not the work you two do but as a
man. Character, temperament and all that. I've heard
on the grapevine that at one time he was doing a job
like mine – running agents into East Germany. Everybody says he was real good.' He shrugged. 'That's all
I know about him.' He smiled. 'And that he's an earl
or a lord or some such jazz.'

'He's a great guy. Easy-going but knows where to draw
the line. Good at his work and I've never met a guy
who I admire and like so much.'

'On our side?'

'Very much so.'

Kaufman sighed and leaned back in his chair. 'Tell me about his family.'

'His father was an earl and when—'

Kaufman leaned forward waving his hand to halt the flow. 'Not that part. His present family. The wife and daughter.'

'She lived in East Berlin when Carling was recruiting agents and informants over there. Very pretty, a semi-professional musician. Younger than Carling. A good loving couple I would say. And the young daughter – also very pretty. I'd guess she'll end up a musician too.'

Kaufman shook his head slowly. 'I wish to God you'd told me that they hated one another and were thinking about getting a divorce.'

'Why the hell should you want that?'

'Because she's a problem, pal. A big, big problem I don't know how to deal with.'

'What's the problem?'

Kaufman pointed to the file in front of him. 'That – is the surveillance file covering a number of years on a Rachel Maria Aarons. Some mystery in the records of who she married. Lived in East Berlin and was having an affair with an unnamed British officer. It may have been just sex but more likely she was an informant. It was confirmed later that the guy worked out of rooms off Kantstrasse and was believed to be SIS. And his name was Carling. Also turns out she was introduced to this guy by a Soviet named Porenski. Yuri Porenski. We've got him down as KGB. When we did a bit of sniffing around on who's who in SIS, Carling was a top man on intelligence in East Berlin and the whole of the Russian Zone. Our source there said he was married but no knowledge of where or when. So our target kisses the frog and changes from Rachel Maria Aarons to Lady Carling. So far, so nothing special.

'The problem came up two weeks ago when we had a walk-in from the KGB detachment in East Berlin. We trotted him around the file on Rachel Maria Aarons and we struck what seemed like oil. Before she met Carling she was the mistress of Yuri Porenski.' He stopped and looked at Henney.

Henney shrugged. 'Not that much of a problem, Al. All in the past. She's a very attractive girl.'

'That's the problem, Hank. It's not all in the past. She's still seeing him, regularly and secretively. On both sides of the Wall.'

'How often?'

'Roughly every ten days. If it were just sex that wouldn't be so worrying but there's every indication that it isn't. Could be sex and informing. Who knows?' He paused. 'I don't know what your operation is with Carling but I'd guess that our friend Yuri Porenski is well informed.'

'Where do they meet?'

Henney pointed at the file. 'There's the file. Read it.'

'Can I take it to my place?'

'No way. It won't take you long. Read it here. I've got things to do in the operations room. Read it and think about it. Tell me what we should do.'

Henney hesitated a long time before he reached for the file and opened it. He didn't want to read it, but he knew he had to.

As Kaufman had said, it didn't take long to read it. He was used to reading such reports on a target undergoing surveillance. There were all those tatty details provided by chambermaids and cleaners that confirmed all too positively that sex took place at most of their meetings. The report also quoted informants who confirmed that the girl had been Porenski's mistress some time before Carling came on the scene. The report inevitably raised the issue of whether the introduction of Carling to the girl was part of a KGB operation. There were some indications that the meeting was fortuitous, but others that it was planned or at least assisted once the relationship developed.

Henney closed the file and pushed it away from him. He wondered how much Carling told her of their game with Philby. If she knew what they were doing and had passed it on to the Russian surely by now Moscow would have taken out Philby. Or were they so sophisticated that they'd rather know what interested London and Washington so much that they risked Philby's life in sending him to Moscow? Or maybe they had turned Philby yet again. Maybe it was just sex and maybe it was just sex for the KGB man too. She was young and very beautiful and he had been her lover before Carling, so she must find him attractive too. He closed his eyes to block out his thoughts and then Kaufman came back. He pulled up his chair and sat down.

'What do you reckon, old pal?'

'I'll need time to think about it.'

'Meantime, what do you want me to do?'

'Let me think about that too. Who else knows about this?'

'Nobody. Just me and my agent. She doesn't know the background. Wonders why I bother about a KGB man screwing a local girl.'

'What do you want to do?'

Kaufman sighed. 'Tell me, how threatening is this?'

'Could be somebody's life.'

'Who's side is the somebody on – ours or theirs?'

'Ours. Could be both.'

'A mole in place?'

'I can't say any more, Al. I'll come back to you to-morrow.' He stopped at the door and turned to look at Kaufman. 'Could your people take out this Porenski guy if it was necessary.'

'No problem, Hank.'

Henney walked to a small park near the CIA HQ and sat watching the mothers with their children in the small playground. He tried not to think of what he had to do. There was no way he could do nothing, but how much did he need to tell George Carling? Was there some way he could warn him without giving any details? He sat there for almost an hour and in the end he knew that he had no choice but to tell Carling what was going on. As he drove back to his own place he was wondering where he should do it, rehearsing how he should start and what he would suggest they should do about it. Carling would be angry as well as hurt but he would be well aware that making the wrong move could endanger Philby, if he wasn't already in trouble. It was going to be messy and there was no way to avoid it. He couldn't do it at Carling's place because the girl would be around and his own place was too crowded with his wife and kids. He'd book a private room at Kempinski's. Neutral territory.

Hank Henney didn't sleep that night.

Carling had listened, sitting quite still in the armchair facing Henney, saying nothing, asking no questions until he'd finished.

For a long time Carling just sat there in silence and then he said quietly, 'You read the reports yourself, Hank?'

'Yes.'

'You think from what you read that they were accurate?'

'I'm afraid so. I'm sorry.'

Carling closed his eyes, thinking, his hands gripping the arms of the chair. With his eyes still closed, Carling said, 'We could cut out the Russian if we moved the operation to London. Would you go along with that?'

'Yes. If it would help you, George.'

'She can't have told him anything about our operation because she doesn't know anything. I've never discussed my work with her, not even when it was routine stuff. I've seen too many men go down the river through careless talk to a mistress or wife.'

Carling opened his eyes and looked at Henney, who said quietly, 'How much will you tell Rachel about what we know?'

Carling smiled. 'Nothing. There's no point. It would make bad worse. Nothing would be gained. She'd be destroyed or wounded. And she doesn't deserve that.' He turned in his chair to look at Henney. 'I owe her a lot, Hank. I love her and I don't intend playing the injured husband. She loves me and she cares about me. The other – well, it's just that. Hormones and maybe genes but not hearts and feelings. Why should I hurt her?'

But Henney was aware of the tears glistening in Carling's big brown eyes.

He said quietly, 'You're a good man, George Carling. A very good man.'

'It's odd, isn't it? Do you know where she is at the moment?'

'No.'

Carling smiled. 'She's at your place with your family with little Rachel. They both love being with your folk.

She's virtually no relatives of her own and your family are her background. I've only got very distant relatives. Most of them I've never met so we're both rather like orphans.'

Henney stood up. 'Let me get you a drink.'

CHAPTER 41

'Was that when you both moved to London?'

'No. It was nearly six months before that happened. First, CIA Langley was agin it but they gave in after a couple of weeks' wrangling from me.'

Mathews said, 'You said first. What else was there?'

Henney sighed. 'Did George tell you about his wife's death?'

'No. I think he mentioned that she died but nothing else.'

'She was killed by a car in Berlin about three weeks before we were to make our move to London.' He paused. 'It was a hit-and-run driver. He was never caught.'

'Was it a KGB operation?'

'No. I was with her at the time. That's how I got my game leg. The car hit her first and then me but mine was a glancing blow, just enough to bust up the hip joint.' He paused. 'You can imagine what that did to Carling. He just wanted to be away from everything. Berlin, SIS, his life. But he couldn't because of the operation with Philby. Another year and we had promised Philby the option of returning and rehabilitation.'

'What happened to his daughter?'

'We took her over, my wife and I. And for the rest of the time in Berlin Carling moved in with us himself. There was no publicity about her death. I think your people and your embassy damped it down.' He sighed. 'I can remember him saying how glad he was that he'd never raised the business with the Russian. Kaufman's informant said later that the Russian hadn't even heard of her death. Still wondering why she didn't contact him. If it had been a KGB revenge operation he would have known.'

'And after this you moved to London?'

'Yeah. Carling took this place in King's Road and the family and I moved in with him and we carried on the operation from an apartment in Gower Street. It went on for just over a year. Philby was going to be brought back about six months later. He was in pretty bad shape by then.'

'Why did he never come back?'

'It was like the whole setup had got a curse on it. Waring, who was then SIS's DG and the only man who knew about the Philby operation, died suddenly of a heart attack. Playing golf at St Andrews. That meant that there was nobody Carling could pass Philby's information to because it didn't officially exist. George passed the news to Philby of Waring's death but he had apparently already read about Waring's death in the London *Times* that he got regularly in Moscow.'

'What was his reaction?'

'Very little. Said he'd carry on and see what could be done to get him back. Didn't seem in any great hurry. And that in itself worried us both. Maybe he'd been playing along with the Russians from when he left Beirut. What was clear was that it was a mess and Carling and I were holding the baby.'

'What was the CIA's reaction?'

'Panic and confusion for two or three days and then I was recalled in a hurry to Langley. A couple of days of so-called debriefing that was aimed solely at making sure that it was I who carried the can. There's an old Russian proverb that says, "Success has a thousand fathers – failure is an orphan." ' He shrugged. 'I went along with what Langley wanted. I had no choice. Had six months' sick leave to see what the medics could do with my hip joint and then they put me in charge of looking over new boys who had jumped all the routine hurdles. Assessing them for loyalty, commitment, background, booze, women and sexual deviation. And after a couple of years I was retired on an enhanced pension and told to keep my mouth shut. I was forbidden to have any contact with George. That's why when you came to see me in New York it caused so much panic.'

'What happened to the little girl, his daughter?'

Henney smiled. 'She's no longer a little girl. She's in her twenties and she's a real doll. She went to the Juilliard and she's now performing all over the world. She uses her mother's name – Aarons. George sees her quite often when she's in Europe. She stayed with us for years but her father bought her an apartment in the Village in New York. That's her base now, but she spends a lot of her time in hotel rooms. Her boyfriend's a musicologist and reviews music for the *New York Times* and is a good partner for her. But she was always daddy's girl and she takes a lot of notice of what he says.' He sighed. 'But even that relationship must be tough on him because she's the spitting image of her mother. Looks, voice, gestures – you can't help noticing it.'

'Where is his wife buried?'

'Somewhere in Berlin. I don't remember where. But the headstone's in her family name of Aarons.' He paused. 'Anything else you want from me?'

'What did Philby do in the end?'

'He seemed to lose interest in coming back. Said he'd rather stay on in Moscow. I think he'd found a new woman who was looking after him.' Henney stood up unsteadily. 'I'd like to head back home on tomorrow morning's flight from Gatwick if that suits you.'

'Of course. I'll drive you there. Julie's made up a few salad things for us. We can all eat together.'

Henney put his hand on Mathews' arm. 'Don't talk to George about any of the things I've told you. He wanted you to hear it from me. He can't bear to talk about it. Just carry on where you two left off.'

Mathews waited with Henney until his flight was called and as they shook hands he said, smiling, 'It's a bit like when Maguire escorted me on to the plane at Kennedy.'

Henney laughed. 'When the CIA panics it does it in a big way. Come and see me any time you want and thanks for your time and listening to me.' As he limped slowly away Henney turned and waved. 'Take care, boy.'

Julie was sorting out the mail on the dining-room table. There were a dozen or so letters for Carling and three for Mathews.

Mathews opened the bulging foolscap envelope and unfolded the document and the letter. He read it hurriedly, the letter first. It was from his solicitor. The decree nisi had gone through and he now had to wait three months for the decree absolute to be granted. The document registered and agreed division of the family's assets. He'd taken Carling's advice and left Pamela the house and all the things she wanted and she hadn't been upset that it hadn't worked out. She seemed as relieved as he was. The other two letters were good news too. A notification that he was promoted a grade and a statement from the bank that was better than he had expected.

Julie had seemed slightly shocked when he invited her to dinner with him at the High Rocks that evening to celebrate his divorce.

When they got back just before midnight, Carling was sitting in the kitchen with a couple of sandwiches that Gabby had made for him, and when Julie went to bed Mathews had stayed on with Carling.

'Freddie Kennedy phoned for you about ten o'clock. Wants to speak to you. I told him you had taken a couple of days' leave.' He paused. 'I thought it would give us time, you and me, to wrap things up.'

'D'you feel it's been a waste of time, all our talking?'

Carling thought for a moment or two. 'No. I don't think so. Depends what Kennedy was after.'

'I think it was just a kind of insurance so that if anything unfavourable to SIS came out in the media he could show that he'd covered everything. Nobody could criticise SIS.' He paused. 'And I think he vaguely wondered if anything *had* been going on recently between you and any Soviet contacts you had in the old days.'

'You're not far out but he'll need a small gift before he can finally close the file.' He smiled. 'I give you my permission to tell him that after I left SIS I acted as a consultant on Soviet matters for the CIA. That'll be something he didn't know. And one more reason why he won't want to keep on raking over the old ground. Explains the CIA's concern about me being harassed and leaving just a small chink for media criticism if he leaked it. Why did SIS let a man go who the CIA subsequently valued as a consultant?' He smiled. 'I've fixed with Langley that if it ever did come out they'd reveal that I gave them a week's advance warning that the Wall was going to come down. They acted on it, London didn't. Then everyone can live happy ever after.'

'Could you tell me about your meeting with the new DG after Waring died?'

Carling threw up his hands. 'An absolute disaster. Tried to suggest that I was mentally ill. Having hallucinations. Nothing I could say would convince him that any of it had happened. The only thing that made him hesitate was when I suggested he checked the source of two or three intelligence items that had been fed into the system by Waring. Where did Waring get them from? I was even interviewed personally by the Attorney-General, a much shrewder man than the DG. I sensed that he didn't intend pursuing the matter too far.' He smiled. 'But it's interesting that GCHQ and SIS and the CIA all use numbers stations even today. Nobody's found a better way of contacting agents in unfriendly countries who can't read Morse. If you're ever bored tune your short-wave radio to 15682 Mh and you'll probably hear a man's voice reading out a series of numbers in English. It sometimes plays a few notes of the song "The Lincolnshire Poacher".' He grinned. 'That was my old frequency but I didn't have any music.'

'Were you worried about Philby not getting what you had promised him?'

'Yes. And thank God the Americans offered to try and smuggle him out. But he didn't seem interested. I think he was tired and ill and totally disillusioned. It ended up with him trying to convince me that none of it mattered. But it mattered to me. So I resigned.' He laughed. 'They were so pleased, so relieved to see the back of me. Farewell parties from SIS and the Foreign Office, full of phoney bonhomie. All chaps together. It was funny, ludicrous and pathetic and now the bastards send you on a fishing expedition in the hope that they can show they're still needed despite the end of the Cold War. Such bloody hypocrites.' He grinned. 'Present company excluded, of course.'

But Mathews knew that he wasn't really excluded in Carling's thinking.

'You're sure you want me to tell Kennedy about you being a consultant for the CIA after you resigned?'

'Oh yes. By all means. It's a titbit and they always appreciate that a chap should earn a buck wherever he can. They'll be doing something similar when their turns come. The days when decent men retired from Broadway to growing roses in West Sussex are long gone.' He paused. 'You'd better have something in mind to suggest to Kennedy as your new posting.'

Mathews smiled. 'Any suggestions?'

'Yes. Investigating Stasis. What they did and what they're doing now after the German reunification. I can give you some contacts if you want.'

'I'm glad all this is coming to an end. But I shall miss being here. It's kind of become home.'

Carling shrugged. 'Come back whenever you want.'

Mathews smiled. 'Julie, Gabby, Carlotta and me. Your waifs and strays.' He laughed. ' "Send these, the homeless, tempest-tost to me . . ." ' He looked across at Carling. 'What made you trust me enough to tell me what really happened?'

'Just instinct, my boy. Just instinct.'

'And nobody would believe me anyway. It's a pity that Philby didn't get his reward.'

'I've left a full account of what happened with my lawyers. It will be published when I'm no longer around, whether it's from natural causes or otherwise.'

'Do you want me to call you and tell you what Freddie Kennedy's reactions were when I tell him about you and the CIA?'

Carling smiled and shook his head slowly. 'No. He'll be glad to close the file.'

'I wish it had been a happier ending for you.'

'There *are* no happy endings in this wretched game. Not if you're good at it. There was a poem by a man named Gosse and there was one line that said it all – "The past is like a funeral gone by".'

As Carling had predicted, Kennedy accepted his 'confession' of acting as a consultant to the CIA. It explained so much of what had happened and he had begun to lose interest in those long-gone days and the players who made them what they were. Several files were closed and Mathews was given a new posting. Not investigating ex-Stasis but as SIS liaison officer to their opposite numbers in ASIO, Australia's own intelligence service. For several years he thought fondly of Carling and his 'family' at the cottage in Kent. He married after a couple of years, a woman officer who was ASIO's anti-sabotage expert. They were not a romantic couple but they got along well together, undemanding and only mildly ambitious.